KING AKBAR'S DAUGHTER

Selected titles from Omega Publications

Spy Princess; The Life of Noor Inayat Khan
by Shrabani Basu

We Rubies Four; The Memoirs of Claire Ray Harper
(Khairunisa Inayat Khan)
by Claire Ray Harper and David Ray Harper

The Complete Sayings of Hazrat Inayat Khan
by Hazrat Inayat Khan

Life is a Pilgrimage
by Pir Vilayat Inayat Khan

Saracen Chivalry; Counsels on Valor, Generosity and the Mystical Quest
by Pir Zia Inayat-Khan

The Story of Layla and Majnun
by Nizami

For a complete listing of Omega titles see
www.omegapub.com

King Akbar's Daughter

Stories for Everyone as Told by

Noor Inayat Khan

Sulūk Press
New Lebanon, New York

Published by
Sulūk Press, an imprint of Omega Publications, Inc.
New Lebanon NY
www.omegapub.com

©2012 Omega Publications, Sulūk Press
All rights reserved. No part of this publication may be reproduced, stored in a retrieval system, or transmitted by any means, electronic, mechanical, photocopying, recording, or otherwise, without prior written permission of the publisher.

Cover photo of Noor Inayat Khan courtesy of David Ray Harper. Background image by Horace Vernet, detail of "Citadel of Cairo," 1819, courtesy of Dover Publications, Inc.
Cover design by Sandra Lillydahl

Translations from the French language by
Sandra Lillydahl with David Harper and Lisa Lillydahl Conley

This edition is printed on acid-free paper that meets ANSI standard X39-48.

Inayat Khan, Noor-un-Nisa (1914–1944)
King Akbar's Daughter
Stories for Everyone as Told by Noor Inayat Khan
Includes biographical notes
1. Tales 2. Sufism
I. Inayat Khan, Noorunisa II. Title

Library of Congress Control Number: 2013930996

Printed and bound in the United States of America

ISBN 978–0930872922

10 9 8 7 6 5 4 3 2 1

Contents

Sources of Illustrations   vii

Introduction by David Harper   xi

Editor's Notes   xv

Stories and Poems For Young Children of All Ages
- The Little Guardian Angel / *Le petit ange guardien*   2
- The Mouse and the Camel / *Le souris et le chameau*   8
- Victor Hugo's Pants / *Le pantalon de Victor Hugo*   12
- The Little Magic Boat / *Le petit bâteau magique*   16
- The Peasant and the Tiger / *Le paysan et le tigre*   22
- The Violet / *Le violette*   28
- The Night / *La nuit*   30
- Nature's Mysteries / *Les mystères de la nature*   32
- Sweet Peas   34

Four Stories for Christmas
- Snowball / *Boule de neige*   36
- When Father Christmas Didn't Come / *Père Noël qui n'etait pas venu*   42
- A Troll's Christmas / *Noël chez les Trolls*   48
- Little Father Christmas and the Two Robins / *Petit Noël et les deux rouge-gorges*   58

From the West
- Echo / *Ce qu'on entend quelquefois dans les bois*   68
- Baldour / *Baldour*   74
- The Kingdom of the Winds / *Au royaume des vents*   80

From the East
   Zeb-un-Nisa / *Zeb-un Nisa*   100
   Mira Bhai / *Mira Bhai*   104
   King Akbar and His Daughter   112

The Story of Renard the Fox / *Le roman de Renard*   118
Huon of Bordeaux / *Huon de Bordeaux*   152

Stories of Hope and Courage
   Princess Wanda   209
   The White Eagles of Poland   212
   Snow Drop / *Perce neige*   214

Memories of Noor *by Pir Vilayat Inayat Khan*   225

Selected Bibliography   229

Sources of Illustrations

pp. ix–x. Photographs of Noor Inayat Khan courtesy of David Ray Harper.

pp. 1, 207. Reproduced from *Owen Jones Decorative Borders*, Own Jones, courtesy of Dover Publications.

pp. 6–7, 35, 64–65, 67, 117, 221. Reproduced from *Decorative Frames and Borders; 396 Copyright–Free Designs for Artists and Craftsmen Selected by Edmund V. Gillon Jr.,* Edmund Gillon Jr., courtesy of Dover Publications.

p. 7. Photograph of Noor Inayat Khan as a child courtesy of David Ray Harper.

p. 7. Reproduced from *Full-Color Decorative Butterfly Illustrations*, courtesy of Dover Designs.

pp. 7, 15, 78–79, 151, 220. *Reproduced from Heraldic Vector Designs*, courtesy of Dover Publications.

p. 10–11, 26–27, 65. Reproduced from *Animal Vector Designs*, courtesy of Dover Publications.

p. 14. French Dragoon adapted from print in the Vinkhuijzen Collection of Military Costume Illustration assembled by H. J. Vinkhuijzen (1843–1910), {{PD-Art}} courtesy of Wikimedia Commons.

pp. 20–21. Reproduced from *Symbols Signs & Signets; A Pictorial Treasury with Over 1350 Illustrations*, Ernst Lehner, courtesy of Dover Publications.

pp. 26–27, 99, 110–111, 115. Reproduced from *Designs from India*, courtesy of Dover Publications.

pp. 40–41. Reproduced from from *Bentley's Snowflakes*, W. A. Bentley, courtesy of Dover Publications.

pp. 46–47, 41, 117, 204, 211. Reproduced from *1,100 Designs and Motifs from Historic Sources*, John Leighton, courtesy of Dover Publications.

pp. 56–57. Reproduced from *Humorous Victorian Spot Illustrations*, edited by Carol Grafton, courtesy of Dover Publications; *P*courtesy of Dover Publications; and *Christmas Vector Motifs*, courtesy of Dover Publications

pp. 72–73. Reproduced from *Ancient Greek Designs*, Marty Noble, courtesy of Dover Publications.

pp. 78–79, 96–97, 213. Reproduced from *Medieval Designs*, Gregory Mirow, courtesy of Dover Publications.

pp. 102–103. Reproduced from *Paisley Designs*, courtesy of Dover Publications.

p. 223. "Ritter und Dame mit Helm und Lanze" L.212, Master ES {{PD-Art}}, courtesy of Wikimedia Commons.

p. 223. Photograph of Noor Inayat Khan in WAAF Women's Auxiliary Air force) uniform courtesy of David Ray Harper.

p. 224. Photograph of Vilayat and Noor Inayat Khan courtesy of David Ray Harper.

Noor Inayat Khan

Noor with vina

Introduction

Who was Noor Inayat Khan?
Sitting among the many mureeds (disciples) that hailed from various lands, she drank in the inspiring words of the great Sufi master. Though only a child, Noor was drawn to the source of eastern mysticism and universal wisdom presented to the western world by the enlightened teacher, poet and musician from India: Pir-o-Murshid Hazrat Inayat Khan who, as it so happened, was also her father.

Raised near Paris, in a household seemingly steeped in oriental tradition, Noor's upbringing was far from the norm. Her American mother, Ora Ray Baker, her exposure to local French schools and the interaction with the many French friends this popular girl had, all contributed to instilling in Noor a unique blend of eastern and western cultures.

As a young child Noor developed a keen interest in poetry, a growing talent that was to be complemented by her passion for music. Taking music lessons, she learned the harp and the piano and began composing songs and classical music in her teen years. Along with her two brothers Vilayat and Hidayat, and her sister Claire, Noor performed regularly in the drawing room of their home at receptions and special events held for the many followers that attended Pir-o-Murshid's classes and seminars.

Noor was just thirteen when her father suddenly passed away. This tragedy incapacitated her mother through such grief and despair that Noor soon assumed responsibility and leadership for her younger siblings. Despite these family

obligations as a "little mother," Noor continued to excel in school, as well as in her artistic pursuits. In her early twenties Noor further developed her literary skills, writing stories for children in both English and French and negotiating an offer to develop her own children's story section in the well-known French newspaper supplement, the *Figaro Littéraire*.

By her mid-twenties, Noor was looking forward to a promising future in the French literary world. She enjoyed the company of her musically talented fiancé, Azeem Goldenberg, who assisted her with her compositions, and Noor became ever more involved in the world of creative writing. Her beautifully illustrated *Twenty Jataka Tales*, a retelling of old Indian moral-focused stories, had been released some years previously which gave Noor the distinction of being a published author of children's stories. Plans and projects for a literary career were gradually developing when the threat of war upturned Noor's future in Paris.

Germany's occupation of France forced the family to flee to England, as they were all British citizens and would not be allowed to remain in the country. An event during their escape prompted Noor to write an inspirational manifesto, calling upon the French to resist and rebel against the enemy.

Once established in England Noor wished to contribute to the war effort in a way in which she could be useful. To this end, she trained with the Royal Air Force as a wireless radio operator and was ultimately recruited by the Special Operations Executive (SOE) to train as a secret agent. Even during training, Noor continued to write: she had befriended a Polish resistance fighter and was inspired to write two short stories about Poland's oppression and its struggle for freedom[1].

Noor kept her involvement with Churchill's SOE task force a completely hidden from her family and friends. In 1943 she was secretly flown to France, behind enemy lines, where she was to aid a British-backed French resistance network.

---

1 *Princess Wanda* and *The White Eagles of Poland*

Introduction

Unfortunately, the network had been infiltrated and the agents arrested by the Gestapo prior to Noor's arrival. Nevertheless she bravely set about helping to establish a new network and, moving from one base to the next throughout the Paris region, faced an ever increasing risk of detection and arrest as time passed. Though Noor's superiors insisted on her return to the safety of England, she valiantly stayed on for months, carrying out missions and relaying valuable information in the preparation for D-Day landing operations.

Just hours before her final replacement by a new agent from England, Noor was betrayed and captured. Throughout the year in which she was imprisoned, starved and tortured, Noor never revealed the secret information with which she had been entrusted. Nor did her spirit break at Dachau concentration camp; kneeling at the feet of her tormentor and knowing her end had come, Noor lifted her head and defiantly retorted: *Liberté!* [2] before being shot. She was thirty years old.

This gentle and selfless yet heroic woman has been remembered thanks to biographies, novels and TV documentaries. Her lofty ideals led her to risk and ultimately sacrifice her young and promising life for the freedom of others. At last Noor's writings have been collected, some translated from French and all carefully compiled in this special tribute to a beautiful being who has been an inspiration to so many.

David Ray Harper
January 2013

---

2 Liberty

Editor's Notes

Most of Noor's stories are traditional myths, fables and legends retold in her own words and embroidered with her unique twists to best serve her purpose of teaching and inspiring children with tales of chivalry, compassion, love, hope and wisdom.

A collection of Noor's stories are presented here in new English translations alongside her original French language versions. Noor's own known English renditions are included in the stories "King Akbar and His Daughter," "Princess Wanda," "The White Eagles of Poland," "Echo," and "Snow Drop." To preserve Noor's unique voice and writing style, only minimal editing has been done, primarily to standardize punctuation and spelling.

In the opening pages of her previously published book, *Twenty Jataka Tales*, Noor acknowledges the sources of her stories. Although we do not have any records from Noor about the exact sources of the stories in the present compilation, we have attempted to trace their origins to the best of our knowledge.

The opening story of "The Little Guardian Angel," comes from Noor's own childhood memories. Noor's father, Hazrat Inayat Khan, was a Sufi teacher from India who lived in Great Britain and France with his American wife Ora Ray Baker and

their four children. Noor's brother Vilayat recalls Inayat Khan telling stories to his children, and several of Noor's stories are Sufi related, such as the "Mouse and the Camel" which is found in the 13th century *Masnavi* of Jalal al-Din Muhammad Rumi. At least three other stories, "Zeb-un-Nisa," "Mira Bhai" and "King Akbar and His Daughter," include also Sufi themes and characters. These stories are meant to illustrate certain ideals and principles rather than to be taken as literal history.

Historically, the Sufi poetess Zeb-un-Nisa was the unmarried daughter of India's 17th century Mughal Emperor Aurangzeb. Prince Dara Shikoh was not her husband but her uncle, the brother of Aurangzeb. Dara Shikoh was put to death at Aurangzeb's command.

Mira Bhai was a 16th century Hindu singer in the devotional *bhakti* tradition, absorbed in the love of Lord Krishna. Many stories have been ascribed to her life, some of which are included in Noor's tale.

King Akbar, a 16th century Mughal emperor of India, was deeply interested in universal religion. In the fictitious story of "King Akbar and his Daughter," the author gives the story teller her own name, Noor. The king's daughter in this tale is also identified with Scheherazade, the storyteller of *The Thousand and One Nights*.

India's *Panchatantra* is the source for "The Peasant and the Tiger," a well-known tale with several versions in different countries, and is a story that was told by Noor's father. Known European sources for other stories in this collection include the Norse *Eddas* ("Baldour"), Ovid's *Metamorphoses* ("Echo"), and *Victor Hugo: Raconté par un témoin de sa vie avec oeuvres inédites de Victor Hugo*, by Adele Hugo and Victor Hugo[1] "Victor Hugo's Pants"). Russian legends of the Snow Maiden are the source for "Snowball," and a possible source for "The Kingdom of the Winds," is "Whirlwind the Whistler, or the

---

1. VII pp.46–47, Les Feuillantines, Paris, 1885, J. Hetzel Cie

Editor's Notes

Kingdoms of Copper, Silver and Gold," from *The Russian Story Book Containing Tales from Song-Cycles of Kiev and Novgorod, and Other Early Sources retold by Richard Wilson*, by Richard Wilson.[2]

Père Noël is the French Santa Claus, and "The Little Magic Boat" includes Japanese names, but it is unknown whether these stories and "The Trolls' Christmas" were from a particular source or were Noor's own creations, as were the four poems. "The Troll's Christmas" was translated by David Ray Harper, who notes that, given the number of anglicisms in the original, this seems to by one or Noor's earlier stories, written before she had fully immersed herself in the French language.

The character of Renard the Fox, a satirical anti-hero, was well known in medieval European literature and appears in additional sources, including the fables of Aesop and Jean de la Fontaine, and the Grimm Brothers' stories. The chivalric tale of Huon of Bordeaux comes from 13th century French *chansons de geste*. "Princess Wanda" and "The White Eagles of Poland" are traditional Polish legends, researched by Noor at the British Museum during her time in London during World War II.

The final story "Snowdrop" also comes from Noor's life, but as a premonition of her own fate. As the first flowers to blossom at the end of winter and the very beginning of spring, snowdrops are considered a symbol of hope. Noor wrote both French and English versions of this story, with the English version found among her technical notes in one of her wireless training notebooks. Like the Sun King's little daughter, Noor (whose name means "light") lived most of her life on earth in the space between the two dark eras of World Wars I and II. In the course of her clandestine wartime work in Paris as a wireless transmitter for Britain's Special Operations Executive (SOE), Noor was betrayed and captured by the Gestapo. Like the Sun King's little daughter, she was held captive by "Fog-Gloom"

---

2. MacMillans, London, 1916

Editor's Notes

or "Night and Fog" (*Nacht und Nebel*), a designation given to certain prisoners, considered dangerous by the Nazi regime, who would be made to disappear by eliminating their names and fates from official records. Noor was executed at Dachau in 1944, and her remains were consigned to an unmarked burial spot. And like the two robins in the story, Noor's brother Vilayat and her SOE superior Vera Atkins searched for Noor across postwar Europe. Her fate was finally revealed in 1950 by an eye-witness to her execution.

In the story, Snow Drop promises to return in a new form, and Noor herself returns to us today in several new forms. As a legend in her own right she is memorialized as an honored recipient of the United Kingdom's St. George Cross and France's *Croix de Guerre* with Gold Star, and her name is engraved in tribute plaques on war memorials in England, France, and Dachau concentration camp in Poland. A bronze statue of Noor now looks over the little park in London's Gordon Square where she used to play as a child and sit quietly with a book as an adult. Books and documentaries commemorate her heroism and help to keep her alive in the hearts and imaginations of the growing number of those who find inspiration and hope in her shining courage and chivalrous self-sacrifice for the cause of liberty. It is our hope that this book of Noor's stories will be another petal in the rose of her memory.

Deep gratitude is due to the late Claire Ray Harper for preserving her sister Noor's stories, to Claire's son David Ray Harper for offering them for publication, and to Noor's surviving brother Hidayat Inayat Khan and her nephew Pir Zia Inayat-Khan for adding their permissions to publish these works. And many thanks to Lisa Lillydahl Conley, George Naughton, and especially to David Ray Harper for their most helpful assistance with proofreading and translations from French to English. Any errors in translation or text remain my own.

Sandra Lillydahl

In my mystery
Deep in my divine Abode
Treasures are bestowed...

*from the poem "The Song of the Night,"
by Noor Inayat Khan*

Stories & Poems for Young Children of All Ages

Le petit ange guardien

CHÈRES lectrices, puisque tout le monde parle d'aventures passées, dans ce monde où nous vivons tous les jours, venez un peu avec moi dans le monde des rêves que je vous raconte les aventures nocturnes d'une toute petite fille.

Il faut d'abord débarquer dans le monde des songes et alors vous la comprendrez.

C'est ce que faisait tous les soirs la fillette lorsque Maman arrangeait ses petites boucles, l'embrassait et fermait la lumière en disant:

"Dors bien mon petit."

Puis, dans le silence poignant de la nuit, lorsque tous dormaient, deux heures sonnaient à la grosse pendule; c'était le signal. La petite se levait, et sur les pointes des pieds elle commencait sa tournée reguliére. Elle ne la faisait pas toujours du même côté de l'immense maison. Quelquefois elle se dirigeait vers le grenier. Une fois elle se pencha par la petite fenêtre et voyant à travers le brouillard londonien, le ciel tout noir et les lumières des reverbères dans la rue, elle dit:

"Comme c'est drôle cette nuit, toutes les étoiles sont tombées sur la terre! Demain matin it faudra que je me réveille très tôt pour les ramasser avant que le cantonnier ne passe."

Puis elle se hasardait dans la grande bibliothèque.

The Little Guardian Angel

DEAR readers, since everyone speaks of past adventures in this world where we live our daily lives, come with me on a visit into the world of dreams, so I can tell you about the night-time adventures of a very small girl.

First we must enter into the world of dreams so that you understand her.

This is what happened to the little girl every evening, when Mama smoothed her little curls, hugged her, and turned off the light, saying:

"Sleep well, my little one."

Then, in the poignant silence of the night, when all were asleep, the hour of two o'clock would chime on the large clock. That was the signal. The little girl climbed out of bed, and on tiptoes began her accustomed rounds. She did not always go to the same part of the large house. Sometimes she went to the attic. One time she leaned out of the little window, and seeing the black sky and lights reflecting in the street through the London fog, she said:

"How funny it is tonight, all the stars have fallen to the earth! Tomorrow morning I will have to wake up very early to gather them up before the street cleaner comes along."

Then she ventured into the large library.

"Les livres sont bien à leur place," disait-elle, "eux ils dorment la nuit. Il n'y a que moi qui veille. Il faudra que je ferme bien la porte sinon eux aussi viendraient faire des petits tours dans la maison. Et puis il y a de la lumière qui vient de cette fenêtre éclairer l'escalier. Pourquoi? D'où vient-elle? Ah! c'est vrai qu'il y a toujours une lumière pour que le petit ange gardien de la maison ne tombe pas dans l'escalier."

Puis doucement, à petits pas, elle se dirigeait vers la grande porte d'entrée et elle essayait les serrures.

"Oui, on n'a pas oublié de bien fermer. Qu'arriverait-il si je ne venais pas toutes les nuits vérifier? Je voudrais tant sortir un peu, mais c'est dur le fer de la serrure, il n'y a que les grandes personnes qui peuvent l'ouvrir. Maintenant montons voir dans les chambres à coucher, ouvrons doucement la porte, Chut! Ne vous reveilles pas, c'est la petite gardienne qui passe! O! Voilà que Maman a oublié de bien fermer sa porte, qu'elle l'a laissé un petit peu ouverte. Qu'arriverait-il si je ne veillais pas la nuit?"

Trois heures sonnent; le signal de retourner au lit.

"Entrons dans ma chambre ... O! quelle merveille, O! comme je suis contente, dans ce lit le bon Dieu m'a mis un nouveau petit frère. O! Vite! que je me reveille demain matin pour dire a Maman qu'un nouveau petit frère est né."

Puis dans la chambre, la nurse anglaise se rèveilla et s'écria:

"Vite au lit, que fais-tu là méchante petite fille?"

Et l'enfant se reveilla et se trouva debout sur le lit de son petit frère. Epouvantée de se retrouver dans la réalité, elle rampa jusqu'a son lit en criant:

"Où suis-je, qu'ai-je fait toute la nuit?!"

Son petit coeur palpita jusqu'a ce que les rayons de l'aube entrèrent à travers les rideaux pour la soulager.

The Little Guardian Angel

"The books are all in place," said she, "They sleep at night. I'm the only one who is awake. I must close the door securely or else they too will set off on little journeys through the house. And here is the light which comes in this window and shines on the stairs. Why? Where does it come from? Ah! There is always a light so that the little guardian angel of the house doesn't fall down the stairs."

Then softly, with tiny steps, she turned towards the large entrance door and tested the locks.

"Yes, no one has forgotten to shut it tightly. What would happen if I didn't come every night to make sure? I would so much like to go outside for a little while, but it would be difficult because of the chain on the lock. Only big people can open it. Now let's go up to the bedrooms, and gently open the door. Shush! Don't wake up; it's the little guardian angel who is coming through. O! See how Mama has forgotten to close her door all the way; she's left it ajar. What would happen if I didn't get up at night?"

The hour of three o'clock chimed the signal to go back to bed.

"Let's go into my room... Oh, how wonderful! Oh how happy I am! Here in this bed, dear God has given me a new little brother. Oh, quickly! I must wake up tomorrow morning to tell Mama that a new little brother is born."

Then, inside the room, the English nurse woke up and cried out: "Go to bed quickly, what are you doing there, naughty little girl?"

And the child woke up and found herself standing on her little brother's bed. Frightened at finding herself back in the world of reality, she crawled into her bed crying:

"Where am I? What have I been doing all night long?"

Her little heart beat rapidly until the rays of dawn entered through the curtains to comfort her.

Le petit ange guardien

Les étoiles se transformèrent en reverbères, les livres en papier et carton, et il n'y avait plus de petit ange gardien. En un clin d'oeil tous les mystères, disparurent. C'était la fin de ces belles aventures et cette hardie petite somnambule ... cétait moi!

The Little Guardian Angel

The stars transformed themselves into streetlights, the books were now just paper and cardboard, and no longer was there a little guardian angel. In the wink of an eye all the mysteries vanished. That is the end of these lovely adventures, and this daring little sleepwalker … was me!

La souris et le chameau

Quel châmeau splendide se promenait à la lisière du grand désert!

Une petite souris le regardait emerveillée. Les rênes du châmeau pendaient à terre car son maître était parti prendre des provisions dans la ville.

"Et pourquoi," pensa Petite Souris, "ne prendrai-je pas les rênes?"

Petite Souris s'approcha, le cœur battant. De ses deux pattes elle prit les rênes, et à son grand étonnement, le grand châmeau partit.

"Ciel!" s'écria Petite Souris, "que je suis donc forte et puissante! Il n'est pas un éléphant sur la terre qui n'obéirait pas à mes ordres!"

Mais Grand Châmeau riait en cachette, pensant à la bonne surprise qui attendait Petite Souris.

Il y avait près de là une rivière aux eaux bonbeuses et profondes.

Grand Châmeau la voyait bien mais Petite Souris était si petite qu'elle ne voyait que les brins d'herbe qui lui barraient le passage.

Mais, arrivée au bord de l'eau Petite Souris s'arrêta brusquement.

"Eh! qu'y a-t-il?" s'écria Grand Châmeau, "on ne s'arrête pas ainsi en pleine route, mon maître a donc quelque malaise?"

The Mouse and the Camel

WHAT a splendid camel strolled at the edge of the great desert!

A little mouse looked at him with amazement. The camel's reins hung down to the ground because his master had gone to gather provisions in the town.

"And why," thought Little Mouse, "shouldn't I take hold of the reins myself?"

Little Mouse approached the camel, her heart pounding. With her two paws she seized the reins, and to her great astonishment, Big Camel started off.

"Heavens!" cried out Little Mouse, "how strong and powerful I am now! There is no elephant on the earth who will not obey my command!"

But Big Camel laughed secretly, thinking of the good surprise that awaited Little Mouse.

Nearby was a river of deep, bobbing waters.

Big Camel saw it clearly, but Little Mouse was so small that she only saw the blades of grass that obscured the path.

But having arrived at the edge of the water, Little Mouse stopped short.

"Hey! What is this?" cried out Big Camel, "One never stops like this in the middle of the journey. Is my master uneasy about something?"

"C'est que," répondit Petite Souris, "la rivière est très profonde."

"La rivière n'est point profonde," répliqua Grand Châmeau en y plongeant ses jambes, "voyez, l'eau ne touche même pas les genoux!"

"Pour vous, grand géant," répondit Petite Souris, la rivière est peu de chose, mais pour moi c'est tout un ocean."

"Alors, jeune amie," répliqua Grand Châmeau, "s'il est une si grande différence entre nous, comment se fait-il que tu veuilles me diriger par les plaines et les déserts. Je ne vois entre nous acun rapport. Puisque tu n'es ni prophète, ni roi, ce n'est pas à toi de conduire et diriger le monde!"

Petite Souris baissa la tête très tristement.

"Grand Châmeau!" dit elle doucement, "je m'en repens, mais puisque nous sommes au bord de l'eau aie pitié et prends moi sur ton dos!"

Grand Châmeau avait très bon cœur et plein de pitié, il prit Petite Souris sur son dos.

"Je pourrais prendre mille comme toi sur mon dos," dit-il en riant.

Petite Souris arriva donc saine et sauve à l'autre rive et, après avoir remercié Grand Châmeau doucement, elle retourna au pays des petites souris et elle y vecut heureuse tout le reste de sa vie.

"It's because," Little Mouse replied, "the river is very deep."

"The river is not so deep at all," replied Big Camel, plunging his legs into it, "see, the water only comes up to my knees!"

"For you, great giant," responded Little Mouse, "the river is a small thing, but for me it's an entire ocean."

"So, my young friend," replied Big Camel, "if there is such a great difference between us, how is it that you wish to lead me through the plains and deserts? I don't see the connection between us. Since you are neither a prophet nor a king, it's not up to you to guide and rule the world!"

Little Mouse very sadly bowed her head.

"Big Camel!" she said softly, "I repent my action, but since we are on the bank of the water, have pity and take me upon your back!"

Big Camel was very good-hearted and, filled with pity, he took Little Mouse upon his back.

"I can carry a thousand like you on my back," he said laughingly.

Little Mouse thus arrived safe and sound on the other side of the river, and after having politely thanked Big Camel, she returned to the land of little mice, and she lived there happily for the rest of her life.

Le pantalon de Victor Hugo

VICTOR HUGO était alors tout petit et comme les garçons de son âge, il avait le caprice de jouer à la guerre. Le champ de bataille était le jardin de leur maison au no. 12 de L'Impasse des Feuillantines à Paris. La place forte était la niche des lapins. C'est là que le jeune commandant Victor se défendait contre son frère Abel, l'ennemi qui assiégeait les remparts de la niche. Tout cela se faisait à coups de bâtons qu'ils trouvaient en déracinant les échalas.

La bataille terminée, les pantalons étaient toujours très bien arrangés et Madame Hugo était bien ennuyée de tous ces lambeaux.

"Il faut des pantalons de cuir à ces enfants-là. Ils auront honte de les porter, mais cela leur apprendrait," pensa-t-elle. Et appelant les deux gamins:

"Mes enfants," leur dit-elle, "si une fois de plus vous déchirez vos pantalons, je vous en ferai en cuir comme aux dragons!"

Bien forte fut la menace et à partir de ce jour les pantalons ne furent plus en lambeaux.

Mais un jour lorsque Victor retournait de l'ecole, un régiment tout orné d'or passa par les rues.

Victor Hugo's Pants

VICTOR HUGO, the famous writer, was once little and, like boys his age, he liked to play war games. The battlefield was the garden of his house at Number 12 on the Alley of the Feuillantines, in Paris. The fort was the rabbit hutch. It was there that the young commander Victor defended himself against his brother Abel, the enemy who besieged the ramparts of the hutch. All this was done with the blows of staffs that they obtained by uprooting the poles that supported hop vines.

When the battle ended, their pants were always torn, and Madame Hugo was very annoyed with all these rags.

"Leather pants are what these children need. They will be ashamed to wear them, but it will serve them right," she thought. And calling the two little imps:

"My children," she said to them, "if you tear your pants one more time, I will make you some leather pants like the ones dragons wear!"

This was a strong threat, so, from that day on, the boys' pants were no longer in rags.

But one day when Victor was returning home from school, a regiment of mounted soldiers resplendent in gold trim passed through the streets.

"Qu'est-ce que c'est?" demanda Victor, "les uniformes sont si beaux!"

"C'est le Régiment des Dragons," répondit la bonne.

Ce soir-là Victor était silencieux comme une souris. Sa maman le chercha partout, il était introuvable. Après bien des recherches, elle le retrouva caché dans un petit coin du jardin, bien tranquillement avec un couteau en train de percer son pantalon.

"Et qu'est-ce que tu fais là?" s'écria la maman.

"Tu m'as dit," répondit Victor, "que si je déchirais mon pantalon, j'en aurais comme les dragons."

"Et alors?" demanda-t-elle.

"Eh bien," répliqua Victor, "c'est que j'ai vu les dragons et je tiens à avoir un pantalon comme eux!"

Dragoon
In French: Dragon

Victor Hugo's Pants

"What is this?" asked Victor, "These uniforms are so handsome!"

"It's the Regiment of Dragoons," replied the maid.

That evening Victor was as silent as a mouse. His mother searched for him everywhere, but he was not to be found. After searching again, she found him hidden in a little corner of the garden, quietly piercing his pants with a knife.

"And what are you doing?" cried his mother.

"You told me," replied Victor, "that if I tore my pants, I would have ones like dragons wear."

"And so?" she demanded.

"Good," replied Victor, "because I have seen the dragons and I want to have pants like theirs!"

Dragon
In French: Dragon

Le petit bâteau magique

"SHHH ... shhh ..." disaient un jour les petites vagues. Le petit Shikao avait laissé sa pelle sur le beau sable d'argent.

"Fée Blanche tarde aujourd'hui," pensait Shikao. "Pourquoi ne vient-elle pas? Il y a beaucoup de gouttes d'argent sur les vagues."

Soudain une vague énorme, bien plus haute que toutes les autres, s'abattit sur le rivage et au-dessus des gouttes d'argent apparut la fée Blanche.

Fée Blanche était la fée de l'écume et chaque matin, lorsque personne n'était encore sur la plage, elle venait jouer avec Shikao. Ils s'ammusaient à faire briller les coquilles, à sauter dans l'eau et à attraper les rayons de soleil.

Mais ce matin-là, Fée Blanche avait deux petites larmes aux yeux.

"Qu'y a-t-il, petite Fée?" demanda Shikao.

"Je dois te quitter, petit ami," dit Fée Blanche; "je dois aller très loin, tout à l'autre bout de la terre, mais je te laisse ce petit bâteau d'argent. Garde le toujours et nul danger ne pourra t'atteindre; tu seras toujours heureux."

A ces mots Fée Blanche disparut dans l'écume et Shikao ne la vit plus jamais. Mais près de lui sur le sable d'argent était un tout petit bâteau d'argent; il n'était pas plus grand qu'une coquille.

The Little Magic Boat

"SHHH … shhh …" said the little waves one day.

Little Shikao left his shovel on the beautiful silver sand.

"White Fairy is late today," thought Shikao. "Why doesn't she come? There are so many silver droplets on the waves."

Suddenly an enormous wave, much higher than all the others, threw itself onto the beach, and above the silver droplets appeared the White Fairy.

The White Fairy was the fairy of sea foam and, each morning, when no one was at the beach, she came to play with Shikao. They amused themselves by polishing the sea shells, leaping in the water, and catching the rays of the sun.

But this morning, White Fairy had two little tears in her eyes.

"What's the matter, little Fairy?" asked Shikao.

"I must leave you, my little friend," said the White Fairy, "I must go far away, to the other side of the Earth, but I am leaving this little silver boat for you. Guard it always, and no danger will be able to harm you; you will always be happy."

At these words, White Fairy disappeared in the sea foam, and Shikao never saw her again. But beside him on the silver sand was the tiniest little silver boat. It was no larger than a sea shell.

Vite, vite il courut le montrer à sa petite Maman, et à ses deux petits amis, Mikou le petit chien, et Kiki le petit chat.

Petite Maman en fut bien heureuse. Mikou remua la queue et Miki cligna des yeux. Bien des mois heureux se passèrent ainsi.

Mais un jour Shikao fut bien malade.

Petite Maman chercha partout le bâteau d'argent. Il était introuvable. De grosses larmes coulaient des yeux de Petite Maman et Kikou et Miki soupiraient an coin du feu.

"J'ai une idée!" s'écria soudain Mikou. "C'est sûrement Grand Ogre qui l'à volé. Il nous faudra le trouver à l'instant même, car notre petit maître est bien malade!"

La fourrure de Miki se dressa tout droit sur son dos quand il entendit prononcer le nom de Grand Ogre, mais bravement il se leva et suivit le gros Mikou. Et ils s'en allèrent tous deux, trottinant.

Ils rencontrèrent bientôt Petit Rat.

"Où allez-vous?" demanda-t-il.

"Nous allons chez Grand Ogre!" répondirent Mikou et Miki. Et ils lui racontèrent tout l'histoire.

"Je vais vous aider!" dit Petit-Rat; "Faites seulement ce que je veus dirai: Pendant que je serai dans le palais de Grand Ogre, restez tous les deux à la porte et criez très fort jusqu'á ce que je revienne!"

Ils arrivèrent chez Grand Ogre et Petit Rat s'enfuit dans le palais tandis que Mikou et Miki crièrent si fort qu'on aurait dit que mille grands ogres hurlaient à la fois.

"Très bien!" dit Petit Rat en sortant du palais. "Au premier cri Grand Ogre a regardé dans sa manche, c'est donc que le petit bâteau y est. Maintenant, je vais vous transformer en petite fille et petit garcon. Vous entrerez dans le palais et demanderez à danser pour Grand Ogre, mais surtout ne vous arrêtez pas de dancer avant que je ne sois sorti du palais!"

Mikou et Miki, transformés en petit garcon et petite fille, allèrent dancer devant Grand Ogre.

The Little Magic Boat

Quickly, quickly, he ran to show it to his little Mother and his two little friends, Mikou, the little dog, and Miki, the little cat.

Little Mother was very happy. Mikou wagged his tail and Miki blinked her eyes. Many happy months passed by.

But one day Shikao was very ill.

Little Mother looked everywhere for the silver boat. It could not be found. Large tears flowed from Little Mother's eyes, and Mikou and Miki sighed in the corner by the fire.

"I have an idea!" Mikou suddenly cried. "Great Ogre has surely stolen it. We must find it right away, because our little master is very ill!"

Miki's fur rose up on her back at the sound of Great Ogre's name, but she bravely rose and followed Mikou. And they went trotting off together.

They soon met Little Rat.

"Where are you going?" he asked.

"We are going to the home of Great Ogre!" replied Mikou and Miki. And they told him the whole story.

"I am going to help you!" said Little Rat. "Do exactly as I tell you. When I am inside Great Ogre's palace, both of you stay at the door and shout very loudly until I return!"

They arrived at the home of Great Ogre, and Little Rat ran into the palace, while Mikou and Miki shouted so loudly that one would have said a thousand great ogres were roaring together.

"Very good!" said Little Rat as he came out of the palace. "At the first shout, Great Ogre looked inside his sleeve, so that is where he keeps the little boat. Now I am going to turn you into a little girl and a little boy. You shall enter the palace and ask to dance for Great Ogre, but above all, don't stop dancing before I have left the palace."

Mikou and Miki, now changed into a little boy and a little girl, went to dance before Great Ogre.

Le petit bâteau magique

Le monstre les reçut de bon gré car il avait eu bien des cauchemars à entendre ces cris dehors; et la venue de deux gentils danseurs lui faisait bien plaisir.

Petit Rat s'était accroché aux plis de la robe de Mikou et lorsque Grand Ogre ne s'en doutait point, il se faufila dans sa manche, enleva le petit bâteau, et fila tout droit hors du palais.

Au même instant Mikou et Miki disparurent. Grand Ogre ne vit plus que deux petites queues s'esquiver par la porte.

Ils retournèrent tous trois portant le petit bâteau, et Shikao, leur gentil petit maître, fut guéri au même instant. Il joua de nouveau avec Mikou, Miki et Petit Rat et ils vécurent toujours heureux.

The Little Magic Boat

The monster received them willingly, because he had been having many nightmares since hearing the shouts outside his palace, and the arrival of two nice dancers made him very happy.

Little Rat hid himself among the folds of Mikou's robe, and when Great Ogre least suspected, Little Rat crept inside Great Ogre's sleeve, grabbed the little boat, and quickly rushed outside the palace.

At the same moment, Mikou and Miki disappeared. Great Ogre saw nothing more than two little tails slipping through the door.

All three returned carrying the little boat, and Shikao, their good little master, was instantly cured. Once again he played with Mikou, Miki and Little Rat, and they lived happily ever after.

Le paysan et le tigre

QUELS sont ces cris? Qu'est-ce donc qui souffre tant à la lisière de la forêt?"

Ainsi songeait un vieux paysan qui marchait près des bois. Bien que ses pauvres pieds fussent las de marcher, il se précipita, le cœur plein de pitié, vers le lieu d'où venaient les appels.

"Non, ce n'est pas un homme!" pensa-t-il tout en courant.

Qu'était donc cette forme qui tournoyait derrière ces étranges barreaux?

"Oh! C'est un tigre pris dans un piège! Pauvre animal!" s'écria le paysan. "Quel sort cruel t'a conduit ici? Ne savais-tu pas qu'en entrant dans cette cage tu ne pourrais plus jamais en sortir? Pauvre tigre, il se peut bien que des petits t'attendent dans la forêt! Je vais ouvrir la porte et tu pourras courir de nouveau!"

Le paysan ouvrit le verrou et laissa sortir l'animal féroce.

"Tu es à moi maintenant!" s'écria le tigre. "Et dans peu de temps tu seras dévoré!"

"Je t'ai donné la vie," répondit le paysan en tombant à genou. "Si je n'avais pas ouvert la porte tu serais encore enfermé. Comment peux-tu donc être si cruel après que je t'ai libéré?"

"C'est vrai," répondit le tigre, "tu as été très bon pour moi. Je te laisse vivre, mais à une condition: c'est que tu demandes

The Peasant and the Tiger

"WHAT are these cries? Who is suffering at the edge of the forest?"

So thought an old peasant who was walking near the woods. Even though his poor feet ached from walking, he hurried along toward the cries, his heart filled with compassion.

"No, this is not a man!" thought he while running.

Then what was that shape turning in circles behind those strange bars?

"Oh! This is a tiger captured in a cage! Poor animal!' cried the peasant. "What cruel fate led you here? Didn't you know, when entering this cage, that you would never be able to get out again? Poor tiger, it may well be that little ones are waiting for you in the forest! I am going to open the door and you will be able to run again!'

The peasant opened the lock and released the fierce animal.

"Now you are mine!" cried the tiger. "And in a short while you will be eaten up!"

"I have given you life," replied the peasant, falling to his knees. "If I hadn't opened the door you would still be locked up. So how can you be so cruel after I have freed you?"

"That's true," responded the tiger. "You have been very good to me. I will let you live, but on one condition: that you

aux trois premiers êtres que tu rencontreras 'qui est le plus cruel, l'homme ou l'animal?' Si parmi les trois, l'un répond que l'animal est le plus cruel, je te laisserai vivre. Mais si tous disent que l'homme est le plus cruel, eh bien, mon cher, tu seras dévoré!"

Le pauvre paysan partit donc, le tigre à son côté, à la rencontre des trois premiers êtres qui seraient sur le chemin. D'abord ils demandèrent à un arbre:

"O! Arbre, roi de la nature, dis-nous qui est le plus cruel, l'homme ou l'animal?"

"Ah!" répondit l'Arbre, en agitant avec rage son feuillage sublime, "qui donc croyez-vous est le plus cruel? Nous, qui étendons éternellement nos bras pour protéger l'homme des rayons brûlants du soleil et lui donner le repos, nous, qui portons pour lui les fruits dont il se nourrit, que recevons-nous en retour? La hache à la main, l'homme vient nous abattre et nos pauvres troncs meurtris tombent à la terre. Non! Aucun animal n'est plus cruel que l'homme!"

Le pauvre paysan, le cœur tremblant, poursuivit son chemin, le tigre à son côté. Bientôt ils rencontrèrent une vache et en s'approchant, le paysan lui dit:

"Ma bonne amie, dis-moi qui est le plus cruel, l'homme ou l'animal?"

"Ne me parle pas de l'homme!" répliqua la vache. "Nous qui lui donnons le lait que nos petits devraient recevoir, lorsque nous vieillissons et ne pouvons plus en donner, au lieu de nous laisser vivre en paix nos dernières années, il vient nous abattre et nous tuer après tout ce que nous lui avons donné. Ah! Non, ne me parle pas de l'homme!"

"Nous verrons ce que dira le troisième," dit le tigre. Et bientôt ils rencontrèrent un renard qui courait derrière les buissons.

Sire Renard réfléchit un instant, puis demanda: "pourquoi me demandes-tu cela?"

Le paysan lui expliqua qu'il avait trouvé le tigre enfermé dans une cage, qu'il lui avait ouvert la porte, et qu'après, le tigre

The Peasant and the Tiger

ask the first three beings you meet 'who is the most cruel, man or animal?' If among these three, one answers that animal is the cruelest, I will let you live. But if all of them say that man is the most cruel, well then, my dear, you will be eaten up."

The poor peasant then set off, the tiger at his side, to meet the first three beings on the road. Accordingly they questioned a tree.

"O! Tree, king of nature, tell us who is more cruel, man or animal?"

"Ah!" replied the Tree, angrily shaking his lofty foliage. "Who then do you believe is the most cruel? We who eternally extend our arms to protect man from the scorching rays of the sun and give him rest, we who bear fruits to nourish him, what do we receive in return? Axe in hand, man comes to cut us down, and our poor trunks fall murdered to the earth. No! No animal is more cruel than man."

The poor peasant, his heart trembling, followed the road, the tiger at his side. Soon they met a cow, and drawing near, the peasant said to him:

"My good friend, tell me who is more cruel, man or animal?"

"Don't speak to me of man!" replied the cow. "We who give him the milk that our little calves should be drinking, when we grow old and are no longer able to provide it, instead of letting us live out our last years in peace, he comes to strike us down and we are killed, after all that we have given. Ah! No, don't speak to me of man!"

"We shall see what the third one will say," said the tiger. And soon they met a fox who was running behind the bushes.

Sir Renard the Fox thought for a minute, then asked: "Why do you ask me that?"

The peasant explained that he had found the tiger locked in a cage, that he had opened the door, and that afterwards the tiger wanted to eat him. But the tiger promised to let him live

voulut le dévorer. Mais qu'il promit de le laisser vivre si parmi trois êtres qu'il rencontrerait sur son chemin, l'un répondrait que l'animal est le plus cruel.

Le renard agita sa queue et prenant l'air bien confus il dit: "Qu'est-ce qu'une trappe? Montrez-moi ce que c'est!"

Le tigre et le paysan accompagnèrent le renard jusqu'à la cage.

Sire Renard fit deux ou trois petits tours, puis il dit: "Je ne comprends pas comment cela c'est passé, comment était mon frère tigre dans la cage? Montrez-moi comment il était."

Sire Tigre, tout fier, rentra dans la cage.

"Et comment était la porte?" demanda le renard.

Le paysan ferma la porte et lui montra qu'elle était ainsi.

Sire Renard poursuivit: "Mais comment? Mon frère tigre aurait pu sortir de là; n'y avait-il pas autre chose sur la porte pour la fermer?"

"Si, le verrou," répliqua le paysan.

"Montrez-moi," dit le renard "comment donc le verrou fermait la porte." Le paysan ferma le verrou et aussitôt sire Renard partit d'un éclat de rire qui retentit dans toute la forêt.

"Voilà mon cher frère tigre," dit-il, "essaye de sortir maintenant, cela t'apprendra à tuer ceux qui te donnent la vie. Adieu, amuses-toi bien!"

Et après avoir remercié le renard, le bon vieux paysan poursuivit son chemin vers le village.

The Peasant and the Tiger

if one of the three beings they met on the road would answer that animal was more cruel.

The fox waved his tail, and adopting a confused manner, said: "What is a cage? Show me what this is!"

The tiger and the peasant accompanied the fox to the cage.

Sir Renard circled around it two or three times, and then he said: "I don't understand how this happened; how did my brother tiger get into the cage? Show me how this happened."

Sir Tiger proudly reentered the cage.

"And how was the door?" asked the fox.

The peasant closed the door and showed him how it was just so.

Sir Renard followed this with: "But how? My brother tiger would be able to get out of that; isn't there something else on the door to fasten it?"

"Yes, the lock," replied the peasant.

"Show me," said the fox, "how the lock fastens the door."

The peasant fastened the lock, and then Sir Renard let loose a burst of laughter that rang through the whole forest.

"And so my dear brother tiger," said he, "try to get out now. This will teach you to kill those who give you life. Farewell, and enjoy yourself!"

And after having thanked the fox, the good old peasant continued his journey to the village.

La violette

Modeste ainsi qu'honnête,
Jolie petite violette,
Qui jette son beau parfum
Dans mon petit jardin.

Elle porte son beau bonnet,
Bleu ou blanc de lait.
Je ne sais quel destin,
L'a mit dans mon jardin

The Violet

Modest and demur,
Pretty little violet,
Casting its beautiful scent
In my little garden.

She wears her becoming bonnet,
Blue or milky white.
I know not what destiny
Placed her here in my garden.

La nuit

Dès que fatigué, monsieur le Soleil,
A fini sa tâche et s'est mis au sommeil,
Madame la lune riante se réveille,
De sa clarté douce,
Elle argente la mousse,
Et les arbres au bord de chemin.

Tout là-haut dans le ciel elle veille
Tandis qu'autour d'elle scintillent
Comme des diamants ses fils et ses filles,
Les fleurettes s'endorment,
Tranquilles jusqu'à l'aurore,
Et les hiboux pleurent dans le mystère.

The Night

With weariness, Mister Sun
Completes his task and falls asleep.
Mistress Moon awakens, laughing;
With her gentle light
She silvers the moss
And the trees along the road.

High in the sky she keeps watch,
While all around, her sons and daughters
Sparkle like diamonds.
The little flowers sleep,
Peaceful until dawn;
And owls cry out in the mystery.

Les mystères de la nature

Que dis-tu joli ruisseau,
Dans ce vallon paisible et doux?
Je chante le roman de l'eau;
Qui de sa source, coule jusqu'au bout.

Que fais-tu joli nuage,
Dan l'azur pur que tu traverses?
Je cours, et dans le rivage,
Je me mire, après une averse.

Oh! charmant bouton de rose,
Que gardes-tu ce jour d'été?
Mes belles mains à peine écloses,
Gardent le secret de ma beauté.

Dis-moi petite pensée,
Que penses-tu dans cette verdure?
Je songe à mon cher passé,
Je rêve de mon joyeux futur.

Nature's Mysteries

What are you saying, pretty stream,
In this peaceful, sweet valley?
I sing the story of the water,
Flowing from its source until the end.

What are you doing, pretty cloud,
In the pure azure through which you pass?
I hurry along, and after the downpour,
I see my reflection in the pools.

Oh! charming rosebud,
What do you guard this summer's day?
My lovely hands, barely budding,
Guard the secret of my beauty.

Tell me, little pansy,
What are you thinking amidst these green leaves?
I muse on my cherished past,
I dream of my joy-filled future.

Sweet Peas

Oh! flowers of my sweetest dream,
In you alone does beauty gleam;
Fairies of an enchanting sphere,
Whisper your secret in my ear.
Sweet peas, who has, with so much skill,
Painted your wings that shiver still?
Such sweet perfume as you exhale,
To produce it, who would not fail?
Treasures of love and purity,
You move my soul to ecstasy.
Like butterflies of distant lands,
What do you hold between your hands?
When morn comes with pure white laces,
Pearls adorn your blushing faces.
Oh! flowers of my sweetest dream,
In you alone does beauty gleam.

English original by Noor Inayat Khan

Four Stories for Christmas

Boule de neige

CRICK — CRACK faisaient les branches, quand le vent glacé soufflait.

Brrr ... qu'il faisait froid! Mais le soir était doré. C'etait la veille de Noël.

Père et Mère marchaient lentement dans la neige, la tête baissée.

Combien de petites lumières sortaient par les fenêtres du village! Tous les carreaux en reflètaient. Sur les branches de sapins, on ne voyait plus que chandelles, fils d'or et fils d'argent. Rien n'existait plus au village sinon les sapins, les poulets et les petits enfants.

Mais Père et Mère marchaient tristement dans la neige, la tête baissée.

Demain ce serait Noël!

"C'est pour moi la toupie! Pour moi la poupée!" Ainsi criaient de petites voix dans les huttes de bois.

Mais Père et Mère ne se regardèrent pas, de peur de pleurer. Inutile de faire un sapin dans leur hutte à eux. Ni le Bon Dieu, ni Père Noël ne leurs avait jamais apporté de petits enfants.

Toutes les mamans et tous les papas du village avaient des petits enfants. Pourquoi n'en avaient-ils pas, eux aussi, un tout

Snowball

CRICK — CRACK, sounded the branches, when the icy wind blew.

Brrr… it was so cold! But the evening was golden. It was Christmas Eve.

Father and Mother walked slowly in the snow, with bowed heads.

How many little lights shone through the windows of the village! They were reflected in all the panes. On the branches of the spruce trees one saw nothing but candles and strings of gold and silver. In the village, there was nothing but the spruce trees, the chickens, and the little children.

But Father and Mother walked sadly in the snow, with bowed heads.

Tomorrow would be Christmas Day!

"The spinning top is for me! The doll is for me!" shouted the little voices in the wooden huts.

But Father and Mother did not look at them, for fear of crying. It was useless to decorate a spruce tree in their hut for themselves. Neither dear God nor Father Christmas had ever brought them little children.

All the mothers and all the fathers of the village had little children. Why didn't they have any themselves? At least one

rond qui pleurait quelquefois et riait à d'autres, qui aimerait les bonbons et les arbres de Noël?

Ainsi songeaient Père et Mère marchant lentement dans la neige.

"Faut pas être triste," dit soudain Père, "On en fera un, nous, un petit bonhomme, un tout rond, tout blanc pour fêter Noël. Tiens, prends de la neige …"

Et heureux comme des gamins et des gamines, ils firent un petit bonhomme de neige.

"Il aura de grands yeux noirs comme Père," disait Mère, "et si c'est une petite fille elle aura de beaux yeux bleus comme la fille de la voisine."

A ces mots Père et Mère regardèrent abasourdis.

O! merveille! Le bonhomme de neige leur souriait et de blondes boucles lui couvrirent soudain la tête. C'était une petite fille ravissante, aux beaux yeux bleus comme ceux de Mère!

Ils n'osèrent pas la toucher. Elle était trop douce, trop tendre, telle que les petits bébés tout neufs que le Bon Dieu apportait.

Mais Père et Mère commencèrent à penser:

"Etait-ce la petite de Fée Neige? Où était-ce bien leur petite à eux? Dormaient-ils? Revaient-ils? Que faire? Qui remercier? Pourquoi donc une petite fille si jolie, pour eux? L'avaient-ils vraiment meritée? Fallait-il la prendre chez eux, dans leur pauvre petite cabane de bois?"

"Non, c'est trop beau, trop joli!" balbutia Mère, les yeux remplis de larmes.

Mais l'enfant neige lui tendit ses tout petits bras et se mit à pleurer comme tous les petits qui viennent au monde. Mère la pressa dans ses bras si doucement et lui sourit si joyeusement que les yeux bleus de l'enfant Neige rayonnaient comme les bougies sur les sapins.

Ils se pressèrent vers la cabane et portèrent la petite fille dans leurs bras.

Snowball

little plump one who sometimes cried and other times laughed; who loved candy and Christmas trees?

Thus pondered Father and Mother, walking slowly in the snow.

"We shouldn't be sad," said Father suddenly, "We can make a little fellow, all round and white, to celebrate Christmas. Here, take some snow…"

And happily, like the little boys and girls of the streets, they made a small snow child.

"He will have big black eyes like Father," said Mother, "and if it's a little girl she will have beautiful blue eyes like our neighbor's daughter."

At these words, Father and Mother looked amazed.

O! How marvelous! The snow child smiled at them, and blond curls suddenly covered its head. It was a delightful little girl, with beautiful blue eyes like Mother's.

They didn't dare touch her. She was too sweet, too tender, like the little newborn babies which were brought by dear God.

But Father and Mother began to think:

"Could this be the little daughter of the Snow Fairy? Or was it really theirs? Were they asleep? Were they dreaming? What should they do? Who could be thanked? Why such a pretty little daughter for them? Did they truly deserve this? Should they take her to their home, into their poor little wooden cabin?"

"No, she is too good, too pretty," cried Mother, her eyes full of tears.

But the snow child reached out both little arms and began to cry, just like all little children who come into the world. Mother held her in her arms so gently, and she smiled so joyously, that the blue eyes of the snow child shone like the candles on the spruce trees.

They hurried to their cabin and carried their little daughter in their arms.

Boule de neige

"Comment l'appelerons—nous?" demanda Père quand ils entrèrent chez eux et s'assirent près du feu pour se réchauffer.

"Boule de Neige," répondit Mère.

"Neige!" s'écria Père, "Notre petite fille est en neige! Et elle fondra ici au chaud!"

Mais la petite Boule de Neige ne fondait point. La chaude lueur du feu avait chauffé son coeur et le sang coulait dans ses veines car Boule de Neige n'était plus de la neige mais transformée en chair et en os comme tous les autres petits enfants.

Père et Mère firent un beau sapin scintillant de mille lumières qui se reflètaient dans leurs yeux et dans ceux de 'Boule de Neige.' Père Noël apporta des cadeaux à la petite fille et ils vécurent tous heureux jusqu'à la fin de leurs jours.

Snowball

"What shall we name her?" asked Father, when they entered their home and sat next to the fire to warm themselves.

"Snowball," answered Mother.

"Snow!" cried Father. "Our little daughter is made of snow! And she will melt here in the heat!"

But little Snowball did not melt. The glowing heat of the fire had warmed her heart and the blood flowed in her veins, because Snowball was no longer made of snow but was transformed into flesh and bones like all the other little children.

Father and Mother set up a nice Christmas tree, sparkling with a thousand lights which were reflected in their eyes and in the eyes of Snowball. Father Christmas brought presents to their little daughter, and they lived happily to the end of their days.

Père Noël qui n'était pas venu

TOUT le monde est occupé au moment de Noël, Maman, Papa et même les petits enfants, mais personne n'est occupé autant que le Père Noël. Il doit passer dans toutes les maisons, chez tous les petits enfants du monde, non seulement dans les villes mais aussi dans les villages, et même dans ces petit villages là-haut dans les montagnes car là aussi l'on attend ses cadeaux.

Il y avait, très haut dans les montagnes lointaines, une toute petite cabane où beaucoup de petits enfants l'attendaient. Pauvre Père Noël, son grand sac sur le dos, escaladait péniblement les rochers où sifflait le vent glacé. Il avait déjà fait le tour du monde et il était très fatigué. Et puis, it faisait noir et de grands précipices s'étendaient au bord du chemin. La neige était haute de trois mètres et Père Noël se mit à trembler. Mais soudain une petite cloche retentit derrière lui. Un gros bonhomme montait la côte dans un traineau qu'un bon petit cheval blanc tirait lentement dans la neige.

"Bonsoir Père Noël," s'écria le gros bonhomme, "viens dans mon traineau, nous pourrons aller aussi loin que le cheval nous conduira."

Père Noël monta dans le traineau et le petit cheval, malgré la neige, se fit un chemin. Mais la montagne montait toute

When Father Christmas Didn't Come

EVERYONE is busy at Christmastime, Mama, Papa, and the little children too, but no one is as busy as Father Christmas. He must visit all the houses, the homes of all the little children in the world, not only in the cities but also in the villages, and also in the little villages high in the mountains, because there, too, the children await his presents.

There was, very high in the faraway mountains, the tiniest little cabin where many little children waited.

Poor Father Christmas, his large sack on his back, painfully climbed up the high rocks where the icy wind whistled. He had already made his journey around the world and he was very tired. And then it grew dark, and great precipices fell away from the edge of the road. The snow was ten feet deep, and Father Christmas began to shiver.

But suddenly a little bell rang behind him. A great big man was climbing the slope, mounted on a sleigh which a nice little white horse pulled slowly through the snow.

"Good evening, Father Christmas," cried the great big man, "come into my sleigh, we can go as far as the horse can take us."

Father Christmas climbed into the sleigh, and the little horse, in spite of the snow, made good progress on the road.

Père Noël qui n'était pas venu

droite et le petit cheval blanc ne put aller plus loin. Le gros bonhomme mit son petit cheval dans une ferme, attacha ses raquettes et dit au Père Noël:

"J'ai encore une heure de route à faire, je n'ai pas vu mes enfants depuis cinq ans car j'ai été loin, très loin chercher de l'or. Et ce soir je retourne chez moi chargé de richesses et de cadeaux. J'ai hâte, bien hâte de les revoir. Mais, où vas-tu Père Noël?"

"Je doit remettre ces derniers cadeaux aux enfants qui habitent la cabane en haut de cette montagne," dit le Père Noël. "Mais je crains ne pas pouvoir y aller."

"C'est justement à ma cabane que tu désires aller!" s'exclama le gros bonhomme. "Et ce sont mes enfants à qui tu veux donner ces cadeaux!"

Tous les petits enfants attendaient patiemment la venue de Père Noël dans leur petite cabane en haut de la montagne.

Maman leur dit "Comme c'est triste un Noël sans Papa! Ça fait plus de cinq ans qu'il est parti, et chaque Noël j'espère qu'il reviendra et restera avec nous."

Les petits enfants furent tristes eux aussi quand ils se souvenaient de leur Papa.

Soudain ils entendirent frapper à la porte. Avant qu'ils eussent même pu ouvrir, un gros bonhomme se tenait à l'entrée. Il était vêtu d'un long manteau rouge avec un col en hermine et un grand bonnet rouge. Il souriait à travers sa grande barbe blanche tandis qu'il posait son grand sac par terre.

"Bonsoir Père Noël!" s'écrièrent les enfants tous à la fois.

"Bonsoir les enfants!" dit le monsieur. "Ceci est pour vous!" Et il leur tendit le grand sac remplit de jouets.

Tout à coup le monsieur retira son bonnet, son manteau rouge, sa longue barbe, et ...

"Papa! Papa!" crièrent les enfants.

"Papa!" cria Maman.

When Father Christmas Didn't Come

But the mountain climbed straight up, and the little white horse could go no further.

The great big man tethered his little horse at a farmhouse, put on his snow shoes, and said to Father Christmas: "I have still one hour to travel. I have not seen my children for five years because I have been far away, very far away, looking for gold. And this evening I return to my home bearing riches and presents. I am eager, very eager to see them again. But where are you going, Father Christmas?"

"I must deliver these last presents to children who live in the cabin at the top of this mountain," said Father Christmas. "But I am afraid I won't be able to reach it."

"That's exactly my cabin that you want to go to!" exclaimed the great big man. "And those are my children that you want give presents to!"

All the little children were waiting patiently for the arrival of Father Christmas in their little cabin on top of the mountain.

Mama told them, "How sad Christmas is without Papa! It's been more than five years since he left, and each Christmas I hope that he will return and remain with us."

The little children also became sad when they remembered their Papa.

Suddenly they heard a knock on the door.

Before they could open it themselves, a great big man let himself inside. He was clothed in a long red cloak with a collar of ermine, and a large red cap. He smiled through his great white beard while he rested his large sack on the ground.

"Good evening, Father Christmas!" cried the children, all at the same time.

"Good evening children!" said the man. "These are for you!" And he gave them the large sack filled with toys.

Suddenly the man pulled off his cap, his red cloak, his long beard, and …

"Papa! Papa!" cried the children.

"Papa!" cried Mama.

"Comme je suis content de vous revoir mes enfants! Père Noël ne pouvait pas venir car il n'avait pas de raquettes pour marcher sur la neige, alors il m'a confié ses cadeaux pour vous les donner ainsi que son costume de rechange pour vous faire cette surprise!"

Ils s'embrassèrent tous, heureux de se retrouver, et ils vécurent heureux ensemble pendant de nombreuses années. Les enfants n'oublièrent jamais ce Noël là, lorsque 'le Père Noël n'était pas venu!'

Father Christmas Didn't Come

"How happy I am to see you again, my children! Father Christmas couldn't come because he didn't have snow shoes to walk over the snow, so he entrusted the delivery of your presents to me along with his spare outfit to give you this surprise!"

They all embraced each other, happy to be together again, and they lived happily together for many years. The children never forgot that Christmas, when Father Christmas didn't come!

Noël chez les trolls

Dans une petite vallée dans les hauteurs des montagnes se trouvait une petite hutte en bois isolée où habitaient Pierre et Anne-Marie avec leurs parents. Chaque jour les deux petits montaient dans les hauteurs pour y jouer.

"Comment oses-tu laisser jouer les enfants tout seuls là-haut?" demandaient les amis en visite chez la mère. "Les trolls pourraient bien les enlever!"

"Mais non," répondit la mère, "ils ont assez à faire avec leurs propres petits, j'en suis sûre!"

Pierre et Anne-Marie en riait aussi: "Les trolls! Nous n'en avons pas peur! Ils sont bien gentils tant qu'on est aimable envers eux."

Puis un jour—c'était la veille de Noël—tandis qu'il jouaient dans les bois les enfants entendirent soudain un formidable fracas venant des hautes montagne provenant de la montagne. Quelqu'un faisait un bruit de tonnerre dans la montagne-même et l'on pouvait facilement deviner que c'était Grand Troll lui-même qui en était la cause.

"Peux-tu entendre ce qu'il dit?" demanda Pierre.

"Viens vite par ici et reste tranquille. Voici une fente dans la roche d'où on entendra bien ce qui se passe!" proposa Anne-Marie.

A Troll's Christmas

In a small valley in the high mountains Pierre and Anne-Marie lived with their parents in a small wooden house. Every day the children climbed up into the high mountain forest to play there.

"How can you possibly let the children play up there all alone?" asked their mother's friends when visiting. "The trolls could easily kidnap them!"

"No, of course not!" replied their mother. "The trolls have enough on their hands with caring for their own children, I am sure of that!"

Pierre and Anne-Marie also laughed at the idea: "The trolls! They don't frighten us! They don't bother you if you stay out of their way."

Then one day—it was Christmas Eve—the children were playing in the woods when they suddenly heard a terrible raucous coming from higher up in the mountains. Someone was making a tremendous commotion inside the mountain itself and they easily guessed that the source of this noise must be Big Troll himself.

Pierre asked his sister, "Can you hear what he is saying?"

"Come this way quickly and stay quiet," suggested Anne-Marie. "There is a crack in the rock through which we can better hear what is happening."

Noël chez les trolls

Les enfants avaient si souvent joué dans les hauteurs et régulièrement entendu parler les trolls à l'intérieur de la montagne, qu'ils arrivaient à comprendre leur langue.

C'était bien Grand Troll qui s'était fâché et qui grondait : "Non, j'ai dit!" cria-t-il en frappant la table d'un tel coup de poing qu'elle s'écroula. "Je ne veux point que vous apportiez de ces sottes nouveautés ici dans notre montagne!"

"Mais, Papa, Noël n'arrive qu'une fois par an," supplièrent les petits trolls en larmes.

"Ça, je le sais bien!" hurla de nouveau Grand Troll, "Ici dans la montagne nous avons déjà fêté Noël depuis des siècles. Nous invitons tous les trolls du voisinage, ainsi que les gobelins, les fées et les gnomes à fêter un Noël traditionnel. Et maintenant vous venez ici et…."

"Mais il faut suivre le cours du temps."

"Cela, je le sais bien!" interrompit la mère troll en continuant à faire sa cuisine. La nourriture commençait à sentir un peu le brulé, ce qui n'était pas bien étonnant vu le fait que son mari était tellement fâché qu'il crachait du feu de tous côtés.

"Suivre le cours du temps! Ma barbe! Je n'ai jamais entendu de telles bêtises! Cela ne suffit peut-être pas que vous receviez vos marmites pleines de vos petits cochons bien gras, ainsi que tant de bière que vous puissiez avaler? Vous ne jugez pas assez amusant d'entendre chanter les gnomes et jouer au violon les nains ou de voir danser les fées? Vous êtes des ingrats, vilains petits trolls!"

"Mais, Papa, pense donc: un sapin de Noël, nous le voudrions tant!"

"Un sapin de Noël!" rugit Grand Troll, "Un arbre de Noël, mon Dieu!" Sur quoi il s'élança vers le coin dans lequel s'étaient réfugiés les petits. Il leur prit par le cou et les jeta hors de la montagne.

"Regarde donc là-bas," dit Pierre à sa sœur en courant vers les deux formes brunes qui gémissaient sur le flanc de la montagne. Ça ne peut pas être de vrais petits trolls, crois-tu?"

A Trolls' Christmas

The children had so often played near the trolls and were so accustomed to overhearing them speak among themselves that they had learned to understand the language of the trolls.

It was indeed Big Troll who was angered and who thundered: "No, I say!" as his fist came crashing down on the table and smashing it to pieces. "I do not want you to bring these idiotic novelties into our mountain!"

"But Papa! Christmas comes just once a year!" begged the little trolls in tears.

"I know that!" roared Big Troll again. "Here inside the mountain we have celebrated Christmas for many centuries. We invite all the trolls of the neighborhood, as well as the goblins, gnomes and fairies to celebrate a traditional Christmas feast with us. And now you come here and want..."

"But one has to keep up with the times."

"That is true!" interrupted the troll mother as she continued to tend to the cooking. The food had begun to smell a bit burned; this was no wonder, as her husband was so angry that he was breathing fire in every direction.

"Keep up with the times! By my beard! I have never heard such nonsense! Perhaps you do not find it enough to receive your cauldrons full of tender fat piglets and as much beer as you can swallow? You don't find it entertaining enough to listen to the gnomes sing and the dwarves play the fiddle or to watch the fairies dance? You are bad, ungrateful little trolls!"

"But, Papa, just think about a Christmas tree, we would so much like to have one!"

"A Christmas tree!" screamed Big Troll again. "A Christmas tree, my God!" Upon which he sprang towards the corner where the little trolls were cowering, took them by the neck and threw them out of the mountain.

"Look over there" Pierre said to his sister as they ran towards the two brown shapes that trembled on the mountainside. "Those couldn't be real little trolls, do you think?

Anne-Marie suivit, puis tout deux s'arrêtèrent étonnés à la vue de deux drôles de petits trolls qui clignotaient des yeux à cause de la forte lumière du jour.

"Qui êtes-vous donc?" demanda Anne-Marie tout en tenant la main de Pierre comme sauvegarde.

"Nous sommes des petits trolls et nous habitons là-dedans," dirent-ils tout en montrant du doigt la pente rocheuse.

"Papa nous a chassé, imaginez-vous, seulement parce que nous lui avons demandé la permission d'avoir un arbre de Noël!"

"Mais n'avez-vous pas tous des sapins de Noël?" demandèrent les deux enfants en même temps.

"Non, nous n'en avons jamais eu, mais nous avons pensé que peut-être ça pourrait changer ce Noël-ci. Nous avons entendu parler de toutes les jolies choses qu'on fait avec un tel arbre. Nous avons demandé très gentiment à Papa mais il s'est mis en colère. Hélas! il semble que nous ne verrons jamais un arbre de Noël décoré," soupirèrent les petits trolls en larmes.

Anne-Marie chuchota quelque chose dans l'oreille de son frère et, après quelques instants d'hésitation, elle avança avec résolution vers les petits trolls et prit l'un d'eux par le bras.

"Ne pleure donc par, petit troll! dit-elle. "Si vous le voulez bien, toi et ton frère, vous pouvez très bien fêter Noël chez nous, car nous aurons un sapin de Noël bien grand et très joli. Venez-donc et vous le verrez."

Les deux petits trolls séchèrent leurs larmes de suite et regardèrent avec effroi nos deux enfants.

"Voulez-vous vraiment dire que vous voulez nous recevoir chez vous?"

"Mais oui ! Quand les cloches de l'église sonneront demain soir nous viendrons vous chercher. Vous n'avez qu'à nous attendre ici."

Les petits trolls hochèrent la tête de joie; puis Pierre et Anne-Marie se hâtèrent de rentrer chez eux et annoncèrent à leur maman qui ils venaient d'inviter pour Noël.

A Trolls' Christmas

Anne-Marie followed him over, but they stopped abruptly at the sight of the two funny little trolls who were blinking their eyes as they were unaccustomed to the bright daylight.

"Who are you?" asked Anne-Marie while holding Pierre's hand tightly for safety.

"We are little trolls and we live in there" as they pointed to the rocky mountainside.

"Our father chased us away just because we wanted permission to have a Christmas tree, can you imagine?"

"But do you not all have Christmas trees?" asked the children in unison.

"No, we have never had any but we thought that it could change this Christmas. We have heard tell of all the beautiful things one can do with such a tree. We asked Father very nicely but he fell into a rage. Alas! It seems like we shall never see a decorated Christmas tree," said the troll children with a heavy sigh and tears in their eyes.

Anne-Marie whispered something in her brother's ear and, after several moments of hesitation, she walked resolutely towards the little trolls and held one of them by the arm.

"Do not cry, little troll!" she said. "If you like, you and your brother can come to celebrate Christmas at our hut because we will have a tall and beautiful tree. Come to us and you will see it for yourselves."

The two little trolls dried their tears straight away and looked at our two children with alarm.

"Do you really wish to invite us to your home?"

"Oh, but yes! When the church bells ring tomorrow evening we shall come to fetch you at this very place."

Joyfully the little trolls nodded their consent, and Pierre and Anne-Marie hurried home to tell their mother about whom they had invited for Christmas.

"Des petits trolls! Je n'ai jamais entendu de chose pareille!" dit Maman tout en levant les bras. Fixant son mari d'un regard interrogatoire, "Eh bien, que dis-tu de cela?"

"Il faut toujours tenir sa promesse," dit Papa d'un ton sérieux, "Surtout à Noël il faut essayer d'apporter autant de joie qu'il nous soit possible, soit aux humains, soit aux trolls."

Jamais l'arbre de Noël n'eut tant de parure que cette année là. Les enfants trouvaient toujours quelque chose de nouveau à y accrocher. Ils avaient envie de le décorer le plus joliment possible pour leurs petits hôtes bizarres.

De la neige tomba ce soir là mais aussitôt que les cloches se mirent à tinter Pierre et Anne-Marie se mirent en route pour chercher leurs invités.

"Petits trolls, maintenant vous pouvez venir!" crièrent-ils à plusieurs reprises dans la montagne. Les petits trolls se précipitèrent pour retrouver nos petits enfants. Ils étaient habillés en tenue de gala et étaient pleins d'émotion. Tous les quatre s'en allèrent vers leur tout petit chalet d'où rayonnait une lueur radieuse par chaque fenêtre.

Vous auriez du voir les petits trolls lorsqu'ils virent le sapin de Noël! Ils restèrent là la bouche ouverte et les yeux pleins d'étonnement et d'admiration. Ils n'avaient jamais pensé qu'il y eût quelque chose d'aussi joli au monde, même dans le monde des humains. Les lumières étincelaient et les couleurs reluisaient autant que les yeux des petits. Maman, Papa et les deux petits enfants prirent les petits trolls par la main et dansèrent autour de l'arbre tout en chantant des chants de Noël.

Ils chantaient vraiment bien ces humains pensaient les petits trolls: c'était bien plus beau que les chants de trolls qu'ils avaient l'habitude d'entendre. Une fois les chansons terminées, ils se mirent à découvrir les cadeaux sous le sapin. Même les petits trolls y trouvèrent un paquet chacun: c'était de drôles de petits pantins qu'on pouvait tordre dans tous les sens.

A Trolls' Christmas

"What? Little trolls? But who ever heard of such a thing?" asked their mother, flinging up her arms in dismay. Throwing her husband a questioning look, she asked "Well, what do you say to all this?"

"One should always keep one's promise," said Papa in a serious tone. "Especially at Christmastime one should try to give as much joy as possible to others, be they human or be they trolls."

Never had their Christmas tree been decorated as beautifully as this year. The children kept on finding new things with which to adorn it. They wanted to make it look as pretty as possible for their funny little guests.

That evening snow had been falling lightly, but as soon as the church bells began to ring Pierre and Anne-Marie set off to fetch their guests.

"Little trolls, you can come out now!" they shouted on the path leading up into the mountains. The little trolls came running down to meet them. They were dressed in their finest and extremely excited. The four of them trotted down to the little wooden chalet from which lights glowed out of each window.

You should have seen the little trolls when they saw the Christmas tree! They stood there with their mouths open and eyes full of wonder and delight. They had never imagined anything could be so beautiful, even in the world of humans. The lights sparkled and the colors glowed just as much as the eyes of the little trolls. Mother, Father and the children led the little trolls by the hand as they danced around the tree, all the while singing Christmas carols.

"They sing really well, those humans," thought the little trolls. These songs were much more beautiful than the troll songs that they were accustomed to hearing. Once the singing was finished, they began to discover the gifts lying under the tree. Even the little trolls found a package for each of them. Inside there were funny little jumping jacks on strings that could be moved every which way.

Mais dans la montagne la mère troll regrettait l'absence de ses enfants. C'était bien dommage qu'ils devaient s'en aller le jour de Noël, pensait-elle. Car, malgré tous les invités amusants et illustres qui étaient venus chez eux, ça ne pourrait jamais être un vrai Noël sans les enfants. A vrai dire elle aussi avait bien envie de voir comment les humains fêtaient Noël et sur cela elle sortit de la montagne et se dirigea vers la cabane de Pierre et Anne-Marie.

Grand Troll vit sa femme sortir et, pris de curiosité, il la suivit. Ce n'est pas surprenant que les enfants trolls entendirent venir leurs parents de loin car les trolls n'ont pas le pas léger! Chaque pas causa un grand fracas et les deux petits trolls se placèrent à l'entrée de la hutte pour montrer leurs cadeaux à leurs parents. La mère troll fut étonnée à la vue des pantins et Grand Troll éclata de rire: "Si vous avez reçu des cadeaux, il faut donner quelque chose en retour!" Sur cela il retira de son bras deux grands bracelets en or et les confia à ses enfants. Tout en jetant un regard par la porte du chalet pour apercevoir le sapin de Noël, il leur dit: "Rentrez et donnez les aux humains! Remerciez-les de vous avoir reçu ce soir. Maintenant que j'ai vu en arbre de Noël dans toute sa beauté que je ne vous en nierais pas une autre fois, ça je vous le jure!"

Grande fut la joie dans la pauvre petite hutte lorsqu'ils reçurent les bracelets du troll.

Et depuis l'on fête Noël avec un sapin chaque année chez les trolls. Les trolls, les gobelins et tous les autres habitants de la montagne dansent autour d'un immense sapin de Noël. Ils sont tous d'accord que sans un arbre de Noël ce n'est pas un vrai Noël, ni chez les humains, ni chez les trolls.

 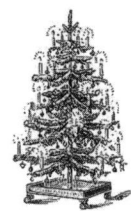 

A Trolls' Christmas

But back in the mountainside the troll mother was beginning to miss her children. What a shame, she thought, that they had to go away at Christmas. Despite all the entertaining and illustrious guests who filled their home, it would never be a real Christmas without the children. To tell the truth, she too very much wished to see how humans celebrate Christmas. The troll mother slipped out of the party and headed towards Pierre and Anne-Marie's cabin.

Big Troll, however, had seen his wife leave and, itching with curiosity, he followed her. It was not surprising that the troll children heard their parents approaching from quite a distance as trolls tread very heavily! Each step made a resonating sound throughout the valley. As the troll parents arrived, the little trolls met them at the door to show them their gifts. The troll mother was very surprised at the sight of her children's amusing toys, and Big Troll burst out laughing. Then, thoughtful, he said "If you have been given presents then we must give something in return!" He then proceeded to remove two large gold bands from his huge arms and handed them to his children. While taking a peek into the chalet to catch a glimpse of the decorated Christmas tree, he told his children "Go inside and give these to the humans! Thank them also for having invited you here this evening. Now that I have seen a Christmas tree in all its splendor I shall not deny you a tree again. This I swear!"

Great was the joy in the little cabin when they received the trolls' precious gifts.

Ever since, the trolls have celebrated Christmas with a tree. The trolls, the goblins and all the other dwellers in the mountain dance around a huge Christmas tree. They all agree that it would not be a real Christmas without a tree: neither for the humans, nor for the trolls.

Petit Noël et les deux rouge-gorges

"PIWI! .....piwi!...." disaient un jour deux petits rouge-gorges dans la forêt.

Que disaient donc les deux petits rouge-gorges?

"Les beaux jours sont partis! Piwi! .....Piwi!"

Il n'y avait pas si longtemps, la terre était encore douce, les feuilles rouges et jaunes, c'est vrai, mais elles tenaient encore aux arbres. Tout était joli, "tiwi!... tiwi!...." et mille compagnons sautillaient sur les branches.

Mais depuis, la méchante Fée Gelée était venue. Elle avait tout durci: la terre, les branches, et l'air était si plein de toutes ses blanches toisons que les gentils rayons n'osaient même pas passer.

Alors, tous les oiseaux avaient ouvert leurs ailes et étaient partis vers des pays lointains où Fée Gelée ne voyageait guère. Et ils laissèrent les deux petits rouge-gorges tout seuls dans la forêt.

La neige commença à tomber, et elle tomba si fort, qu'une couche bien épaisse recouvrait les bois.

Pauvres petits rouge-gorges! Ils avaient beau sautiller, chercher, il ne restait plus un coin de terre où trouver à manger...

Et il était si silencieux, ce bois, sans les babillages habituels, le grand vent soufflait si fort... leurs petites plumes furent toutes ébouriffées tant ils avaient peur tout seuls, tous les deux.

Little Father Christmas and the Two Robins

"PIWI!... piwi!..." said two little robins in the forest one day. What did the two little robins say?

"The good weather has gone! Piwi!... piwi! ..."

It was not so long ago that the earth was still soft, the leaves red and yellow, it's true, but they still clung to the trees. Everything was pretty, "tiwi!... tiwi!..." and a thousand companions hopped upon the branches.

But then the naughty Frost Fairy had come. She made everything hard: the earth and the branches. And the wind was so full of all her white fleeces that the gentle rays of the sun didn't dare to come out.

Then all the birds unfolded their wings and left for faraway lands where the Frost Fairy never came. And they left the two little robins all alone in the forest.

Snow began to fall, and it fell so heavily that a thick layer covered the trees.

Poor little robins! In vain they hopped and searched, but there was no patch of ground left where they might find something to eat...

And it was so silent in these woods without the usual twittering, and the great wind blew so strongly. The birds were so

Petit Noël et les deux rouges-gorges

Comme quelques miettes leur auraient fait du bien!

Mais ils étaient loin, très loin du village et leurs pauvres ailes gelées n'avaient pas la force de voler.

Il y avait pourtant dans le bois une toute petite cabane et certainement quelqu'un y habitait car lorsque la forêt devenait toute noire, une toute petite lumière se montrait par le carreau.

Pourquoi ne pas y frapper?

Et tic ... tic ... frappèrent leurs becs sur le carreau.

Mais le vieux bonhomme de la cabane n'ouvrit même pas, tant il avait peur du froid.

La sombre nuit descendit alors. Les deux petits rouge-gorges laissèrent tomber leurs têtes et se mirent à pleurer. Personne ne les entendait dans le silence du bois.

Mais soudain, tout fut éclairé. De petites lumières de chandelles apparaissaient sur les branches des sapins. On entendait des cloches, des flûtes ...

Les deux petits oiseaux levèrent la tête.

Comme tout était joli! "Tiwi! ... Tiwi!" Et la neige n'était plus froide!

Mais quelles étaient ces lumières qui passaient entre les branches?

Des milliers de fées vêtues de nuées blanches portaient de petites torches dans les mains. Elles travaillaient éperdument. Pourquoi se pressaient-elles ainsi?

C'était de longs fils d'argent qu'elles attachaient aux arbres ... Tout cela devait être prêt avant minuit.

A peine eurent-elles achevé la besogne que le grand ciel s'ouvrit et un cortège splendide descendit sur la terre.

Il y avait des fées, les milliers de fées, et un homme à la longue barbe blanche les conduisait.

Comme il était beau! Il portait un manteau rouge vermeil, un col en hermine blanc et sur son dos pendait une grande corbeille.

Little Father Christmas and the Two Robins

frightened that their little feathers were all ruffled up, for they were alone, just the two of them.

How good a few crumbs would be!

But they were far, very far from the village and their poor frozen wings hadn't the strength to fly.

There was, however, a tiny little cabin in the woods, and certainly someone lived there, because when the forest grew completely dark, a tiny little light showed itself through the windowpane.

Why not knock there?

And tic... tic... their beaks knocked on the window.

But the old man in the cabin didn't open it, because he was afraid of the cold.

Then gloomy night fell. The two little robins lowered their heads and they began to cry. No one heard them in the silence of the woods.

But suddenly, everything was illumined. Little candlelights appeared on the branches of the fir trees. Bells and flutes were heard ...

The two little birds lifted their heads.

How pretty everything was! "Tiwi! ... tiwi!" And the snow was no longer cold!

But what were these lights that were flickering through the branches?

Thousands of fairies robed in white clouds carried tiny torches in their hands. They worked urgently. Why were they in such haste?

They were stringing long threads of silver to the trees... Everything had to be made ready before midnight.

Scarcely had they completed their task when the great heavens opened and a splendid procession descended to the earth.

There were fairies, thousands of fairies, and a man with a long white beard was leading them.

How beautiful he was! He wore a crimson red cloak with a collar of white ermine, and on his back hung a great basket.

Petit Noël et les deux rouges-gorges

Les fées lui parlaient doucement. Elles l'appelaient Petit Noël.

Elles aussi portaient des corbeilles, moins grandes que celle de Petit Noël mais toutes pleines de sucres d'orge et de jouets! Car c'était la nuit de Noël et des milliers de petits enfants sur terre les attendaient.

Combien de souliers il y avait à remplir ... et en une seule nuit! Elles se pressaient donc, et entouraient Petit Noël de mille tendresses pour qu'il ne soit pas trop fatigué.

Le cortège avançait vers les bois.

Les oiselets n'avaient plus faim. Ils sautillaient émerveillés de branche en branche.

Puis le cortège disparut si loin, derrière les pins, qu'on ne vit plus qu'une longue file dorée survolant les cheminées du village.

Mais dans la forêt tout était an fête. Là-bas les fées grimpaient les rayons de lune, ... se laissaient glisser jusqu'en bas. Et là, entre les branches, elles faisaient des chaînes interminables. D'autres jouaient à cache-cache et d'autres à la ronde. C'étaient des rondes rapides et sans trêve. D'autres, déjà fatiguées, sommeillaient doucement sous les champignons.

Mais les rouge-gorges songeaient tristement.

"Demain," pensaient-ils, "elles seront toutes parties. La neige sera froide et nous aurons faim ..."

Bientôt la petite file dorée reparut au loin, derrière les pins. Elle s'avançait toujours plus grande vers les bois. Les oiseaux sautillaient de joie.

Oui, Petit Noël avait fait le tour du grand monde, et il savait que deux petits oiseaux restaient dans la forêt.

Il s'approcha d'eux et leur parla doucement.

"Rouge-gorges, mes petits," leur dit-il, "j'ai rempli les souliers de tant de petits enfants au monde. Je savais ce qu'ils voulaient, mais vous, gentils oiseaux, que puis-je faire pour vous?"

Little Father Christmas and the Two Robins

The fairies spoke softly to him. They called him Little Father Christmas.

They also carried baskets, smaller than Little Father Christmas', but filled to the brim with barley sugar candy and toys! For this was Christmas Eve, and thousands of little children in the world were waiting for them.

How many shoes there were to fill… and in a single night! Then they hurried along and encircled Little Father Christmas with a thousand encouraging and endearing words so that he would not grow weary.

The procession advanced towards the woods.

The little birds hungered no more. They hopped in amazement from branch to branch.

Then the grand procession disappeared so far behind the pine trees that nothing more could be seen other than one long line of gold flying above the chimneys in the village.

But within the forest everything was in state of celebration. Over there the fairies climbed rays of moonlight, … and let themselves slide back down again. And there, skipping among the branches, they wove endless chains. Others played hide and seek, and others danced in a circle. They danced very fast and never stopped for a rest. Others, already tired, slept sweetly beneath the toadstools.

But the robins sang sadly.

"Tomorrow," they thought, "they will all be gone. The snow will be cold, and we will be hungry…"

Soon the little golden procession reappeared in the distance, behind the pine trees. It came towards the woods, growing ever larger. The birds hopped with joy.

Yes, Little Father Christmas had completed his tour of the big world, and he knew that two little birds were waiting in the forest.

He approached them and spoke softly to them.

"My little robins," he said to them, "I have emptied the baskets for all the little children of the world. I knew what they wanted, but you sweet birds, what can I do for you?"

Petit Noël et les deux rouges-gorges

"Prends-nous avec toi! Piwi! Piwi!" répondirent tous les deux à la fois. "On nous a laissés seuls, il fait froid ... nous avons faim! Prends-nous avec toi, Petit Noël, nous chanterons pour toi au ciel, chaque fois que tu voudras dormir."

Et Petit Noël les prit avec lui.

Ils s'envolèrent tous là-haut où il ne fait jamais froid et vécurent heureux au ciel.

Et "tiwi! tiwi!" chantaient les deux rouge-gorges chaque fois que Petit Noël voulait dormir.

Little Father Christmas and the Two Robins

"Take us with you! Piwi! Piwi!" replied both at the same time. "We have been left alone, it's cold and we are hungry! Take us with you, Little Father Christmas, and we will sing for you in heaven whenever you wish to go to sleep."

And Little Father Christmas took them with him.

They flew high away where it is never cold, and they lived happily in heaven.

And "tiwi! tiwi!" the two robins sang whenever Father Christmas wanted to go to sleep.

From the West

Ce qu'on entend quelquefois dans les bois

BIEN, bien des siècles passés vivaient des nymphes sur la cime d'une haute montagne. Il y avait aussi des nymphes sur la terre, mais celles des montagnes étaient plus belles que toutes les autres, car elles buvaient le miel des jonquilles qui couvraient les pentes, et vivaient si près du ciel là-haut sur les rochers qu'elles en respiraient tous les parfums.

Aussi, recueillaient-elles tous ces parfums, les mélangeaient à ceux des pins, des branches de laurier, et lorsque Mistral, le roi des vents, passait par la montagne, elles les lui donnaient pour les répandre sur la terre.

Parmi les nymphes, il en était une plus jeune que toutes les autres. On l'appelait Echo. C'était la plus petite, sa voix était plus douce, plus tendre que celle des autres, mais elle avait deux grands défauts.

D'abord, elle ne parlait jamais la première, c'était son habitude. Il fallait toujours qu'une autre lui dise d'abord bonjour.

Mais une fois la conversation commencée, elle ne cessait de babiller, car elle était bavarde, plus bavarde même que les pies et les cigales.

Un jour, une des nymphes allant porter à Mistral les parfums qu'elle avait recueillis, rencontra Echo sur le chemin.

"Bonsoir, Echo, ma petite sœur," lui dit-elle.

Echo

MANY, many centuries ago nymphs lived on top of a high mountain. There were also nymphs on the earth, but those on the mountain were more beautiful than all the others, because they drank the honey of the jonquils which covered the slopes, and they lived so close to the sky up there on the high rocks that they breathed all the fragrances.

They also gathered all the fragrances, mixing those of pine trees and bay laurel branches, and when Mistral, the king of the winds, passed through the mountain, they gave them to him to spread upon the earth.

Amongst the nymphs who lived on a high mountain slope was a little one who talked and talked and jabbered and chattered, even more than the crickets in the grass, and more than the sparrows in the trees. Her name was Echo.

One evening, as one of the nymphs was walking up the cliffs, taking the scent of the mountain flowers to Evening Breeze who passed to fetch them every night at the peak, Echo stopped her on the way.

"Good evening, little sister," she said.

"Good evening, Echo," replied the nymph; and Echo started telling all the tales of the flowers on the mountainside, and she jabbered so long that Evening Breeze passed by the peak before the little nymph reached the top. Her tiny feet flew over

"Bonsoir!" répondit Echo. Et aussitôt commencèrent les babillages. Et ils durèrent si longtemps, si longtemps que Mistral passa par la cime avant que la nymphe ait pu y arriver.

Si grande fut la colère de Mistral ce soir-là qu'il souffla quatre fois plus fort, et les arbres se penchèrent, le sable des rochers s'envola, et sur toute la terre on n'entendit plus que soupirs.

Toutes les nymphes de la montagne étaient déjà rentrées dans les creux des rochers, mais la pauvre nymphe qu'Echo avait retardée courait éperdument, portant les baumes vers la cime.

Et Mistral, qui l'aperçut de loin, lui souffla du sable dans les yeux pour la punir.

Pauvre petite nymphe! Elle s'assit et sanglota jusqu'à ce que le grand soleil disparût et qu'elle s'endormit sous les sapins.

Mais le lendemain, en retrouvant Echo sur son chemin, la colère lui monta au gosier.

"Echo! méchante Echo!" s'écria-t-elle, "c'est toi qui m'as retardée par tes bavardages interminables! La terre n'a pas reçu les parfums du soir et Mistral m'a durement punie! Et tu crois que je vais oublier tout le mal que tu as causé! Non, désormais, tu ne pourras que répéter les derniers mots de ce qu'on te dira, et ainsi tu ne pourras plus retarder personne sur le chemin."

Aussitôt, la malheureuse Echo fut ravie de sa parole.

Elle se blottit sous les sapins tout au bord d'un sentier et se mit à sangloter amèrement.

"Tout parle," pensait-elle, "la source qui descend là-bas sur le rocher, le sapin qui ne cesse d'agiter ses branches ... Que raconte-t-il? Les histoires interminables des nymphes, de Mistral, du grand soleil ..."

Et pendant qu'elle songeait ainsi à tout le bonheur qu'elle n'avait pas, un bruit de pas approchait doucement.

C'était Narcisse, le jeune berger.

"Un homme de la terre, si beau!" pensait Echo, "certes il est le fils de quelque nymphe car il est beau comme le lever du soleil."

Echo

the hard rocks as fast as they could go, but Evening Breeze had passed and gone away.

The world received no perfume that night, and Evening Breeze was very angry, so angry that he blew and blew in fury until all the nymphs hid in the hollows of the rocks, all but the one who was late carrying the scent. She sat alone at the peak wondering whether Evening Breeze had passed. He swiftly returned and to punish her, he blew sand into her eyes.

She cried but no one heard, for the others were hiding in the rocks. She wept all night till the sun rose again and the nymphs came out to play.

"Echo, you naughty child!" she cried as Echo passed, "how long shall we suffer your unseemly chattering! Why did you detain me to listen to your endless tales! Evening Breeze passed by the peak before I could reach the top. The world received no scent and Evening Breeze punished me cruelly!"

The sobs choked her.

"Senseless one!" she continued, "no one shall suffer your restless tongue again. From this moment you shall speak no more!"

Echo tried to answer but she could not. Something kept silent in her tiny throat. Her speech was lost. Tears filled her tiny, hazel-colored nymph-eyes and she wept bitterly. So much did she weep that the nymph felt sorry for her and said: "You shall speak again, only to repeat the words that are spoken to you!" Having said this, she left her alone.

Echo ran away, far away, down into the valley. And as she sat under the oak trees in the woods, she thought and thought. "Everything speaks," thought she, "the birds speak, the trees tell all that happened in the past, the little stream at my feet tells all the tales of the speechless rocks. Only rocks don't talk. Maybe I shall turn into a rock. Poor little Echo, not even a soul passing by so that you could repeat their words!"

Hardly had she thought this than the sound of footsteps reached her ears. A tall shepherd passed through the trees.

Ce qu'on entend quelquefois sans les bois

A peine était-il passé à travers les sapins, qu'Echo suivit ses pas tout doucement.

"Qui est derrière moi?" s'écria Narcisse.

"Moi!" répondit Echo, qui se cachait derrière un sapin.

"Pourquoi fuis-tu?" s'écria Narcisse.

"Pourquoi fuis-tu?" répondit Echo.

"Attends que je te trouve ... je viens!" dit Narcisse.

"Je viens", répondit Echo.

Et à ces mots, elle fendit l'épais feuillage et parut devant Narcisse. Ses larmes étaient séchées et ses grands yeux brillaient comme des pervenches.

Mais Narcisse en la voyant tourna sur ses pas et s'enfuit.

Elle resta seule sous les sapins et pleura si longtemps qu'elle se transforma en rocher.

Il ne resta d'Echo que sa voix.

Et cette voix s'entend encore dans les montagnes et les bois.

Lorsqu'on appelle, elle répond et sa voix est encore toute triste, car elle pense à Narcisse qui la laissa seule un jour, sous les sapins.

Echo

"How handsome!" thought Echo, "no doubt he is the son of a nymph, for his look is too fine to be mortal and his steps have the rhythm of a deer's gait." She hid behind the oak and waited. The leaves rustled.

"Who is hiding behind the tree?" called the shepherd.

"Who…hiding…tree…" replied a little voice through the bushes.

"Who are you?" called the shepherd.

"Who…are…you?" repeated Echo.

"Come out," called the shepherd.

"Out!" replied the tiny little voice, and Echo appeared between the leaves.

"You would mock me!" said the shepherd, and with these words he turned away.

Echo sat down and wept. She wept so long that she turned into a rock.

But if you talk she still repeats your words, and if you call she still answers, for she thinks it may be the shepherd who once passed by in the woods.

Following the first two paragraphs, the English version is by Noor Inayat Khan

Baldour

LE grand Wotan régnait autrefois sur toute la terre. Son souffle était le souffle du monde. On l'entendait dans le vent; dans la brise.

Zzzzz ... Zzzzzzz ... sifflait le vent lorsque Wotan était en colère. Les nuages noirs se rassemblaient et il chevauchait parmi eux sur un char de feu.

Son épouse, la belle Frigga aux tresses d'or régnait au paradis. Elle avait là un jardin magnifique planté de pommes d'or.

Wotan et Frigga avaient un fils nommé Baldour.

Baldour était le plus beau des êtres.

Là où il passait, tout devenait clair et beau, et les hommes, les animaux et les plantes devenaient heureux. Mais, lorsqu'il s'éloignait, tout devenait triste et obscur.

Les habitants de la terre et ceux du paradis l'aimaient donc tendrement.

Seul un être ne l'aimait pas car il était noir comme les ténèbres que Baldour chassait. Il s'applelait Loki.

Un jour, Baldour s'endormit profondément et il eut un triste rêve. Il alla donc trouver sa douce mère Frigga.

"Mère," lui dit-il, "toi seule tu peux consoler Baldour affligé. Ecoute donc ce que je vais te dire: j'ai rêvé que je devais

Baldour

GREAT Wotan once ruled the whole Earth. His breath was the breath of the world. It was heard in the wind and in the breeze.

Zzzzz… Zzzzzzz… whistled the wind when Wotan was angry. Black clouds gathered together, and he rode among them on a chariot of fire.

His wife, beautiful golden-haired Frigga, ruled Paradise. There she had a marvelous garden in which grew golden apples.

Wotan and Frigga had a son named Baldour.

Baldour was the most beautiful of all beings.

Wherever he went, everything became light and beautiful; people, animals and plants grew happy. But when he went away, everything became sad and gloomy.

And so the inhabitants of Earth and of Paradise loved him dearly.

Only one being didn't love him, for he was dark like the shadows that Baldour drove away. He was called Loki.

One day, Baldour slept deeply and had a sad dream. He then went to find his sweet mother, Frigga.

"Mother," he said to her, "only you can console Baldour in his distress. Listen then, to what I am going to tell you: I

mourir et qu'après ma mort toute la terre serait plongée dans les ténèbres."

Frigga écouta tristement ce récit et dès qu'il eût parlé, elle descendit sur la terre.

Elle parla d'abord à tous les hommes.

"Promettez-moi," dit-elle à chacun d'eux, "que vous ne causerez jamais de mal à Baldour, mon fils chéri."

"O! Reine aux tresses d'or," répondirent-ils "Jamais nous ne causerons de mal à Baldour car nous l'aimons; et comment aurions-nous de joie sur terre s'il ne nous l'apportait pas?"

Elle alla ensuite parler aux animaux:

"Promettez-moi, compagnons," dit-elle à chacun "que vous ne causerez jamais de mal à Baldour, mon fils chéri."

"Auguste Frigga," répondirent-ils, "nous ne causerons jamais de mal à Baldour car nous l'aimons, et comment trouverions-nous de nourriture sur terre s'il ne venait pas éclairer les chemins?"

Frigga alla ensuite parler à toutes les plantes.

"Petite plante," dit-elle à chacune d'elles, "promets-moi de ne jamais causer de mal à Baldour, mon fils chéri."

"Douce Frigga," répondirent-elles, "nous ne causerons jamais de mal à Baldour car nous l'aimons et comment nos cœurs seraient-ils pleins de miel sans les rayons d'or qu'il nous porte sur la terre."

Les habitants du paradis se réjouirent, sachant que rien ne pouvait causer de mal à Baldour qu'ils aimaient tant, et, pour s'amuser, ils lui lançaient des branches d'arbres, des fruits, mais rien ne pouvait le blesser.

Cependant, Frigga avait oublié de parler au gui car il poussait si haut dans les chênes qu'elle ne l'aperçut point. Mais Loki, le méchant, avait remarqué que Frigga l'avait oublié. Il en coupa une branche et la porta au paradis.

"Prends cette branche et jette-là à Baldour," dit-il à un vieil aveugle qui se nommait Hodour.

Hodour la lui jeta.

A peine la branche l'eut-elle touché que Baldour tomba à terre blessé mortellement.

dreamed that I died, and after my death the whole Earth was plunged into darkness."

Frigga listened sadly to this story, and after it had been told, she descended to Earth.

Then she spoke to all the people.

"Promise me," she said to each of them, "that you will never harm Baldour, my beloved son."

"O! Golden-haired Queen," they answered, "we will never harm Baldour because we love him. And how would we have happiness on Earth, if he didn't bring it?"

She then went and spoke to the animals.

"Promise me, my friends," said she to each of them, "that you will never harm Baldour, my beloved son."

"Noble Frigga," they replied, "we will never harm Baldour because we love him. And how would we find nourishment on Earth, if he didn't come to light the way?"

Frigga then went to speak to all the plants.

"Little plant," she said to each of them, "promise me that you will never harm Baldour, my beloved son."

"Sweet Frigga," they replied, "we will never harm Baldour because we love him. And how would our hearts be full of honey, without the golden rays which he brings to Earth?"

The inhabitants of Paradise rejoiced, knowing that nothing would cause harm to Baldour, whom they loved so much. And, to amuse themselves, they threw tree branches and fruit at him but nothing could hurt him.

However Frigga had forgotten to speak to the mistletoe, because it grew so high in the oak trees that she never saw it. But Loki, the wicked one, had noticed that Frigga had forgotten it. He cut a branch and carried it to Paradise.

"Take this branch and throw it at Baldour," he said to old blind Hodor.

Hodor threw the mistletoe.

The branch had hardly touched Baldour when he fell to the earth, mortally wounded.

Baldour

De grands nuages noirs couvrirent alors le monde. Wotan déchira le ciel de ses éclairs et toute la terre trembla de sa colère.

De grosses larmes tombèrent des nuages car Frigga sanglotait amèrement.

Et depuis, elle pleure toujours et toute la nature pleure avec elle la nuit quand la lumière est partie.

C'est pour cela que le matin la terre est toujours pleine de rosée.

Baldour

Large black clouds then covered the world. Wotan whipped the sky with his lightning, and the whole Earth shook from his anger.

Great tears fell from the clouds because Frigga sobbed bitterly.

Ever since then she weeps, and all nature weeps with her in the night, when the light has departed.

And this is the reason that Earth is always full of dewdrops in the morning.

Au royaume des vents

JE vais vous conter, petits enfants, les exploits merveilleux du jeune Ivan, qui vainquit un jour le terrible roi des vents.

C'était dans un pays très lointain, tout au bout du monde, là où la Volga prend sa source.

Le roi qui y régnait se nommait Beljanin; et la reine, la douce Nastia aux tresses d'or était si belle qu'on ne savait en la voyant si elle était de la terre ou du ciel.

Ils avaient trois fils. Ivan était le plus jeune et les deux aînés se nommaient Pierre et Vasil.

Un jour, Nastia aux tresses d'or se promenait dans les jardins du palais. Une grande tempête éclata soudain et le vent souffla si fort que Nastia fut soulevée dans les airs et emportée loin, loin à travers les nuages.

Bien des larmes remplirent les yeux du pauvre roi et des ses fils. En vain ils suppliaient les vents, mais Nastia était déjà loin, si loin qu'on ne la voyait plus.

Hélas! les années passaient et dans tout le royaume on n'entendait plus que soupirs et sanglots. Car tout le monde aimait Nastia aux tresses d'or et depuis qu'elle était partie, c'était comme si le soleil ne brillait plus.

Un jour, lorsque Pierre, Vasil et Ivan étaient devenus grands, leur père Beljanin les appela auprès de lui.

The Kingdom of the Winds

ONCE there was a country very far away, at the edge of the world, where the Volga River finds its source.

The king who reigned there was named Beljanin, and the queen, sweet golden-haired Nastia was so beautiful that anyone who saw her couldn't tell if she was from the earth or the heavens.

They had three sons. Ivan was the youngest, and the two oldest were named Peter and Vasily.

One day, while golden-haired Nastia walked in the gardens of the palace, a great tempest suddenly burst forth and the wind blew with such force that Nastia was lifted into the air and carried far, very far away over the clouds.

Many tears filled the eyes of the poor king and his sons.

In vain they pleaded with the winds to bring her back, but Nastia was already far away, so far away that she could no longer be seen.

Alas! The years passed, and throughout the kingdom one could hear nothing but sighs and weeping.

Because everyone loved golden-haired Nastia, and since she was gone, it seemed as if the sun no longer shone.

One day, when Peter, Vasily and Ivan had grown tall, their father Beljanin called them to him.

"Enfants," leur dit-il, "vous êtes grands et forts et vos coeurs sont pleins de courage. Quel est donc celui d'entre vous qui est prêt à partir sur un long voyage, retrouver Nastia, votre douce mère aux tresses d'or?"

"Père," répondirent les deux aînés, "nous sommes des hommes et nos bras sont forts. Nous irons dès l'aube sur nos chevaux, retrouver notre douce mère."

Et dès que le jour fut levé ils partirent sur leurs beaux chevaux tandis qu'Ivan resta seul avec son père.

Mais Ivan ne dormait plus. Il songeait à sa mère que les vents avaient emportée quand il était tout petit encore.

"Bayou, bayoushka,
Ivanoushka!"

lui chantait-elle chaque soir. Et Ivan l'aimait tendrement.

"Je voudrais la retrouver!" pensait-il. Et il alla trouver son noble père.

"Père," lui dit-il "je veux aller retrouver ma mère."

"Ivan, mon fils," dit le roi, "ne me quitte pas. Tes deux frères sont déjà partis; ne me laisse donc pas seul."

Mais chaque jour Ivan le suppliait de plus en plus et son père consentit enfin.

"Va, mon fils," dit-il, "je ne puis te retenir; que le bon Dieu soit avec toi. Adieu!"

Et il l'embrassa tendrement.

Ivan quitta le palais et chevaucha longtemps à travers les forêts.

Là il trouva un jour sous les arbres, un vieillard, beau comme le jour. Sa grande barbe blanche comme les paquerettes des prés, tombait jusqu'à terre.

Ivan descendit de son cheval et alla vers lui.

"Qui es-tu, jeune homme?" lui demanda la vieillard, "et où vas-tu ainsi dans les bois?"

"Je suis le Prince Ivan," répondit-il, "fils du Roi Beljanin et de Nastia aux tresses d'or. Je vais ainsi chevauchant par les bois

The Kingdom of the Winds

"Children," he said to them, "you are tall and strong, and your hearts are full of courage. Which one among you is ready to depart on a long journey to bring back Nastia, your sweet golden-haired mother?"

"Father," replied the two oldest, "we are men and our arms are strong. We will go at dawn, upon our horses, to bring back out sweet mother."

And as soon as the day began, they departed on their beautiful horses, while Ivan remained alone with his father.

But Ivan didn't sleep. He was thinking of his mother whom the winds had carried off when he was still little.

"Bayou, Bayoushka,
Ivanoushka!"

she sang to him each evening. And Ivan loved her tenderly.

"I would like to bring her back," thought he. And he went to find his noble father.

"Father," he said, "I want to go and find my mother."

"Ivan, my son," said the king, "Do not leave me. Your two brothers have already left; do not leave me alone."

But each day Ivan pleaded more and more and his father finally consented.

"Go, my son," said he, "I cannot hold you back; may the Good Lord be with you. Farewell!"

And he embraced him tenderly.

Ivan left the palace and rode for a long time through the forest.

There in the woods one day, he found an old man, as handsome as the day. His great beard, white like the nearby daisies, fell down to the earth.

Ivan climbed down from his horse went towards him.

"Who are you, young man?" asked the old fellow, "and where are you going in the woods?"

"I am Prince Ivan," he answered, "son of King Beljanin and golden-haired Nastia. I am riding through the woods to bring

pour retrouver ma douce mère. Pourrais-tu me dire, Oncle, où je la trouverai dans ce vaste monde?"

Le vieillard sourit et répondit:

"Je ne puis te le dire; mais je te donne cette petite balle en bois. Fais la rouler devant toi et suis-la toujours; elle roulera même sur les pentes abruptes des rocs. Dans la caverne d'un des rocs tu trouveras des crochets en fer. Tu les attacheras à tes pieds et à tes mains et tu pourras ainsi grimper les hautes montagnes et peut-être un jour retrouveras-tu Nastia, ta mère aux tresses d'or."

Ivan remercia chaleureusement le vieillard, et prenant la balle, il la jeta devant lui. Le coeur battant de joie, il la suivit nuit et jour par les sentiers.

Après plusieurs jours il arriva dans une grande vallée. Deux hommes étaient assis sous un arbre, la tête baissée tristement. Ivan les reconnut. C'étaient ses frères, Pierre et Vasil et il se jeta dans leurs bras et les embrassa tendrement.

"Frères," leur dit-il, "pourquoi êtes vous si tristes?"

"Nous ne pouvons retrouver notre douce mère;" répondirent-ils, "nous avons chevauché jusqu'à la mer et nous ne savons plus où aller."

Ivan leur montra alors la petite balle merveilleuse et tous les trois partirent ensemble à la recherche de Nastia aux tresses d'or.

La petite balle roula jusqu'aux montagnes et, là elle commença à monter. Les trois frères la suivaient toujours.

Mais devant eux de grands rochers abrupts montaient vers le ciel et Pierre et Vasil en eurent très peur.

"Tu peux continuer si tu veux," dirent-ils à Ivan, "mais nous ne grimperons plus."

"Attendez-moi ici," leur répondit Ivan,"et gardez les chevaux. Attendez-moi trois mois, frères, et si je ne reviens pas, ne m'attendez plus!"

Ivan partit seul, se cramponnant aux rochers et tout le grand monde s'étendait à ses pieds. Bientôt il atteignit la caverne dont lui avait parlé le vieillard. Il y trouva les crochets en fer et les attacha à ses mains et à ses pieds.

back my sweet mother. Can you tell me, Uncle, where I will find her in this wide world?"

The old man smiled and replied:

"I cannot tell you that; but I give you this little wooden ball. Roll it before you and always follow it; it will roll just the same over steep rocky slopes. In the cavern inside one of the rocks you will find iron hooks. You will attach them to your feet and to your hands, and in this way you will be able to climb the high mountains and perhaps one day you will bring back Nastia, your golden haired mother."

Ivan warmly thanked the old man, and taking the ball, he threw it before him. His heart beating with joy, he followed it night and day along the pathways.

After many days he arrived in a large valley. Two men were seated beneath a tree, with heads bowed down in sorrow. Ivan recognized them. They were his brothers, Peter and Vasily, and he threw himself in their arms and embraced them tenderly.

"Brothers," he said to them, "why are you so sad?"

"We cannot find our sweet mother," they replied. "We have ridden as far as the ocean and we don't know where else to go."

Ivan then showed them the marvelous little ball and all three left together to search for golden-haired Nastia.

The little ball rolled up to the mountains and began to climb. The three brothers always followed.

But in front of them a great steep cliff rose up to the heavens, and Peter and Vasily were much afraid.

"You can continue if you wish," said they to Ivan, "but we will climb no further."

"Wait for me here," Ivan answered them, "and guard the horses. Wait for me for three months, brothers, and if I don't return, don't wait for me any longer!"

Ivan departed alone, clinging to the high rocks, and the whole wide world spread out at his feet. Soon he reached the cavern which the old man had told him about. There he found the iron hooks and attached them to his hands and to his feet.

Le roc suivant montait droit dans les nuages. Ivan grimpa à pic jusqu'au sommet, et là devant lui se dressait dans le ciel un palais magnifique en cuivre rose. Ses tours rayonnaient tant, que les nuages tout autour en étaient roses et sur la terre on les voyait à l'aube et au crépuscule.

Le jeune Ivan alla droit vers la porte. De grands serpents gardaient l'entrée, et, en voyant Ivan, ils se mirent à siffler si fort que tout le ciel les entendit.

Mais tout près de là se trouvait une fontaine et une cruche en cuivre rose. Ivan remplit la cruche et donna à boire aux terribles serpents. Ceux-ci furent si contents qu'ils se penchèrent à terre pour le laisser passer. Aussitôt la jeune Reine du Palais de Cuivre accourut au devant de lui.

"Qui es-tu, jeune homme?" demanda-t-elle. "Et qu'est-ce qui t'amène dans ce palais?"

"Je suis le Prince Ivan," répondit-il; "et je suis à la recherche de Nastia, ma mère aux tresses d'or. Un jour les vents l'emportèrent je ne sais où et c'est pour cela que je la cherche nuit et jour. Pourrais-tu me dire, O! Noble Reine, où je pourrai la trouver?"

"Je ne puis te le dire," répondit-elle, "mais je te donne cette balle en cuivre. Tu la jetteras devant toi et elle roulera jusqu'au palais de ma soeur qui règne sur le Royaume d'Argent. Et si jamais tu es vainqueur du Roi des Vents et tu retrouves ta mère aux tresses. d'or, n'oublie pas la pauvre Reine du Royaume de Cuivre que ce même roi a emprisonnée ici. Reviens me trouver et porte-moi dans le grand monde sur la terre!"

Ivan fit le serment qu'il la délivrerait et il partit en suivant la petite balle de cuivre.

Bientôt il arriva an Royaume d'Argent. La palais était d'argent si blanc que toute la nuit en était éclairé. On le voyait sur la terre et on l'appelait 'Lune'.

Pareils que ceux qui gardaient le palais de cuivre rose, d'énormes serpents se tenaient à la porte et sifflaient si fort qu'on les entendait même à cent lieues de là.

The Kingdom of the Winds

The rock continued upwards, straight into the clouds. Ivan climbed a peak up to the summit, and there before him, rising into the sky, was a magnificent palace of red copper. Its tower shone so that the clouds all around were colored red, and on the earth they are seen at dawn and at dusk.

Young Ivan went straight to the door. Great serpents guarded the entrance and, on seeing Ivan, they hissed at him so forcefully that all the heavens heard it.

But close by there was a fountain and a pitcher of red copper. Ivan filled the pitcher and gave it to the terrible serpents to drink from. They became so satisfied that they lay down on the ground to let him pass. At once the young queen of the Copper Palace ran up to him.

"Who are you, young man?" she asked. "And what brings you to this palace?"

"I am Prince Ivan," he replied, "and I am searching for Nastia, my golden haired mother. One day the winds carried her off, I don't know where, and this is the reason that I search night and day. Can you tell me, O Noble Queen, where I can find her?"

"I cannot tell you that," she answered him, "but I can give you this copper ball. Throw it in front of you, and it will roll to the palace of my sister who rules the Kingdom of Silver. And if ever you vanquish the King of the Winds and find your golden-haired mother, do not forget the poor Queen of the Kingdom of Copper whom that same king has imprisoned here. Come back to find me and carry me to the great world of the earth!"

Ivan declared that he would rescue her and he departed, following the little copper ball.

Soon he arrived at the Kingdom of Silver. The palace was of silver so white that it shone all through the night. One sees it from the earth and calls it "Moon."

Enormous serpents, like those which guarded the Palace of Copper, positioned themselves at the door and hissed so forcefully that it could be heard a hundred leagues from there.

Mais à coté du palais était une fontaine et une petite cruche d'argent.

Ivan remplit la cruche et donna à boire aux serpents. Ceux-ci se baissèrent aussitôt pour laisser passer Ivan.

Et la Reine du Royaume d'Argent accourut en le voyant:

"Sois le bienvenue!" s'écria-t-elle; "Viens-tu de la terre, jeune homme? Connais-tu mon doux pays?"

"Oui, je viens de la terre," répondit-il. "Je suis Ivan, le fils de Beljanin et je suis à la recherche de ma mère. O! Noble Reine, connais-tu peut-être Nastia aux tresses d'or?"

"Non, je ne la connais pas," répondit-elle; "et je ne sais où elle est. Mais je te donne cette petite balle d'argent; fais la rouler; elle te conduira au palais de ma soeur, la belle Reine du Royaume d'Or. Son palais est en or et tu le verras de très loin, tant il est brillant. Et si jamais tu es vainqueur du Roi des Vents, souverain de ce monde, n'oublie pas la pauvre Reine du Royaume d'Argent, que ce roi a emprisonnée. Reviens me délivrer et porte-moi là-bas sur la terre!"

Ivan remercia la Reine et fit serment de retourner un jour, et il partit vers le Royaume d'Or.

Il le vit bientôt au loin dans le ciel. Le palais était d'or si rayonnant qu'on le voyait même de la terre et on l'appelait 'Soleil'.

De grands serpents gardaient l'entrée et des flammes sortaient de leurs bouches.

Mais îl y avait tout près de là une fontaine et une petite cruche en or. Ivan le remplit d'eau, donna à boire aux terribles serpents qui en furent si contents qu'ils se penchèrent à terre pour laisser passer Ivan.

La belle Reine du Palais d'Or accourut en le voyant:

"Qui es-tu, jeune homme?" demanda-t-elle; "Viens-tu de la terre que j'aime tant?"

"Je suis Ivan," répondit-il, "fils de Beljanin et de Nastia aux tresses d'or. Je viens de la terre et je voyage par les royaumes chercher ma douce mère."

The Kingdom of the Winds

But next to the palace there was a fountain and a little silver pitcher.

Ivan filled the pitcher and gave it to the serpents to drink from. At once they lowered themselves to let Ivan pass.

And seeing him, the Queen of the Kingdom of Silver ran to him.

"Be welcome!" she cried, "Do you come from the earth, young man? Do you know my sweet country?"

"Yes, I come from the earth," he replied. "I am Ivan, the son of Beljanin, and I am here searching for my mother. O! Noble Queen, do you perhaps know golden-haired Nastia?"

"No, I don't know her," she replied; "and I do not know where she is. But I give you this little silver ball; roll it along, it will guide you to the palace of my sister, the beautiful Queen of the Kingdom of Gold. Her palace is golden and you will see it from very far away because of its radiance. And if you ever vanquish the King of the Winds, sovereign of this world, do not forget the poor Queen of the Kingdom of Silver, whom that king has imprisoned. Return to save me and carry me down to the earth!"

Ivan thanked the Queen and declared he would return one day, and he departed for the Kingdom of Gold.

He soon saw it far off in the sky. The palace was gold, so radiant that one could see it from the earth, and it was called "Sun."

Great serpents guarded the entrance and flames came out of their mouths.

But there was a fountain close by and a little golden pitcher. Ivan filled it with water, gave it to the terrible serpents who became so satisfied that they bent down to the earth to let Ivan pass.

The beautiful Queen of the Golden Palace rushed out on seeing him:

"Who are you, young man?" she asked; "Do you come from the earth that I love so much?"

"I am Ivan," replied he, "son of Beljanin and golden-haired Nastia. I come from the earth and I travel through the kingdoms to search for my sweet mother."

"Je sais où elle est," dit la reine aux yeux d'azur, "elle n'habite pas loin d'ici. Le grand Roi des Vents l'a enfermée là-bas dans son palais. Je te donne cette petite balle d'or; fais-la rouler et suis son cours; elle te conduira droit au palais du Roi des Vents et tu trouveras ta mère aux tresses d'or. Et si jamais tu es vainqueur du Roi des Vents, n'oublie pas la pauvre Reine du Royaume d'Or; reviens la trouver et porte-la là-bas sur la douce terre!"

Ivan suivit la petite balle d'or et elle roula jusqu'à un magnifique palais entouré de nuages blancs.

Il entra dans le palais; passa par des couloirs interminables et tout au milieu du palais, dans une immense salle, était sa mère, sa douce mère, assise sur un trône.

"Toi, mon petit Ivan!" s'écria-t-elle en le serrant dans ses bras; "Comment es-tu venu jusqu'ici?"

"Je viens te délivrer, O! ma mère aux tresses d'or!" repondit-il.

"Ivan, mon fils," dit Nastia, "le temps presse. Le Roi des Vents doit venir bientôt après avoir soufflé sur le monde. Suis-moi, Ivan, jusqu'à la cave du palais."

Il s'y trouvait deux tonneaux, tous deux remplis d'eau; l'un était à droite et l'autre à gauche.

"Bois de l'eau du tonneau de droite," lui dit Nastia, "car cette eau donne la force."

Et lorsqu'Ivan eut bu, it sentit en lui une telle force qu'il aurait bien pu briser des grandes montagnes.

"Lorsque viendra le Roi des Vents," lui dit ensuite sa mère "il voudra boire du tonneau de droite pour se rendre fort et te combattre, mets donc le tonneau de gauche à droite car l'eau dans le tonneau de gauche enlève les forces et après en avoir bu, on devient faible comme un roseau."

Ivan changea les tonneaux de place et ensuite ils montèrent tous les deux dans la grande salle.

The Kingdom of the Winds

"I know where she is," said the blue-eyed queen, "she lives not far from here. The great King of the Winds has locked her up over there, in his palace. I give you this little golden ball; roll it along and follow its path; it will guide you straight to the palace of the King of the Winds, and you will find your golden-haired mother. And if ever you vanquish the King of the Winds, do not forget the poor Queen of the Kingdom of Gold; come back to find her and carry her down there to the gentle earth!"

Ivan followed the little golden ball and it rolled to a magnificent palace encircled by white clouds.

He entered into the palace, passed through endless corridors and, in the middle of the palace, in an immense room, was his mother, his sweet mother, seated upon a throne.

"You, my little Ivan!" she cried, pressing him in her arms; "How have you come here?"

"I come to rescue you, O! my golden-haired mother!" he replied.

"Ivan, my son," said Nastia, "time is short. The King of the Winds will come soon after having blown on the world. Follow me, Ivan, to the cellar of the palace."

There were two barrels, both filled with water; one was on the right and the other on the left.

"Drink the water from the barrel on the right," Nastia told him, "because this water gives strength."

And when Ivan had drunk, he felt strong enough to break great mountains.

"When the King of the Winds comes," his mother then told him, "he will want to drink from the barrel on the right to make himself strong and fight you; so place the barrel from the left on the right, for the water in the barrel of the left removes strength and after having drunk it, one becomes as weak as a reed."

Ivan switched the places of the barrels, and after that they both went up into the great room.

Bientôt un amazon souffla autour du palais et un fracas de tonnerre fit trembler les murs. Le Roi des Vents avait fait son entrée.

Il regarda autour de lui bien courroucé.

"Qui est entré par ici?" s'écria-t-il.

Ivan se jeta alors sur lui.

De ses bras puissants le roi le repoussait mais Ivan se cramponnait à lui avec une telle force que mille géants n'auraient pu l'en enlever.

Le Roi des Vents s'envola alors par la fenêtre. Mais Ivan ne le quitta pas et resta accroché à ses bras. Ils volèrent ainsi tout autour du monde.

Mille fois le roi furieux s'efforça de faire tomber Ivan dans l'espace mais le jeune enfant ne céda point. .

Après avoir ainsi voyagé, le grand roi sentit peu à peu ses forces s'épuiser. Il se dirigea droit vers le palais et, prenant l'eau du tonneau de droite, il en but à grandes gorgées. Tout à coup il trembla de tous ses membres. Le peu de force qui lui restait disparut et il se sentit plus faible que le plus faible des roseaux.

Ivan le jeta alors à terre; il s'affaissa et disparut.

Bien grande fut la joie de Nastia lorsqu'elle vit son enfant vainqueur. Et ils partirent tous les deux vers les trois royaumes trouver la Reine du Royaume d'Or, la Reine du Royaume d'Argent et la Reine du Royaume de Cuivre Rose.

Ivan les conduisit toutes au bord du rocher par lequel il était monté.

Il suspendit une corde par laquelle on pouvait glisser jusqu'en bas où attendaient ses frères Pierre et Vasil.

"Ivan a retrouvé notre mère!" s'écrièrent-ils en les voyant sur le sommet.

Et une grande jalousie s'empara alors de leurs cœurs.

"Lorsque notre mère sera arrivée ici," dit Pierre à Vasil, "coupons la corde pour qu'Ivan ne descende pas. Nous le laisserons dans les montagnes et nous dirons à notre père que nous avons trouvé notre mère et qu'Ivan ne put revenir."

The Kingdom of the Winds

Soon a mighty wind blew around the palace and a clap of thunder made the walls tremble. The King of the Winds made his entry.

He looked angrily around him.

"Who has entered here?" he cried.

Ivan then threw himself on top of him.

The king pushed him away with powerful arms, but Ivan climbed on him with such strength that a thousand giants would not have been able to remove him.

The King of the Winds then flew through the window. But Ivan would not let go and remained hanging onto his arms. They flew like this all around the world.

A thousand times the furious king endeavored to make Ivan fall into space, but the youth would not give up.

After having thus journeyed, the great king felt that, little by little, his strength was weakening. He steered himself straight to the palace and, taking the water from the barrel on the right, he drank in great gulps. Suddenly he trembled in every limb of his body. The little strength that he still had disappeared, and he felt weaker than the weakest reed.

Ivan then threw him to the ground, and he sank down and disappeared.

Nastia's joy was very great when she saw her son triumph. And they departed together toward the three kingdoms to find the Queen of the Kingdom of Gold, the Queen of the Kingdom of Silver, and the Queen of the Kingdom of Copper.

Ivan guided all of them to the edge of the rock which he had climbed.

He suspended a rope by which one could slide down to the bottom, where his brothers Peter and Vasily were waiting.

"Ivan has brought back our mother!" they cried, seeing them on the summit.

And a great jealousy then seized their hearts.

"When our mother arrives here," said Peter to Vasily, "let us cut the rope so that Ivan cannot descend. We will leave him in the mountains, and we will tell our father that we have found our mother and that Ivan was unable to return."

Vasil approuva cette idée.

La douce Nastia descendit alors, puis la Reine du Royaume d'Or, celle du Royaume d'Argent et celle du Royaume de Cuivre Rose, et Ivan commença à descendre à son tour. Tandis que Nastia embrassait Pierre et que les trois autres reines se penchaient à la douce terre pour l'embrasser aussi, Vasil lança son poignard inaperçu vers Ivan. Le couteau coupa la corde juste en-dessous du jeune Ivan et le pauvre garçon dut remonter au sommet.

"La corde s'est cassé!" crièrent Pierre et Vasil, "Et notre cher frère ne pourra jamais redescendre!"

Ivan resta seul sur le rocher, et malgré les pleurs de la pauvre Nastia, ils emportèrent les quatre reines sur les chevaux et galopèrent au loin.

Là haut dans les sombres rochers, Ivan erra tristement.

Il n'y avait ni homme, ni oiseau, ni même une fleur; rien que des nuages eternels et des rochers.

Il marcha jour et nuit.

Il arriva finalement à un palais transparent tout construit de diamants et il appela. Deux petits bonshommes, pas plus hauts que des champignons, apparurent aussitôt.

"Que pouvons-nous faire pour vous?" lui demandèrent-ils, "Nous n'avons plus notre roi qui commandait les vents; nous voulons donc vous servir."

"Je veux retourner au palais de mon père." dit Ivan doucement.

Les petits bonshommes aux longues barbes blanches lui donnèrent une petite flûte toute en diamant.

"Joue de cette petite flûte." lui dirent-ils alors.

Et aussitôt qu'il joua, it se retrouva au palais près de son père et de sa douce mère.

Nastia le serra dans ses bras et l'embrassa mille et mille fois.

Mais Pierre et Vasil baissèrent la tête de honte et avouèrent leur faute.

The Kingdom of the Winds

Vasily approved this idea.

Sweet Nastia then descended, and then the Queens of the Kingdom of Gold, and of the Kingdom of Silver, and of the Kingdom of Copper, and Ivan began to descend in his turn. While Nastia was embracing Peter and the three other queens lowered themselves to the gentle earth to kiss the ground also, Vasily, unseen, flung his dagger toward Ivan. The knife cut the rope just below young Ivan, and the poor boy had to climb back to the summit.

"The rope has broken!" cried Peter and Vasily, "and our dear brother will never be able to come down!"

Ivan remained alone on top of the high rock, and in spite of poor Nastia's tears, they carried off the four queens on the horses and galloped faraway.

High up on the dark rock ledges, Ivan was filled with sorrow.

There was neither man nor bird, nor so much as a flower; nothing but eternal clouds and rocks.

He walked day and night.

Finally he arrived at a transparent palace constructed wholly of diamonds and he called out. Two little men, not even as tall as toadstools, soon appeared.

"What may we do for you?" they asked him. "We no longer have our king who commanded the winds; so we wish to serve you."

"I wish to return to the palace of my father," said Ivan gently.

The little men with long white beards gave him a little flute of diamond.

"Play this little flute," they said to him.

And as soon as Ivan played it, he found himself back in the palace next to his father and his sweet mother.

Nastia pressed him in her arms and embraced him thousands and thousands of times.

But Peter and Vasily bowed their heads in shame and acknowledged their misdeed.

Le Roi Beljanin ordonna alors que les deux méchants frères fussent jetés en prison.

Mais Ivan s'agenouilla devant le roi.

"Père," lui dit-il doucement, "ne punis pas Pierre et Vasil. Ils sont mes frères et je les aime, et bien des larmes couleraient de mes yeux si je les savais enfermés dans un sombre donjon!"

Beljanin earessa tendrement la tête d'Ivan.

Le lendemain de grandes noces furent celebrées.

Ivan épousa la belle Reine du Royaume d'Or, Vasil épousa la Reine du Royaume d'Argent, et Pierre, la Reine du Royaume de Cuivre Rose.

Et les trois frère s'aimarent tous les jours de leur vies et tout le royaume se réjouit car Nastia aux tresses d'or était retrouvée et le soleil brillait de nouveau sur le pays.

The Kingdom of the Winds

Then King Beljanin commanded that the two wicked brothers be thrown in prison.

But Ivan kneeled before the king.

"Father," he said gently, "do not punish Peter and Vasily. They are my brothers and I love them, and many tears would flow from my eyes if I knew they were locked in a dark dungeon!"

Beljanin tenderly caressed Ivan's head.

The next day, great weddings were celebrated.

Ivan married the beautiful Queen of the Kingdom of Gold, Vasily married the Queen of the Kingdom of Silver, and Peter, the Queen of the Kingdom of Copper.

And the three brothers loved each other all the days of their lives, and all the kingdom rejoiced because golden-haired Nastia had returned, and the sun shone once more upon the land.

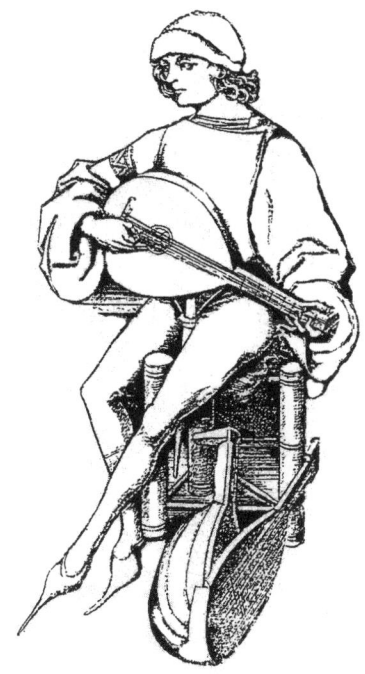

From the East

Zeb-un-Nisa

ON dit que les poètes sont enfants de la douleur.
Combien de poètes la Perse n'a-t-elle pas donné, de poètes dont les vers miraculeux viennent d'on ne sait quelle source inconnue, de poètes illustres aux chants épiques ardents et merveilleux.

Mais parmi tous ces poètes dont les noms celèbres se sont répandus dans le monde au 16ème siècle, il en était une qui les a tous surpassé.

C'était une jeune fille nommée Zeb-un-nisa. Elle était maigre, les yeux profondément noirs.

Fille de l'Empereur Aurengzeb, elle ne connut du monde que le palais aux murs de pierres précieuses et aux jardins enchanteurs.

Mais cette joie trop douce et paisible pour ce monde, ne dura pas plus longtemps que son enfance. A peine la jeune enfant eut-elle regardé par la grille du jardin du palais, quelquechose frémit en elle. La voix des passants accablés sous le poids de leurs charges, la fit baisser la tête sous le poids d'un destin qui la menaçait sourdement. C'est ainsi que naquit la jeune poètesse dont les vers brûlants ont valu à la Perse cette gloire que les Indes lui envient. Car elle écrivit en perse.

Elle épousa un jeune prince, Darus Shikoh qu'elle aimait tendrement mais ce prince était trop noble pour un palais

Zeb-un-Nisa

IT is said that poets are the children of sorrow.
No one knows how many Persian poets there are whose miraculous verses come from an unknown source, illustrious poets of epic songs, passionate and marvelous.

But among all these famous poets spread across the world of the sixteenth century, there was one who surpassed all the rest. This was a young girl named Zeb-un-Nisa. She was slender, her eyes were deep black.

Daughter of the Emperor Aurangzeb, she knew nothing of the world except for the palace with its walls of precious stones and enchanting gardens.

But that joy was too sweet and peaceful for this world, and it lasted no longer than her childhood. Scarcely had the young child looked through the gate of the palace garden, when something in her shuddered. The voice of the dejected ones, passing along beneath the weight of their burdens, made her lower her head beneath the weight of insensible fate. And thus was born the young poetess whose burning verses are treasured in Persia, a glory envied by India. For she wrote in Persian.

She married a young prince, Dara Shikoh, whom she loved tenderly, but this prince was too noble for a palace strewn with

jonché de courtisans, trop fort pour être gendre d'un roi indigne et faible. L'Empereur le fit empoisonner.

Zeb-un-nisa resta seule dans le palais.

Elle vécut dans une tour, une de ces tours blanches dont le sommet pointe dans les nuages.

Sans doute se sentait-elle là plus près de son bien-aimé. Et les larmes qui jaillisaient de son coeur se transformèrent en vers miraculeux.

Les plus grands poètes de l'époque furent appelés auprès d'elle. On dit que les paroles qu'elles prononcaient même dans les discours étaient en vers, tant son inspiration était grande et continuelle.

courtiers, too strong to be the son-in-law of an unworthy and weak king. The emperor had him poisoned.

Zeb-un-Nisa remained alone in the palace.

She lived in a tower, one of those white towers whose peak was a speck in the clouds.

No doubt she felt closer to her beloved. And the tears which gushed from her heart were transformed into miraculous verses.

The greatest poets of the era were named after her. It is said that the words which she spoke in conversation were also in poetic verse, so great and lasting was her inspiration.

Mira Bhai

VOULEZ-VOUS, mes soeurs, que je vous conte la vie d'une jeune princesse hindoue dont le nom est inscrit dans le cœur de toutes les femmes hindoues, dont la douceur a éte chantée par bien des poètes, et la musique jouée dans toutes les Indes.

C'était au temps de l'Empereur Akbar, dans un des riches états que gouvernait un roi, vassal de l'Empereur.

Mira-Bhai, la fille du roi, avait alors cinq ans.

La ville était en fête, les cloches sonnaient aux cous des éléphants, les rues étaient couvertes de fleurs et l'air vibrait au son des flûtes de Pan.

"Quelle est donc cette fête?" demanda la petite princesse à sa mère.

"C'est qu'il y a de grandes noces dans la ville," répondit la noble reine, "Vois-tu à l'ombre des Boudas, la jeune mariée et son époux?"

"Et qui sera mon époux?" demanda Mira.

La reine se tourna vers une statue dans la palais et, la montrant du doigt à sa fille:

"Krishna!" répondit-elle.

C'est ainsi qu'à l'âge de cinq ans, l'amour naquit dans le coeur de Mira,

Mira Bhai

MY sisters, would you like me to tell you the story of the life of a young Hindu princess whose name is inscribed in the hearts of all Hindu women, whose sweetness is sung by many poets, and whose music is played in all of India?

It was the time of the Emperor Akbar, in one of the richest states governed by a king, a vassal of the emperor.

Mira Bhai, the daughter of the king, was then five years old.

The city was celebrating, the bells jingling on the necks of elephants, the streets were covered with flowers and the air resonated with flutes.

"What is this celebration?" the little princess asked her mother.

"It's for a great wedding in the city," replied the noble queen. "Do you see the young bride and her groom there, in the shade of the Buddha statues?"

"And who will be my husband?" asked Mira.

The queen turned towards a statue in the palace and, pointing to it with her finger,

"Krishna!" she replied.

So it was, that at the age of five years, love was born in Mira's heart.

Depuis ce jour tout avait changé pour elle.

Le soleil brillait avec moins d'éclat que les yeux de Krishna; les fleurs n'avaient de parfum que pour fêter Krishna, le palais n'avait de splendeurs que pour l'abriter.

Adieu les jouets, les poupées, les escapades par les sentiers du parc! Désormais, devant la statue de Krishna, Mira passait ses jours et ses nuits,

Parfois elle croyait voir un sourire sur ses lèvres, et son propre petit visage s'illuminait de joie, parfois il lui paraissait triste, et les yeux de Mira se remplissaient de larmes.

Ainsi grandit la jeune princesse, et dans son jeune coeur, l'amour grandit aussi.

Tout son être en était imprégné; ses yeux où toute la souffrance et la joie des humains semblaient reflétées, sa voix légèrement vibrante, ses doigts qui créaient des sons magiques sur son instrument, la vina.

Mais, pendant qu'aveugle au monde, elle chantait chaque jour au temple de Krishna, tout le pays chantait ses louanges. Car, ainsi que la plante nourrie produit des fleurs sans pareilles, sa voix acquit une beauté incomparable.

Son talent était déjà célèbre aux Indes et innombrables étaient ses admirateurs et les princes qui demandaient sa main.

Mais les notes sonnaient sous ses doigts pour Krishna seul. Pour lui elle jouait, pour lui elle composait des chants infiniment tendres et purs.

Mais le jour vint où les visites nocturnes au temple de Krishna durent cesser. Mira dut abandonner ses rêves et épouser finalement le radja d'Udaipur, un des princes qui demandaient sa main.

Bien à contre-coeur, fut ce mariage qu'elle accepta, par obéissance et devoir. Néanmoins, nulle femme n'aurait pu témoigner plus de bonté envers son époux. Mais la joie d'aimer dans le coeur de Mira avait laissé place à de sombres nuages,

Son époux était bien trop pris par les plaisirs du palais pour comprendre Mira, et comme elle ne goûtait pas les

Mira Bhai

Since that day everything changed for her.

The sun shone with less brilliance than the eyes of Krishna, the flowers had perfume only to celebrate Krishna and the palace had splendors only to provide shelter for him.

Farewell to toys, dolls and romps along the garden paths. From that time on, Mira spent her days and nights in front of the statue of Krishna.

At times she believed she saw a smile on his lips, and her entire little face was illumined with joy. At times he seemed to be sad, and Mira's eyes filled with tears.

And so the young princess grew, and in her young heart, love grew as well.

Her whole being was quickened by love; all the suffering and the joy of humanity seemed to be reflected in her eyes, her voice was lightly resonant, her fingers created magic sounds on her instrument, the vina.

Blind to the world, she sang each day at the temple of Krishna while the whole country sang her praises. For just as the watered plant produces unrivaled flowers, her voice acquired an incomparable beauty.

Her talent was already famed in India, and she had innumerable admirers and princes who asked for her hand.

But the notes that sounded beneath her fingers were for Krishna alone. For him she played; for him she composed songs of infinite tenderness and innocence.

But the day came when the nocturnal visits to the temple of Krishna had to end. Mira had to abandon her dream and, in the end, marry the raja of Udaipur, one of the princes who had asked for her hand. Against her wishes she was constrained to accept this marriage out of obedience and duty. Even so, no woman could have demonstrated more kindness towards her husband. But the joy of love in Mira's heart had been replaced with dark clouds.

Her husband was too occupied with the pleasures of the palace to understand Mira, and because she had no taste for the

mêmes plaisirs que lui, une certaine distance s'établit entre eux. Aussi, la jalousie s'empara de lui, car il la soupçonnait de mille trahisons.

Mira, de son côté, se consolait dans son amour caché que la séparation ne faisait qu'accroître. Et, en secret elle invoquait son bien-aimé.

"Seigneur," dit un jour au radja, un des intendants du palais, "il m'est douloureux de vous apprendre une nouvelle, mais le devoir m'oblige à vous la faire savoir. Mira vous trahit. Chaque nuit, elle cache quelque amant auprès d'elle, car on l'entend prononcer des paroles douces et des aveux interminables."

Le prince furieux s'élança vers la chambre de Mira, armé d'une épée pour tuer son rival.

Il écouta à la porte.

"Mon bien-aimé," disait Mira doucement, "combien de temps encore me faudra-t-il cacher mon amour? Bientôt je retournerai au temple te retrouver, je chanterai pour toi quand toute la terre sera plongée dans le sommeil."

A ces mots, le prince fondit sur la porte avec ses hommes et parcourut la chambre, les yeux flambant de rage.

Il n'y avait personne! .. Mira était seule.

"A qui parlais tu?" s'écria-t-il.

"A Krishna," répondit-elle.

Des éclats de rire remplirent la chambre; le prince resta stupéfait.

Depuis ce jour-là, il l'abandonna désormais à ses désirs. Elle s'enfuit du palais et vécut dans le temple de Krishna.

Là son talent se développa. Elle acquit une technique sur la vina jusque-là inconnu des musiciens hindous, at la nouvelle se répandit de plus en plus. Les musiciens accouraient de toutes parts pour l'entendre et ses chants furent joués dans les cours des rois.

Un jour l'Empereur Akbar les entendit à sa cour. Si grande fut sa surprise et son émotion qu'il se décida à aller lui-même an temple de Krishna pour entendre la grande musicienne,

same pleasures as he did, a certain distance developed between them. In addition, jealousy took hold of him, because he suspected a thousand betrayals.

As for Mira, she consoled herself in her hidden love that separation had only increased. And in secret, she invoked her beloved.

"Sire," said a palace attendant to the raja one day, "it grieves me to tell you this news, but duty obliges me to inform you. Mira is betraying you. Each night, she hides a lover beside her, and one hears sweet words spoken, and endless vows."

The furious prince rushed to Mira's chamber, armed with a sword to kill his rival.

He listened at the door.

"My beloved," said Mira sweetly, "how much longer must I hide my love? As soon as I return to the temple to find you again, I will sing for you when the whole world will be deep in slumber."

At these words, the prince knocked down the door with his men and searched the chamber, his eyes burning with rage.

No one was there! ... Mira was alone.

"Whom were you speaking to?" he cried.

"To Krishna," she answered.

Bursts of laughter filled the room, and the prince was stunned speechless.

Since that day, he abandoned her to her desires. She fled from the palace and lived in the temple of Krishna.

There her talent developed. She acquired a technique on the vina that was until then unknown to Hindu musicians, and the news of this spread further and further. Musicians came from everywhere to hear her, and her songs were played in the courts of kings.

One day the Emperor Akbar heard them at his court. So great was his surprise and emotion that he decided to go himself to the temple of Krishna to hear the great musician.

Il demanda à Tansen, le célèbre musicien de sa cour, de l'accompagner, et tous les deux partirent vers Udaipur, déguisés en mendiants.

Durant des heures ils restèrent à écouter la jeune reine agenouiliée devant la statue du prophète.

En quittant le temple, l'Empereur y laissa son collier de perles. Elle le posa autour du cou de celui qu'elle aimait.

Mais un jour le radja d'Udaipur se rendit an temple.

Il trouva le collier et il reconnut que c'était celui de l'Empereur Akbar, le collier que toutes les richesses des Indes ne pourraient payer.

La jalousie l'emporta et dans une colère violente il exila son épouse loin, loin de son royaume.

Elle s'en alla vivre loin du monde et seuls les oiseaux et les ruisseaux répétaient ses chants d'amour.

Elle y resta jusqu'à la fin de ses jours.

Ses chants ont été notés et sont restés jusqu'à nos jours les plus pures merveilles de la musique hindoue. Son nom est inscrit dans l'histoire immortelle des Indes, et le soir, sur les terrasses, sa vie demeure le thème principal des contes et des légendes.

Car l'époque de Mira Bhai fut la période la plus florissante aux Indes. Le grand Tansen avait alors porté la musique hindoue à sa plus belle apogée.

Et depuis, ni Tansen ni Mira Bhai n'ont jamais été égalés, mais leurs voix ont laissé une trace aux Indes que les âges ne pourront jamais éffacer.

Mira Bhai

He asked Tansen, the famous musician of his court, to accompany him, and together they left for Udaipur disguised as beggars.

During the hours while they listened, the young queen knelt before the statue of the prophet.

In departing the temple, the Emperor left her his necklace of pearls. Mira hung it around the neck of the one whom she loved.

But one day the Raja of Udaipur visited the temple.

He found the necklace and he recognized it as belonging to Emperor Akbar; the necklace that all the wealth of India could not buy.

Jealousy carried him away, and in a violent rage he exiled his wife far, far away from his kingdom.

She went to live far from the world, and only the birds and rushing streams repeated her songs of love.

She remained there until the end of her days.

Her songs have been written down, and have lasted until our present time as the purest marvels of Hindu music. Her name is inscribed in the immortal history of India, and in the evenings, on the terraces, her life lives on as the main theme of stories and legends.

This is because the time of Mira Bhai was the era of India's greatest blossoming. The great Tansen had carried Hindu music to its most beautiful peak.

And since then, neither Tansen nor Mira Bhai have ever been equaled, but their voices have left a mark on India which the ages could not erase.

King Akbar and His Daughter

DEAR little friends, listen to my story for it tells the tale of the great emperor Akbar who reigned over the far off land of India when all the glory and grandeur were on its soil.

Glorious were his marble palaces, which seemed to reach the blue heavens with their resplendent towers of lace. Glorious were the gardens where the flowers were of precious stones. Glorious were the majestic elephants with jewels hanging on their necks.

Such was the kingdom of Akbar the Great.

One day as he was travelling on the sea in a large vessel he saw floating above the waves a little box. And eagerly he sent the sailors swimming to fetch the box. It was soon brought on the ship and King Akbar himself opened the little box. And inside, as a little pearl in an oyster shell, was a tiny little baby girl. Thrilling with joy, Akbar held the little one in his arms, and said,

"Dear little one, lost in the waves of the sea, I have found thee, and thou shalt be my little daughter and thy name shall be Nur."

Nur grew up in the palace as a happy and loved princess. And one day, when she was quite grown up, Akbar came to her and said,

King Akbar and His Daughter

"My daughter, to whom do you owe that your life has been saved? To whom do you owe all the riches and happiness which you have enjoyed? To whom do you owe that you are the envied princess of India?"

And pointing upwards she said,

"To God."

Akbar became furious at the answer, feeling that all her life she owed to him. And overflowing with wrath, he exiled Nur far away from the palace.

For days and nights she walked far far away till she reached the gates of a city, an unknown city. Two guards stood at the gate, and seeing Nur, told her not to enter the gates for danger would await her inside the city walls.

She said to them,

"Pray tell me, who is the king of this city? What are the inhabitants, and what danger could befall a wanderer like me, harmless, penniless, roaming far away from home?"

Then they told her the whole story:

"O! unfortunate one, who but cruel fate could have guided you to these gates? Alas! Queen for one day and one night, and then no more to see the light; such is the fate of each fair daughter in this land. Heartless is the king of this country; neither the tears of a mother, nor the pleas of a daughter will he hear. Each day another is brought to the palace with the crown of a queen on her drooping forehead, and the next day must perish by the will of the monstrous monarch. O! fair one, enter not these gates. Danger awaits within the city walls."

Such were the words of the guards.

But heedless she entered within. Hardly did her eyes behold the city and her feet tread a few steps, she was taken by the soldiers and brought into the palace. Adorned with glittering garments and jewels she was brought before the king, and he said,

"Whomsoever thou be, unknown daughter from an unknown land, today thou shalt be my queen."

King Akbar and His Daughter

She said, "O! king, thou shallst first listen to my story. And when the story has come to an end, then only shall I be your queen!"

Such were her words, and the monarch was compelled to consent.

"This evening shall I hear thy story!" said he.

The evening came about and the silver moon, from its lofty abode, sent its soothing rays upon the head of Nur. She sat, telling her story to the monstrous sovereign who lay on the cushions listening in the deepest interest. Her voice was so soft and melodious that it lulled the king to sleep.

And the next day he said,

"Today, thou shallst be queen!"

But she said,

"O King, sleep came over thee and thou didst not hear the end of the story."

So the next evening he listened again, and again in the midst of the story he was lulled to sleep by her voice. And so it went on for a thousand and one nights, and the stories which she told were called *The Thousand and One Nights*, and the lives of a thousand and one daughters were saved.

At the end of the thousand and one nights, Nur escaped and did not become the queen of the monstrous sovereign. She returned to the palace of Akbar the Great, and falling into his arms, she said,

"O! Father, who has saved my life when I was far away from thee, who has protected me from danger, who has given me to eat and watched over my wandering steps?"

And Akbar, clasping his daughter in joy and rapture, pointing upward towards the sky, said,

"God!"

English original by Noor Inayat Khan

The Story of Renard the Fox

Le roman de Renard

UN jour, Renard, toujours habile dans son métier, se promenait près d'un village.

Il faisait très beau, l'air était plein de toutes sortes de bruits et Renard avait grand envie de quelque aventure.

Il s'en fut donc tout droit vers la plus grande ferme du village. Il y avait là des poules, des coqs et des canards qui ne se doutaient jamais d'une visite aussi importante.

Renard grimpa sur la haie, étira ses pattes, et se préparait à sauter et à atterrir en plein milieu de la basse-cour. Mais, pensait-il, les poulets auront bien vite fait de se sauver, il faudra trouver un autre moyen.

Des choux étaient plantés tout près de là et, sur la pointe des pattes, Renard se glissa dans les choux.

Mais les petites demoiselles poulets l'avaient bien aperçu et elles s'enfuirent éperdument vers la maison.

Messire Chanteclair (c'était ainsi que se nommait le coq souverain de la ferme), se dressa d'un air très indigné.

"Petites filles," s'écria-t-il, "qu'avez-vous à filer ainsi?"

"C'est que," expliqua dame Pinte qui était la plus sage, et qui pondait les œufs les plus gros, "nous avons eu grand peur car nous avons vu une grosse bête sauvage se cacher près d'ici!"

"Comment l'avez-vous vu?" demanda Chanteclair.

The Story of Renard the Fox

ONE day Renard, always cunning in his work, went for a stroll near a village.

It was a beautiful day, the air was full of all sorts of sounds, and Renard had a great desire for some adventure.

So he ran right up to the largest farm in the village. There were hens, roosters and ducks who did not suspect they were about to have such an important visit.

Renard climbed up on the hedgerow, stretched out his paws, and prepared to leap and land right in the middle of the farmyard. But then he thought, "The hens will be very quick to run away; I'll have to find another way."

Some cabbages were planted nearby and, on the tips of his paws, Renard slid down among the cabbages.

But the little maiden hens had clearly seen this and they desperately rushed off towards the house.

Sir Chanticlair (this was the name of the rooster, the sovereign of the farm), assumed an indignant air.

"Little girls," he cried, "why are you running off like this?"

"It's because," explained Lady Pinter, who was the wisest of the hens and who laid the largest eggs, "we are very much afraid because we have seen a large wild animal hide nearby!"

"How did you see him?" asked Chanticlair.

"Les feuilles des choux ont tremblé," répondirent-elles toutes en chœur, et la bête s'est blottie en dessous !"

Et Chanteclair parti d'un grand éclat de rire.

"Mais de quoi avez-vous peur?" s'écria-t-il, "il n'est ni renard ni rat qui oserait entrer ici lorsque j'y suis! Retournez donc où vous étiez et ne vous emportez pas ainsi pour rien!"

Après ce discours très sage, Chanteclair, bien content de lui-même, se percha sur le toit, ferma un œil, puis l'autre, et s'endormit.

Il eut un rêve, un rêve bien triste. Il vit en songe la basse-cour qui était pourtant bien fermée de tous les côtés et quelque chose de bien étrange s'avançant vers lui. A ce moment-là il frissonna de toutes ses plumes.

Et ce quelque chose avait une fourrure couleur des feuilles après l'été, et cette chose vint vers lui, le saisit et l'emmena sur son dos. Chanteclair fut bien en détresse et il avait tant envie de crier qu'il s'éveilla.

Il alla tout droit vers Pinte, la bonne dame.

"Pinte," lui dit-il, "je viens d'avoir un songe très fâcheux et c'est pour cela que tu me vois si pâle: quelque chose, je ne sais quoi exactement, venait vers moi. C'était quelque chose avec une fourrure couleur des feuilles après l'été. Et cette chose me jeta sur son dos. C'était très triste, Pinte, et j'en suis tout confus."

"Pauvre Seigneur," dit Pinte, "ne t'en prends qu'à toi-même car je te dis que sous ces choux il se cache un goupil qui se jettera sur toi quand tu ne t'y attendras pas!"

"Pinte ! Méchante Pinte!" s'écria Chanteclair, "ne me parle pas ainsi. Il n'est point possible qu'un malheur m'advienne à la suite de ce rêve! Non, Pinte, tu n'es pas gentille!"

Et Chanteclair s'en alla de nouveau sur le toit et se remit à dormir.

Pendant ce temps, Renard s'impatientait sous les choux.

The Story of Renard the Fox

"The cabbage leaves were shaking," they replied in a chorus, "and the beast is crouched underneath."

Then Chanticlair let out a great burst of laughter.

"But what do you have to fear?" he cried, "no fox or rat would dare enter while I am here; so return to wherever you were and don't get carried away over nothing again!"

After this very wise speech, Chanticlair, pleased with himself, perched on the roof, closed one eye and then the other, and fell asleep.

He had a dream, a very sad dream. In his dream, the rooster saw the farmyard which was, as usual, safely enclosed on all sides, and yet something very strange was advancing towards him. At that moment he ruffled all his feathers.

And that something had a coat of fur the color of leaves after the end of summer, and that thing was coming towards him and flung him across the fur on its back. Chanticlair was most distressed and had such a desire to scream that he awoke.

He went straight to Lady Pinter, the good hen.

"Pinter," he said to her, "I have had a very upsetting dream, and that's why you see me looking so pale: something, I don't know what exactly, was coming towards me. It was something with fur the color of leaves after the end of summer. And that thing flung me across the fur on its back. It was very sad, Pinter, and I am utterly confused."

"Poor Sire," said Lady Pinter, "no one is to blame but you yourself, because I told you that, hidden beneath the cabbages, was a fox who would jump on you when you were least expecting it!"

"Pinter! Wicked Pinter!" cried Chanticlair, "Do not speak to me like this. It's impossible that misfortune will come to me as a result of that dream! No, Pinter, you are not kind!"

And Chanticlair returned to the roof and went back to sleep.

During all this time, Renard was becoming impatient beneath the cabbages.

D'un bond il sauta, mais, tout en dormant, Chanteclair sauta si bien de côté que Renard en resta tout ébahi.

Comme il était en assez mauvaise posture, il parla à Chanteclair d'une voix douce et mélodieuse.

"Chanteclair, mon ami, pourquoi me crains-tu? Ne sais-tu pas que je suis ton cousin germain? Te souviens-tu de Chanteclin, ton père? Sa voix était si belle et si forte qu'on l'entendait à trente fermes d'ici. Tu lui ressembles, Chanteclair, tes plumes sont couleur du soleil comme les siennes et je t'assure que si je suis venu ici c'est que j'ai entendu ta voix de loin!"

"Tu veux me flatter," dit Chanteclair.

"Mais tu ne me comprends pas," répliqua Renard, "c'est que je veux t'entendre chanter. Allons, je suis venu de si loin pour cela et tu as vu comme j'ai sauté de joie en te voyant ! Chanteclair, sois gentil et chante pour moi, et pour me faire plaisir, cligne tes yeux, c'est si émouvant!"

"Si tu veux que je chante," dit Chanteclair, "retire-toi un peu en arrière."

Puis, gonflant le gosier, un œil ouvert et l'autre fermé, Chanteclair poussa un grand cri.

"Ah ! Comme ton père chantait mieux que toi!" dit Renard. "Sa voix était forte et suave. Les yeux fermés, et prenant son souffle, il lançait son fausset à trente villages d'ici."

Chanteclair n'en pouvait plus. Il se dressa sur ses pattes, ferma les yeux, prit une longue haleine et se mit à chanter à tue-tête.

Aussitôt Renard bondit.

On n'entendait plus Chanteclair. Il était pris.

Pinte et les petits poulets se mirent à crier.

"Ciel!" s'écrièrent-ils, "que ferons-nous? Notre bon seigneur est pri !"

C'était l'heure où le soleil s'en allait derrière les champs. La bonne fermière sortit pour appeler les poulets et, en voyant le goupil emporter Chanteclair, elle poussa des cris de désespoir.

The Story of Renard the Fox

He leaped with one bound but, still sound asleep, Chanticlair jumped aside so easily that Renard was astounded.

Since he now found himself in an embarrassing situation, the fox spoke to Chanticlair in a sweet and melodious voice.

"Chanticlair my friend, why are you afraid of me? Don't you know that I am your first cousin? Do you remember Crowcleer your father? His voice was so beautiful and so strong that one could hear it thirty farms from here. You resemble him, Chanticlair: your feathers are the color of the sun, like his, and I assure you that if I have come here, it's because I heard your voice from far away!"

"You're trying to flatter me," suggested Chanticlair.

"But you don't understand," replied Renard, "it's because I longed to hear you sing. That is why I came from so far away, and you have seen how I leaped for joy upon seeing you! Chanticlair, be so kind and sing for me, and to please me, blink your eyes; it's so moving!"

"If you wish for me to sing," said Chanticlair, "step back a little."

Then, inflating his gullet, with one eye open and the other closed, Chanticlair uttered a great cry.

"Ah! Your father sang better than you!" exclaimed Renard. "His voice was strong and sweet. With closed eyes, and taking a deep breath, he projected his falsetto thirty farms away."

Chanticlair could wait no longer. He raised himself up high on his toes, closed his eyes, drew in a long breath and began to crow his head off.

Immediately Renard sprang, and Chanticlair was no longer to be heard.

He had been captured.

Lady Pinter and the little chickens cried out.

"Heavens," they gasped, "What shall we do? Our good sire is captured!"

It was the hour when the sun sank behind the fields. The good farmwife came out to call in the chickens and, seeing the fox carry off Chanticlair, she let out a cry of despair.

Aussitôt les fermiers accoururent de toutes parts.

"Qu'y a-t-il, petite fermière? Qu'y a-t-i?" s'écrièrent-ils.

"Par ce chemin, là-bas," répondit-elle, "Renard emporte Chanteclair!"

De gros bâtons à la main et en jetant des cris, les fermiers se mirent sur la piste du goupil.

"Sire Renard," dit Chanteclair, "n'entends-tu pas comme on crie? Quand on est goupil, on ne se laisse pas insulter ainsi! Pourquoi ne leur réponds-tu pas: 'vous ne m'aurez pas cette fois-ci!'?"

C'en était trop pour la dignité de Renard.

"Cette fois-ci vous ne m'aurez pas!" s'écria-t-il. Et aussitôt qu'il ouvrit la bouche, Chanteclair batta les ailes et s'envola.

Il se percha sur un pommier et partit d'un rire que l'on entendait à dix lieues de là…..

Pour une fois, ce fut Renard le trompé et non le trompeur.

II

Tibert était là. Tibert son ennemi qui, en dépit de toute la ruse dont Renard était célèbre, avait réussi tant de fois à le duper. Renard grinçait des dents de rancune.

Pauvre goupil! Il avait si faim. Comme il aurait bien voulu saisir ce chat!

Mais Tibert avait des griffes comme n'en ont pas tous les chats et ses prouesses dans les combats étaient connues.

"Renard, mon ami," dit Tibert, "qu'est-il donc arrivé pour que tu sois fâché? J'ai grande peine à te voir ainsi."

"Tibert," répondit-il, "ne me pose pas de questions mais écoute plutôt ce que j'ai à te dire: Je vais déclarer la guerre à Ysengrin, mon ennemi. J'ai déjà plusieurs alliés qui se préparent au combat; si tu veux venir aussi, nous conclurons ensemble un pacte de fidélité."

Immediately the farmers came running from every direction.

"What is it, little farmwife? What is it?" they cried.

"By the road, over there," she replied, "Renard is carrying off my dear Chanticlair!"

Stout staffs in hand and uttering shouts, the farmers followed the fox's trail.

"Sir Renard," said Chanticlair, "don't you hear the shouts? When one is a fox, one cannot allow them to insult you like this! Why don't you answer them: 'You shall not get me this time!'?"

This was too much for Renard's pride.

"You shall not get me this time!" he shouted. And as soon as he opened his mouth, Chanticlair flapped his wings and flew away.

He perched atop an apple tree and let out a laugh which one could hear ten leagues off...

For once, Renard was the tricked one and not the trickster.

II

Tiber sat there. Tiber his enemy, who, in spite of all the cunning for which Renard was famous, had succeeded so many times in fooling him. Renard gnashed his teeth in frustration.

Poor fox! He was so hungry. How he would have liked to seize that cat!

But Tiber had claws like no other cat, and his prowess in battle was renowned.

"Renard, my friend," said Tiber, "what has happened to make you so cross? I am greatly pained to see you like this."

"Tiber," he replied, "don't ask me questions but rather listen to what I have to suggest to you: I am going to declare war on my enemy, Ysengrin the wolf. I already have several allies who are preparing themselves for combat; if you wish to come too, we'll make a pact of loyalty to each other."

"Bien volontiers," répondit Tibert, "je suis en bonne santé, mes griffes sont aiguisées et, par la foi que je dois à mon chef, je jure de rester loyal!"

Le pacte fut donc conclu et ils marchèrent côte à côte tout le long du sentier.

Néanmoins, Renard n'avait pas oublié sa rancune. Il aperçut soudain à quelque distance sur la route un piège qu'un homme avait construit. Renard sursauta en le voyant.

"Compagnon," dit-il à Tibert, "à peine le soleil s'était-il levé ce matin que j'ai commencé à m'exercer au combat, car il faut pouvoir courir à toute allure. Et toi, tu n'as rien fait pour cela. Cours donc un peu afin que je voie de quoi tu es capable!"

Tibert baissa la tête, visa son but et partit d'une course invraisemblable.

"Il sera pris!... il sera pris!..." pensait Renard tout heureux de son triomphe.

Mais, arrivé au bord du piège, Tibert, le malin, s'arrêta. Il comprit alors la trahison de Renard et franchit d'un bond le piège.

Au même moment, deux chiens ayant vu le goupil, se mirent à le poursuivre sans relâche. Renard courait, mais il touchait le piège. Que faire? Les chiens étaient à gauche, à droite, et Renard dans son émoi, fit un faux pas. La clé du piège sauta et le pauvre goupil fut pris.

"Sire Renard," cria Tibert, "te voilà donc bien hébergé! Je te souhaite une bonne nuit et des rêves charmants. Adieu! Je m'en vais au combat!"

Ah! Quelle détresse, que de mésaventures! Renard n'avait jamais tant souffert de sa vie.

Mais il n'était plus temps de pleurer. Un homme, un grand homme qui suivait les chiens, accourut portant une hache. Au moment où il l'abaissa pour frapper le goupil, la hache fendit le piège et Renard s'échappa.

Son pied blessé, boitant comme un vieillard, il fila néanmoins à toute allure. Et bien que tout heureux de s'être sauvé, Renard tremblait encore en pensant à la hache.

The Story of Renard the Fox

"Willingly," replied Tiber, "I am in good health, my claws are sharpened, and by the faith which I give to my master, I swear to remain loyal."

The pact was then concluded and they walked side by side along the path.

Nevertheless, Renard had not forgotten his bitterness.

Suddenly, at some distance away on the road, Renard noticed a man-made trap.

"Companion," said he to Tiber, "scarcely had the sun risen this morning than I began to train for combat, because one must be able to run at top speed; and you, you have done nothing for that. Now run a little so that I can see what you are capable of doing!"

Tiber lowered his head, set his sights into the distance, and raced off at incredible speed.

"He will be caught!... He will be caught!..." thought Renard, utterly pleased with his victory.

But approaching the edge of the trap, cunning Tiber managed to stop. He then understood Renard's betrayal, and jumped over the trap.

At the same moment, two dogs had seen the fox and they set out to pursue him relentlessly. Renard ran ahead with the dogs on either side: one to the left and one to the right. Renard, in his fear, made a mistake. The latch of the trap was released, and the poor fox was captured.

"Sir Renard," cried Tiber, "you are well lodged there! I wish you a good night and lovely dreams. Farewell! I am going off to the battle!"

Ah! What miseries! What misadventures! Renard had never suffered so much in his life.

But it was no longer time to cry; a man — a large man who followed the dogs — ran up carrying an axe. At the moment when he lowered it to strike the fox, the axe broke the trap, and Renard escaped.

With his paw wounded, hobbling like an old man, he nevertheless fled at top speed. And though he was well pleased at having been saved, Renard still trembled, thinking of the axe.

"O Ciel!" s'écria-t-il, "ne m'envoie pas tant de malheurs! De grâce! Je ne ferai plus aucun mal de ma vie!"

Mais à peine eût-il prononcé son doux repentir que mille pensées de vengeance lui passèrent par la tête.

D'ailleurs, qu'était-ce donc qui remuait là-bas sur les branches?

Renard se blottit à quelques pas de là, le museau entre ses pattes et attendit.

III

Les feuilles s'entrouvrirent doucement et Tiècelin, le corbeau, apparut, un grand fromage blanc au bec.

"Tiècelin, mon ami," dit Renard, "vois-tu comme je suis blessé? Oui, la vie est bien triste, les hommes ne pensent qu'à nous faire du mal. On ne peut même plus courir dans les bois sans qu'un piège soit posé à chaque pas."

Tiècelin hocha la tête en signe d'approbation.

"Tiècelin, mon doux ami," continua Renard, "comment se fait-il que tu ne chantes plus? Toi qui a la voix si douce, l'as-tu donc perdue pour toujours?"

"Point du tout," répondit Tiècelin sans pourtant lâcher son fromage, "c'est qu'à présent j'ai un fromage qui m'occupe."

Ah! qu'il était blanc ce fromage!

"Ami," dit Renard, "l'autre soir j'écoutais Rossignol qui s'est fait, comme tu le sais, une grande renommée durant ces dernières années. Ses trilles étaient si merveilleux que tous les habitants du bois en restèrent muets."

C'en était trop pour Tiècelin! Il ouvrit son bec, poussa un cri, et le fromage tomba à terre.

Mais, tout en chantant, Tiècelin s'en souvint et arrêta brusquement sa chanson.

"Oui, coquin," dit-il à Renard, "c'est mon fromage que tu veux me voler!"

The Story of Renard the Fox

"Oh Heaven!" he cried, "Do not send me such misfortune, please! I will never do another bad thing in my life!"

But scarcely had he pronounced his sweet repentance than a thousand thoughts of revenge passed through his head.

Besides, who was moving up there, in the top branches?

Renard crouched several steps away, his snout between his paws, and he waited.

III

The leaves parted gently, and Tiecelin the raven appeared, holding a large white cheese in his beak.

"Tiecelin, my friend," said Renard, "look how wounded I am. Yes, life is very sad, men think of nothing but wickedness against us. One can no longer run in the woods without a trap being placed at each step."

Tiecelin nodded his head to signal agreement.

"Tiecelin, my sweet friend," said Renard, "why is it that you don't sing anymore? You, who have such a sweet voice, have then lost it forever?"

"Not at all," said Tiecelin without dropping his cheese, "it's because at present I am busy with a cheese."

Ah! How white the cheese was!

"Friend," said Renard, "the other evening I heard Rossignol the nightingale who has become, as you know, greatly famous during these last years. His trills were so marvelous that all those who dwell in the woods remained silent."

This was too much for Tiecelin!

He opened his beak, gave forth a cry, and the cheese fell to the ground.

But in the midst of singing, Tiecelin remembered and abruptly stopped his song.

"Yes, you rascal," he said to Renard, "it's my cheese you wish to steal from me!"

"Moi? Non!" répondit Renard. "Je n'aime point le fromage et je me sens trop mal pour manger. Viens, compagnon, prends-le, ne crains pas un pauvre malade qui a le pied blessé!"

Tiècelin, se sentant rassuré, descendit de sa branche altière. Le rusé bondit alors sur lui!

"Vieux félon!" s'écria le corbeau, "prends le fromage si tu veux, mais moi, tu ne m'auras point, c'est certain!"

Renard baissa la tête bien tristement. Comme il aurait bien voulu les deux !

Et il partit en pleurnichant, le fromage entre les dents.

Non loin de là une belle fourrure avec de longues moustaches remuait entre les feuilles, et deux grands yeux guettaient le chemin.

"Encore Tibert!" soupira Renard.

Et Tibert, en voyant le goupil, sentit un grand frisson lui passer sur le dos.

Il aiguisa ses griffes, se mit en bonne posture et attendit.

"N'aie pas peur, Tibert," dit Renard, "je ne t'en veux pas, tu sais. Au fond, tu as été très méchant de me laisser seul en si grand péril. J'ai été durement blessé dans le piège mais je te pardonne."

Tibert fit de doux yeux car il se sentait un peu coupable.

"Tibert, mon ami," dit le goupil, "la vie est très triste. On ne voit autour de soi que ruse, que trahison. On cherche toujours à se causer du mal l'un à l'autre. Je parle de ce monstre d'Ysengrin à qui je vais faire la guerre."

Et ils trottèrent ainsi, côte à côte en parlant des choses de ce monde.

A peu de distance sur le sentier était une anguille, qu'une paysanne avait dû laisser tomber de sa corbeille. Qu'elle était bonne et longue!

Renard et Tibert ouvrirent bien grand les yeux.

"Nous la mangerons ensemble, n'est-ce pas?" dit Renard.

"Certes!" répondit Tibert.

"Me? No!" said Renard, "I don't like cheese at all and I am feeling too sick to eat. Come, friend, take it, don't be afraid of a poor sick one who has a wounded paw!"

Feeling reassured, Tiecelin descended from the height of his branch.

The trickster then pounced upon him.

Tiecelin was agile and managed to escape, but a good many of his feathers remained between the teeth of the fox!

"You old crook!" cried the raven, "take the cheese if you like, but you cannot have me at all; I am sure of that!"

Renard lowered his head sadly. How he had wanted both!

And he departed whimpering, the cheese between his teeth.

Not far from there a beautiful fur coat with long whiskers moved among the leaves, and two large eyes observed the road.

"Tiber again!" sighed Renard.

And Tiber, seeing the fox, felt a great shudder pass over his back.

He sharpened his claws, assumed a ready stance and waited.

"Don't be afraid, Tiber," said Renard, "I don't want you, you know. In reality, you were very wicked to leave me alone in such great danger. I have been badly wounded by the trap, but I forgive you."

Tiber gave the fox a coy look because he felt a little guilty.

"Tiber, my friend," said the fox, "life is very sad. One sees nothing but trickery and betrayal; one always searches for the cause of one evil or another. I am speaking of that monster Ysengrin, whom I am going to fight."

And they trotted off like this, side by side and speaking of the things of this world.

A short distance along the path lay an eel, which a peasant had dropped from her basket.

How good and long it looked!

Renard and Tiber opened their eyes wide.

"We will eat it together, won't we?" said Renard.

"Certainly!" replied Tiber.

Et Renard la prit entre ses dents.

"Portons-la plus loin," dit le goupil, "nous y serons bien plus tranquilles!"

Mais Tibert ne fut point tranquille à ce sujet et se mit à froncer les sourcils.

"Tu la portes mal," dit-il à Renard, "regarde comme tu la traînes par terre!"

"Et comment donc faut-il la porter?" demanda le goupil.

"Attends que je te montre," dit Tibert, et Renard, en voyant ses griffes, la lui passa sans mot dire.

Tibert prit soigneusement un bout entre ses dents et lança le reste sur son dos.

"Voilà!" s'écria-t-il, "et maintenant à qui le premier!"

Et il partit si vite qu'il ne touchait guère le sol. Renard courait après lui.

Tibert arriva le premier et sauta sur un pieu qui mesurait un peu plus que la hauteur du nez de Renard. Le goupil trembla de fureur.

"Pendant sept ans je resterai ici s'il le faut, mais tu ne m'échapperas pas!" s'écria-t-il.

"Je ne vois pas très bien Sire Renard jeûner pendant sept an!" dit Tibert en avalant son anguille.

Des rumeurs inquiétantes venaient de loin : des aboiements approchaient. Renard dressa les oreilles. Il était poursuivi!

Il écouta, puis s'enfuit et disparut derrière les chênes.

Et Tibert, en le voyant s'éloigner, riait à en perdre le souffle.

"A bientôt!" cria-t-il au goupil.

IV

Mais Renard oublia bien vite ses chagrins car il trouva non loin de là une charrette toute pleine de poissons.

Il y fourra le museau et sans s'inquiéter ni de bête, ni d'oiseau, il en mangea tout un panier.

And Renard seized it between his teeth.

"We'll carry it further," said the fox, "we will be safer over there!"

But Tiber was not at all easy about this, and he frowned.

"You are carrying it badly," said he to Renard, "look how you're dragging it on the ground."

"And how then should it be carried?" demanded the fox.

"Wait while I show you," said Tiber, and Renard, seeing his claws, handed it over without saying a word.

Tiber carefully took one end between his teeth and tossed the rest over his back.

"There!" he cried, "And now let's see who will be the first!"

And he took off so quickly that he barely touched the ground. Renard ran after him.

Tiber arrived first and leaped upon a post that was a little taller than the height of Renard's nose.

The fox trembled with fury.

"I will stay here for seven years if necessary, but you will not escape me!" he cried.

"I cannot imagine good Sir Renard fasting for seven years!" said Tiber while gulping down his eel.

Alarming noises came from afar: the barking drew nearer. Renard pricked his ears. He was being pursued!

He listened, and then he fled and disappeared behind some oak trees.

And Tiber, seeing him running into the distance, laughed until he was out of breath.

"So long!" he cried to the fox.

IV

But Renard quickly forgot his troubles, for not far from there he found a cart filled with fish.

He foraged there with his muzzle, and without disturbing beast or bird, he ate a whole basketful.

Puis il en emporta de bien frais sur son dos, des roses, des argentés et des blancs. Il fit un petit salut au charretier qui arrivait brandissant son bâton, et retourna à son château à Maupertuis.

Il y trouva sa gentille femme Hermeline au nez pointu et ses deux petits Percehaie et Malebranche.

Dame Hermeline était en pleurs car elle s'inquiétait beaucoup de cette longue absence de Renard.

Il s'assit au coin du feu, Malebranche et Percehaie lui essuyèrent la fourrure mouillée, et mit les poissons à griller.

Comme ils doraient bien! Et quels doux arômes sortaient par la cheminée!

Ysengrin, le loup, qui passait par là ne pouvait pas y résister.

"Il faut à tout prix que j'en goûte!" pensa-t-il, "mais comment?"

Il alla à la porte et frappa doucement.

"Qui est là?" demanda Renard.

"C'est ton frère!" répondit Ysengrin.

"Quel frère?" demanda Renard.

"Ton frère Ysengrin, ne me reconnais-tu pas?"

"Je ne peux pas t'ouvrir tout de suite car nous sommes à table," répondit le goupil.

"Est-ce qu'on laisse son frère ainsi à la porte sans même l'inviter?" dit Ysengrin. "Au moins pourrais-tu me dire si c'est de la viande grillée qui sent si bon!"

"C'est du poisson," répliqua Renard. "Il y a des truites, des brochets et des harengs."

"Qu'est-ce donc que le poisson?" demanda Ysengrin. "Est-ce que c'est bon?"

Renard lui en jeta deux ou trois par la fenêtre.

Le loup les avala d'un trait. Comme ils étaient bons!

"Si tu en veux," dit Renard, "je te montrerai où et comment on en trouve, mais attends que j'aie fini de dîner."

Ysengrin s'assit bien patiemment à la porte et attendit.

The Story of Renard the Fox

Then he carried off the fresh fish on his back: some red, some silver and some white ones. He gave a little bow toward the cart driver who arrived brandishing his staff, and scurried back to his castle in Maupertuis.

There he found his kind wife Hermeline who had such a lovely pointed muzzle, and their two little ones: Hedge-Holer and Malebranche.

Lady Hermeline was in tears because she was most upset over Renard's long absence.

He sat in a corner by the fire, drying his wet fur, with Malebranche and Hedge-Holer nearby. The fish were placed on the grill.

How nicely golden they turned! And what sweet aromas went up the chimney!

Ysengrin the wolf, who was passing by, could not resist the aroma.

"I must have a taste at any price!" thought he, "but how?"

He went to the door and knocked politely.

"Who is there?" asked Renard.

"It's your brother!" replied Ysengrin.

"What brother?" asked Renard.

"Your brother Ysengrin; don't you recognize me?"

"I can't open the door for you right away because we are at the table," replied the fox.

"Does one leave his brother at the door like this without inviting him in?" said Ysengrin. "At least can you tell me if it's roasted meat that smells so good?"

"It's fish," answered Renard. "There is trout, pike and herring."

"What is fish?" asked Ysengrin, "Is it good?"

Renard threw a couple of them out the window.

Ysengrin gulped them down in a flash. How tasty they were!

"If you wish," said Renard, "I will show you where and how I found them, but wait till I finish eating."

Ysengrin sat patiently at the door and waited.

Renard sortit bientôt et ils s'en allèrent côte à côte en parlant de leurs grandes prouesses.

Un petit lac était là parmi les arbres.

Renard y conduisit son illustre compagnon.

"C'est ici, vois-tu," lui dit-il, "que l'on trouve des poissons."

Un seau se trouvait au bord de l'eau.

"Tiens!" dit Renard, "c'est avec ceci qu'on les prend."

Et, avec beaucoup de soin, il attacha le seau à la queue du loup.

"Plonge-le," dit Renard, "et attends que tous les poissons soient dedans."

Ysengrin tourna le dos au petit lac et plongea sa queue dans l'eau.

Le goupil s'en alla dormir au pied d'un arbre et épia Ysengrin du coin de l'œil.

Mais il faisait très froid, la bise soufflait et l'air était plein de brouillard.

Bientôt tout le lac fut gelé et la queue d'Ysengrin fut prise dans la glace.

Il attendit.

Le soleil disparaissait déjà et le grand monde devenait obscur.

Ysengrin attendait toujours….

Comme la nuit était longue! Elle n'avait jamais été si longue de toute sa vie!

Ysengrin soupirait et gémissait.

Enfin le matin apparut et le pauvre loup avait les yeux mouillés.

"Compagnon," dit-il à Renard, "le seau est si lourd, il me pèse à la queue, je crois qu'il est plein de poissons."

"Retire-le donc!" dit le goupil.

Ysengrin tira, mais hélas ! sa queue était prise!

Au même moment Renard se redressa. Des cris lointains approchaient.

Il partit d'un bond et fila droit vers le bois.

The Story of Renard the Fox

Renard came out soon, and they went off side by side, speaking of their great deeds.

A little lake nestled among the trees.

Renard guided his illustrious companion there.

"It's here, you see," he said, "that one finds fish."

A bucket was discovered at the edge of the water.

"Take it!" said Renard, "With that, one can catch them."

And, very carefully, he tied the bucket to Ysengrin's tail.

"Plunge it in," said Renard, "and wait until all the fish are inside of it."

Ysengrin turned his back to the little lake and immersed his tail in the water.

The fox went to sleep at the foot of a tree and watched Ysengrin out of the corner of his eye.

But it grew very cold, the north wind blew and the air was full of mist.

Soon the whole lake froze, and Ysengrin's tail was stuck in the ice.

He waited.

The sun had already disappeared and the large moon became hidden in the fog.

Ysengrin still waited... ...

How long the night was! There had never been such a long night in all his life!

Ysengrin sighed and groaned.

Finally the morning appeared, and the poor wolf's eyes were wet.

"My friend," he said to Renard, "the bucket is so heavy, it weighs on my tail and I believe it's full of fish."

"Then pull it out!" said the fox.

Ysengrin pulled but alas! His tail was stuck!

At the same moment, Renard rose up on his haunches.

Far off, cries were approaching.

He departed in one bound and ran off straight towards the woods.

Mais Ysengrin avait beau tirer, la glace était trop dure.

Les cris étaient tout près. C'étaient des cris d'hommes, des pas de chevaux, des aboiements interminables de chiens.

"Au secour!" criaient-ils. "Au loup!"

Pauvre Ysengrin ! Il était entouré d'hommes, de chevaux et de chiens.

Il se défendit comme un guerrier qui a toute l'expérience de ces assauts.

Et dans la lutte, un des hommes leva sa faux, mais au lieu de frapper Ysengrin, la faux perça la glace et Ysengrin put retirer sa queue: il était libre!

D'un bond il sauta par-dessus les chiens, le seau encore suspendu à sa queue. Et Ysengrin s'enfuit ainsi dans les bois.

Il s'arrêta enfin lorsque le danger était passé et se jeta à terre tremblant et hors d'haleine.

Petit singe Cointereau l'avait vu. Il descendit donc de la branche où il était et lui détacha le seau de la queue.

Cependant, Dame Hersent, la bonne louve, et les quatre petits louveteaux n'avaient pas dormi de la nuit car Ysengrin n'était pas rentré le soir au logis, et ce matin-là, ils erraient par la forêt en poussant des cris désespérés.

Mais bientôt ils trouvèrent leur père, qui était en train de discuter de graves questions avec Cointereau et d'autres amis.

Aussi Dame Hersent avait bien du chagrin en le voyant, car son dos était plein de blessures. Les petits louveteaux lui frottèrent le museau et l'entourèrent de mille tendresses.

"Doux Seigneur," lui dit Hersent, "qu'est-il donc arrivé? J'ai bien de la peine à te voir ainsi."

Ysengrin tremblait encore, et d'une voix pleine de sanglots, il raconta le triste récit.

Cependant, de tous les coins de la forêt venaient mille petites têtes.

On vit arriver Brichemer, le cerf et maréchal à la Cour, Belin le mouton, Beaucent le sanglier, Blanchépine, le lapin, puis Léopard et Panthère.

The Story of Renard the Fox

But although Ysengrin pulled hard, the ice was too hard.

The cries were quite close. There were the cries of men, the hooves of horses, the endless barking of dogs.

"Help!" they cried. "A wolf!"

Poor Ysengrin! He was surrounded by men, horses and dogs.

He defended himself like a warrior who was thoroughly experienced in these attacks.

And in the struggle, one of the men raised his scythe, but instead of striking Ysengrin, the scythe broke the ice, and Ysengrin was able to pull out his tail: he was free!

With a single bound he leaped over the dogs, the bucket still hanging from his tail. And Ysengrin ran off into the woods.

He finally stopped when the danger was past and collapsed trembling on the ground, completely out of breath.

A little monkey, Cointereau, saw him. He climbed down from the branch where he sat and he untied the bucket from Ysengrin's tail.

Meanwhile, Dame Hersent, the good she-wolf, and her four little wolf cubs hadn't slept during the night because Ysengrin hadn't returned home in the evening, and that morning they ran through the forest, uttering desperate cries.

But soon they found him, deep in discussion with Cointereau and other friends.

Dame Hersent was filled with dismay seeing Ysengrin like this, for his back was full of wounds. The little wolf cubs rubbed his muzzle and cuddled up to him affectionately.

"Sweet Sire," Hersent said to him, "what has happened? It pains me to see you like this."

Ysengrin trembled again, and in a sobbing voice he told the sad story.

Meanwhile, a thousand little heads appeared from all corners of the forest.

One could see Brichemere the deer and the Marshall of the Court; Belin the sheep; Beaucent the wild boar; Blanchepine, the hare; then Leopard and Panther.

Vinrent aussi les corbeaux et les petits tourtereaux, et tout le monde écouta le récit.

Beaucent commença à grogner, Blanchépine à frapper du pied, Brichemer à baisser ses cornes et tout ce monde fut bien courroucé des actions de Renard, le rusé.

On décida donc de porter plainte à la Cour de Noble, le lion, roi de toute la forêt.

Tous, grands et petits, furent donc appelés à s'assembler à la Cour.

Ce fut Sire Hibou qui veille toujours sur la plus haute branche, qui lança l'appel dans la nuit.

Et tous accoururent sauf Sire Renard, qui se chauffait les pattes au coin du feu dans son château à Maupertuis.

V

Noble, le grand roi, prit place sur son trône.

A sa droite était Brichemer, le cerf, premier maréchal à la Cour, et à gauche, Rousselet, l'écureuil.

Toute la Cour fut donc assemblée; seul Musard, le chameau, que de graves affaires politiques retenaient dans une autre partie de la forêt, arriva en retard.

Le roi donna d'abord la parole à Ysengrin car le malheureux avait si mauvaise mine que Noble en avait grande pitié.

Ysengrin fit alors une grande révérence et commença sa plainte.

"Grand roi," dit-il, "voyez mes blessures! Ce n'est pas la première fois que je suis victime des ruses du seigneur Renard, le plus traître de tes sujets. Il m'a conduit à un lac, attaché je ne sais quoi à ma queue et m'a fait passer la nuit ainsi, la queue prise dans la glace. Tout cela, soi-disant pour prendre des poissons. Et c'est par miracle que me voilà sauvé après avoir lutté contre je ne sais combien d'hommes et de chiens. Vraiment, mon roi, s'il y a justice sur cette terre, je mériterais de recevoir de grands honneurs et Renard d'être durement châtié!"

The ravens also came, as well as the little turtledoves, and everyone listened to the story.

Beaucent the boar began to snort, Blanchepine the rabbit thumped her foot, Brichemere the deer lowered his antlers and everyone was angered by the actions of Renard, the trickster.

Then they decided to take their complaint to the Court of Noble the lion, king of the whole forest.

All of them, large and small, called for an assembly at the Court.

It was Sir Hibou the owl (who was always watching on top of the highest branch) who gave out the call in the night.

And everyone came running except for Sir Renard, who warmed his paws in a corner by the fireside in his castle at Maupertuis.

V

Noble, the great king, took his place on the throne.

At his right stood Brichemere the deer, the first Marshall of the Court, and at his left, Russet the squirrel.

The whole court was assembled, except for Musard the camel, who was engaged in serious political affairs in another part of the forest and would arrive late.

The king then gave Ysengrin the first chance to speak, for the unfortunate one had such a miserable appearance that Noble felt pity for him.

So Ysengrin gave a deep bow and began his complaint.

"Great King," said he, "look at my wounds. This is not the first time I have been a victim of the tricks of Sir Renard, the most treacherous of your subjects. He led me to a lake, attached I-don't-know-what to my tail, and had me spend the night like that, so that my tail froze in the ice. All this was supposedly to catch fish. And it is by a miracle that I am here safe, after having fought against I-don't-know-how-many men and dogs. Truly, my King, if there is justice on this earth, I deserve to receive great honors, and Renard deserves to be severely punished."

Hersent approuva ce récit par de grands hochements de tête, mais Noble écouta sans mot dire car tout au fond du cœur il avait un petit point de sympathie pour Renard qui était, à vrai dire, un des chevaliers les plus habiles du royaume.

"Quelqu'un d'autre a-t-il quelque chose à dire?" demanda-t-il.

"Moi!" dit Tiècelin en battant ses ailes. "Moi!" dit Tibert, en sortant ses griffes. "Moi!" dit l'ours Brun, en montrant ses crocs. Et ils criaient tous à la fois.

"Silence!" rugit alors Noble en frappant du pied, "il n'y a donc pas de bonnes manières en ce pays! Taisez-vous ou vous aurez affaire à Tigre et Panthère!"

Il y eut un grand silence et ils se serrèrent les uns contre les autres.

"A toi, Tibert," dit Noble ensuite.

Et Tibert parla d'une toute petite voix.

"Grand roi," dit-il, "c'est par un miracle du ciel que je puis parler aujourd'hui. Hélas ! ma fourrure se dresse encore quand j'y pense. Je marchais avec Renard un jour le long d'une route et il imagina les moyens les plus rusés pour me faire tomber dans un piège. Hélas! si je n'étais pas malin de par ma naissance, que me serait-il donc arrivé!"

Et Tibert se mit à gémir.

Puis Tiècelin, d'une voix très aigue, raconta comment ce félon prit non seulement son fromage, mais aussi la moitié de ses plumes.

"Voyez!" dit-il, "mon beau manteau tout déchiré! C'est pour cela que je tremble à chaque coup de brise."

"Tu n'avais qu'à ne pas chanter!" dit Grimbert, le blaireau.

Puis Brun, le grand ours, parla.

"Moi, qui aime tant le miel," dit-il, "ce goupil promit de m'en donner et me conduisit sous ce prétexte dans une ferme. Ah ! J'y fut durement blessé, et cependant, malgré ma graisse, j'ai réussi à m'échapper."

Noble écouta tous ces récits en se tirant la barbe.

The Story of Renard the Fox

His wife Hersent agreed with this account with vigorous nods of her head, but Noble listened without saying a word, because at the bottom of his heart he felt some sympathy for Renard who was, to tell the truth, one of the most cunning knights in the kingdom.

"Who else has something to say?" he asked.

"Me!" said Tiecelin the raven, flapping his wings, "Me!" said Tiber the cat, flashing his claws. "Me!" said Brown the bear, baring his fangs. And they all shouted at the same time.

"Silence!" roared Noble, stamping his feet, "Are there no manners in this country? Be silent or you will deal with Tiger and Panther!"

There was a great silence, and they huddled against each other.

"It is your turn, Tiber," said Noble, the king.

And Tiber spoke in a very soft voice.

"Great King," said the cat, "It's a miracle from heaven that I am able to speak today. Alas! My fur stands on end again when I just think of it. I was walking along a road with Renard one day, and he thought up the trickiest ways to make me fall into a trap. Alas! Were I not clever from birth, what would have happened to me?"

And Tiber began to wail.

Then Tiecelin, in a very shrill voice, told how that crook not only took his cheese, but also half of his feathers.

"Look!" said the raven, "my handsome coat is all torn up! Because of this I shiver with each gust of a breeze."

"You don't have to crow about it!" said Grimber the badger.

Then Brown, the big bear, spoke.

"And as for me, who loves honey so much," said he, "that fox promised to give me some, and under that pretext led me into a farm. Ah! I was severely wounded — however in spite of my fat, I succeeded in escaping."

Noble listened to all these accounts while pulling on his whiskers.

"Tant de griefs," dit-il, "sont bien fâcheux, mais n'y attachez pas d'importance. Chacun a ses défauts sur cette terre, oublions donc un peu ceux du goupil. Il y a des choses plus importantes dans ce royaume!"

A ces mots, Ysengrin se redressa, Beaucent grogna, Panthère rugit, Tibert réfléchit. Et pendant que toute la foule se révoltait, une petite procession s'avança.

C'étaient Chanteclair et Dames Pinte, Blanche, Noire et Roussette et toutes les petites demoiselles, et elles étaient toutes en pleurs.

"Seigneur," dit Dame Pinte, "Renard a tué la petite cousine que nous aimions tant ; elle était toute rose et blanche!"

A ces mots les autres demoiselles se mirent à pleurer, et les plus grands même à la Cour en eurent les larmes aux yeux.

Noble se leva de son trône, Ysengrin dansait de rage, Tibert fit les yeux doux.

Mais le moment le plus émouvant fut lorsque Chanteclair alla seul vers le grand roi, s'agenouilla devant lui et fondit en sanglots.

C'en était trop! Couart, le lièvre, en eut la fièvre pendant deux jours et Noble même en eut les yeux mouillés.

"Qu'on m'amène Renard en ce lieu à l'instant même!" s'écria-t-il. "A toi, Grimbert, de porter le message."

Grimbert fit un grand salut bien que sa peau se hérissait de peur, et il se mit en marche vers Maupertuis.

La cheminée chez Sire Renard fumait toujours, il s'y chauffait les pattes, et en entendant la voix de son cher cousin, il ouvrit vivement la porte.

"C'est toi, Grimbert!" s'écria-t-il, "quel bon vent t'amène donc ici?"

Le blaireau baissa la tête tristement.

"Viens donc t'asseoir," dit le goupil, "et raconte-moi ce qui se passe en ce grand monde."

Ils s'assirent au coin du feu, et Malebranche et Percehaie se cachèrent dans un coin et écoutèrent le blaireau, les yeux grands ouverts.

The Story of Renard the Fox

"So many grievances," said he, "are very troubling, but don't attach any importance to them. Each one has his faults on this earth, so then let us forget those of the fox, as there are more important things in this kingdom!"

At these words, Ysengrin rose up again, Beaucent snorted, Panther roared, Tiber gave a pleading glance. And while the whole crowd rebelled, a little procession came forward.

There were Chanticlair the rooster and Lady Pinter the hen, along with other lady hens: Blanche, Noire and Roussette and all the little maiden hens; and they were all in tears.

"Sire," said Lady Pinter, "Renard killed the little cousin whom we loved so much; she was so pretty: all red and white!"

At these words, the other maidens started to cry, and even the largest of the animals at the Court had tears in their eyes.

Noble rose up from his throne, Ysengrin danced with rage, Tiber simply looked coy.

But the most moving moment occurred when Chanticlair went alone up to the great king, knelt before him and burst into sobs.

That was too much! Sprinter, the hare, was feverish for two days because of it, and Noble himself had moist eyes.

"Bring Renard here to me right now!" he cried, "It's your job, Grimber, to carry this message."

Grimber gave a great bow even though his coat bristled with fear, and he set off walking to Maupertuis.

The chimney at Sir Renard's home was still smoking, and he was warming his paws there. Hearing the voice of his dear cousin, he opened the door promptly.

"It's you, Grimber!" cried he, "What good wind leads you here?"

The badger lowered his head sadly.

"Then come and sit down," said the fox, "and tell me what is happening in this large world."

They sat by the fireside, and Malebranche and Hedge-Holer hid themselves in a corner and listened to the badger, their eyes wide open.

"Le roi te demande," dit Grimbert. "A l'instant même tu dois paraître devant la Cour. C'est une affaire très grave, cousin Renard, il faut que nous partions de suite. Toute la race des quadrupèdes et celle des oiseaux est contre toi, sauf tes cousins et cousines. Renard, mon ami, j'ai grand pitié de toi!"

"Ah! Cousin!" dit Renard, "que la vie est donc triste! Oui, j'ai mal agi bien des fois et c'est pour cela que je reste au coin du feu à me repentir jour et nuit. Enfin, partons, s'il le faut."

Il embrassa tendrement la gentille Hermeline, Malebranche et Percehaie, et ils s'en allèrent tous deux dans les bois.

"Vois-tu, cousin," dit Grimbert, "à quoi te servent toutes tes ruses? Tout le monde est contre toi, même Noble, le roi. Frère, ne fais donc plus ces choses."

"Je te promets, par ma foi," dit Renard, "que jamais plus je ne ferai aucun mal."

Mais Renard trébuchait à chaque pas et son cœur n'avait jamais battu si fort de sa vie.

"Cousin," dit Grimbert, les larmes aux yeux, "je savais bien que tu n'étais pas si méchant."

Ils arrivèrent bientôt à la Cour.

"Approche, Renard!" dit le roi.

Renard s'approcha et s'agenouilla devant le grand lion.

"Roi," dit-il, "tu m'as appelé et me voici. Je te demande humblement pardon, Seigneur, car je ne suis point venue à l'assemblée de la Cour. Vois-tu, la vie m'est très dure. Ceux qui m'étaient les plus chers sont maintenant contre moi. Hélas! J'ai pourtant montré à Ysengrin comment on trouve des poissons; à Brun comment on trouve du miel; à Tibert j'ai donné une anguille."

Noble, en écoutant ces paroles, s'attendrit un peu.

Ysengrin se redressa alors, Tiècelin battit des ailes, Beaucent grogna et toute la foule se révolta.

"Que le combat commence!" s'écria Noble.

Ysengrin s'avança fièrement. Tibert s'esquiva sans que personne ne le vît car il n'aimait pas assez Ysengrin pour se battre

The Story of Renard the Fox

"The King demands," said Grimber, "that you appear before the Court right now. This is a very serious matter, cousin Renard, we must leave immediately. The whole race of four-footed creatures and that of the birds is against you, except for your cousins. Renard, my friend, I am very sorry for you!"

"Ah! Cousin," said Renard, "how sad life is! Yes, I have done wicked deeds many times, and this is why I stay by the fireside and repent my misdeeds day and night. Well, let's go, if we must."

He tenderly embraced good Hermeline, Malebranche and Hedge-Holer, and they went off together into the woods.

"Do you see, cousin," said Grimber, "how all these tricks have served you! Everyone is against you, even Noble the King. Brother, don't do any more tricks."

"I promise you, by my faith," said Renard, "that I will never do another wicked thing."

But Renard stumbled at each step, and his heart had never beaten so strongly in his life.

"Cousin," said Grimber, with tears in his eyes, "I knew that you were not so bad."

Soon they arrived at the Court.

"Approach, Renard," said the King.

Renard approached and knelt before the great lion.

"King," he said, "you have called me, and here I am. I humbly beg your pardon, Sire, for I did not come to the assembly of the Court. See how very difficult life is for me. Those who are dearest to me are now against me. Alas! Nevertheless, I showed Ysengrin where to find fish; and Brown how to find honey; and I gave an eel to Tiber."

Listening to these words, Noble softened a little.

Then Ysengrin rose up, Tiecelin flapped his wings, Beaucent snorted, and the whole crowd rebelled.

"Let the battle begin!" cried Noble.

Ysengrin advanced proudly. Tiber slipped away without anyone noticing him because he didn't like Ysengrin enough to

à ses côtés et le souvenir de son pacte avec Renard lui faisait un peu mal au cœur. Il fit donc le dos rond et s'assit sur une branche pour regarder le combat.

Du côté de Renard étaient Taupe, Dame Nore, la marmotte, le loir, le martre, Sire Furet, Petit Rat et Grimbert, le bon blaireau.

Mais à côté d'Ysengrin il y avait Roonel le chien, commandant de l'armée royale, et les meilleurs des héros, Passelièvre, Heurtevilain, Passe-Avant, Trottemenu, Genterose, Primevère. Ce n'était pas tout. Il y avait aussi Beaucent, le sanglier, qui grognait à faire trembler le monde, Tigre et Panthère.

On lança le signal pour annoncer l'attaque.

Ysengrin bondit, et Renard tourna aussitôt les pattes et fila droit devant lui.

Toute la troupe royale en resta ébahie.

Il monta sur une colline, se dressa fièrement sur la cime et s'écria:

"Amis, courez si vous voulez, je retourne à mon château!"

"Le traître!" s'écrièrent-ils, "poursuivons-le!"

Renard alors éclata d'un rire si fort que toute la forêt en résonna.

Et Chanteclair à la tête, puis Ysengrin, Belin, Brichemer, Cointereau, Beaucent, Roonel, Passe-Avant, Percelièvre, Couart, Panthère, Tigre, Léopard, Tiècelin, Primevère, Genterose, Brun et Pinte et Blanche et Roussette et mille autres de la grande forêt partirent à sa poursuite.

On ne vit plus Renard, ni le lendemain, ni tout l'hiver.

On le vit après, mais comme un éclair passant par les buissons, au loin, riant aux éclats.

Et petit Renard rit encore, et rira toujours, chaque fois qu'on voudra le prendre.

The Story of Renard the Fox

fight at his side, and the memory of his pact with Renard made him uneasy in his heart. Then he arched his back and sat on a branch to watch the combat.

On Renard's side was Taupe the mole, Dame Nora the marmot, the dormouse, the martin, Sir Ferret, Little Rat, and Grimber the good badger.

But on Ysengrin's side there was Roonel the dog, commander of the royal army, and the best of its heroes: Piercehare, Thumpvillain, Runahead, Tinytrott, Gentlerose, Primula. That was not all. There also Beaucent, the boar, who grunted enough to make the world tremble, as well as Tiger and Panther.

The signal was given to begin the attack.

Ysengrin bounded, and at once Renard whirled on his paws and ran away from the melee.

All the royal company was astounded.

Renard climbed a hill, standing proudly on the summit, and cried:

"Friends, run after me if you wish; I am returning to my castle!"

"The traitor!" they cried, "Follow him!"

Renard then let out a burst of laughter so strong that the whole forest resounded with it.

And Chanticlair in the lead, then Ysengrin, Belin, Brichemere, Cointereau, Beaucent, Roonel, Piercehare, Couart, Thumpvillain, Runahead, Tinytrott, Gentlerose, Primula, Sprinter, Panther, Tiger, Leopard, Tiecelin, Brown, Pinter, Blanche, Roussette and a thousand others from the great forest set out in pursuit.

Renard was seen no more—not the next day; not the whole winter long.

He was sighted afterwards, but only as a passing flash among the bushes, faraway, laughing heartily.

And little Renard laughs still, and will laugh always, each time someone tries to capture him.

Huon of Bordeaux

Huon de Bordeaux

Le grand Charlemagne était déjà vieux. Sa longue barbe était blanche, mais des larmes coulaient de ses yeux et son cœur était rempli de chagrin, car son fils, le gentil Prince Charlot avait été tué.

Il réunit donc tous ses nobles vassaux, les ducs, les barons, et les chevaliers courageux pour découvrir qui l'avait tué.

Or, un nommé Amaury de Laon se leva et dit:

"Gentil roi, nobles et francs, écoutez-moi. Le coupable est Huon de Bordeaux. C'est lui qui assassina Charlot au Clair Visage dans la forêt."

Ainsi parla Amaury, mais ses lèvres tremblaient et son regard n'était ni fier, ni droit, car il avait menti.

Alors le jeune Huon parla. Son regard était vif et puissant.

"Grand roi et seigneurs," dit-il, "je ne suis point coupable. Par ma foi, je vous le jure, je ne savais pas que l'homme que j'ai tué était le fils du Roi! Il m'a attaqué, et je me suis défendu."

"Ses paroles semblent vraies," murmurèrent les nobles.

Alors un tournoi eut lieu entre Huon et Amaury.

Le noble Huon se revêtit de jambières blanches aux fleurs de lys, d'un beaume aux éclats de feux et du haubert que lui donna son père. Il suspendit l'écu et entra dans la lice. Amaury

Huon of Bordeaux

GREAT Charlemagne had grown old. His long beard was white, but tears flowed from his eyes and his heart was full of sorrow because his son, noble Prince Charlot, had been killed.

The king then met with all his noble vassals, the dukes, the barons and the courageous knights, to discover who had killed the prince.

One named Amaury of Laon rose up and said:

"Good King, noblemen and freemen, listen to me. The guilty one is Huon of Bordeaux. He is the one who assassinated Charlot of the Bright Face in the forest."

Thus spoke Amaury, but his lips trembled and his glance was neither proud nor virtuous, because he had lied.

Then young Huon spoke. His glance was ardent and strong.

"Great King and lords," said he, "I am not at all guilty. By my faith, I swear to you that I did not know that the man I killed was the son of the king! He attacked me, and I defended myself."

"His words seem true," murmured the nobles.

And so a tournament was held between Huon and Amaury.

Noble Huon clothed himself in white leggings decorated with lilies, a helmet sparkling with fiery light and a hauberk, a shirt of chain mail, given to him by his father. He hung his

entra à son tour tandis que Charles à la Barbe Fleurie regardait le combat.

Maintes et maintes fois le fier Huon fut blessé mais nul n'aurait pu égaler le jeune chevalier en courage et en prouesse.

Les poitrails des chevaux se heurtèrent, les tronçons de lances volèrent de tous côtés, les écus s'entrechoquèrent. Huon fut rejeté de son cheval et s'affaissa. Mais il revint à lui et frappa Amaury si fort que celui-ci tomba à terre mourant. Ce fut la victoire!

Avant de mourir Amaury parla à Huon.

"Jeune seigneur," dit-il d'une voix tremblante, "c'est moi le coupable. J'ai entraîné Charlot dans le bois profond pour te tuer, toi et ton frère. Hélas! aujourd'hui c'est moi qui meurt. Viens, prends mon épée!"

Huon s'approcha pour la recevoir, mais lorsqu'il se pencha pour la prendre, le traître le frappa au bras. Huon ne fut pas blessé car les mailles du haubert ne se déchirèrent point.

"Misérable!" s'écria Huon, "C'est la dernière fois que tu m'e tromperas!"

Huon et ses compagnons se dirigèrent alors vers Paris.

La forêt était vaste et profonde. Les ombres, les feuilles, tout jouait à leur passage, mais Huon souffrait de maintes blessures et il avait faim et soif. Soudain un tout petit homme, beau comme un rayon de soleil, surgit de la forêt. Son mantelet était brodé de toutes les couleurs des ruisseaux et des fleurs, et orné de trente fils d'or. Il portait un arc à l'épaule et au cou pendait un cor d'ivoire et d'or, que les fées lui avaient rapporté d'une île lointaine. Le petit homme, en voyant les preux dans l'immense forêt, fit résonner son cor.

"Compagnons!" s'écria Huon, "Je ne sais pourquoi mes douleurs disparaissent et ma faim et ma soif sont apaisées. Voyez, je ne souffre plus!"

Puis un autre son de cor perça de nouveau la forêt et sans savoir pourquoi, tous les compagnons se mirent à chanter. Ils chantaient si gaiement que toute la forêt en retentit de joie.

shield and entered the tournament. Amaury entered in turn while Charles of the Flowing Beard watched the combat.

Again and again proud Huon was wounded, but no one could match the young knight in courage and skill. The horses' breastplates crashed together, shafts of lances flew on all sides, shields clashed against each other. Huon was thrown from his horse and fell prostrate. But he recovered himself and struck Amaury so hard that Amaury fell dying to the earth. It was victory!

Before dying, Amaury spoke to Huon.

"Young lord," said he in a trembling voice, "it is I who am guilty. I lured Charlot into the deep woods to kill you and your brother. Alas! Today I die. Come and take my sword!"

Huon approached to receive it, but when he bent down to take hold of it, the traitor struck his arm. Huon was not wounded because the chain mail of the hauberk did not tear.

"You wretch!" cried Huon, "That is the last time you will deceive me!"

Afterwards, Huon and his companions set off for Paris.

The forest was vast and deep. The shadows, the leaves, and everything danced at their passage, but Huon suffered from many wounds and he was hungry and thirsty. Suddenly a tiny little man, beautiful as a ray of the sun, sprang from the forest. His cloak was embroidered with the colors of the streams and the flowers, and adorned with thirty golden threads. He carried a bow on his shoulder, and from his neck hung a horn of ivory and gold, which fairies had brought to him from a faraway island. Seeing the valiant knights in the immense forest, the little man sounded his horn.

"Companions!" cried out Huon, "I don't know why but my pains are disappearing and my hunger and thirst are quenched. See, I suffer no more!"

Then another sounding of the horn penetrated the forest anew, and without knowing why, all the companions began to sing. They sang so gaily that all the forest echoed with joy.

Le nain apparut devant eux et cria:

"Hommes qui parcourez ma forêt, le Roi du Monde vous salue!"

Mais les hommes ne répondirent point tant ils avaient peur d'entrer en son pouvoir, et ils s'enfuirent à travers les buissons.

Une tempête éclata soudain. Les arbres les plus altiers furent secoués et jetés à terre, le vent poussait les nuages à une folle allure à travers le ciel noir, et le tonnerre retentit si fort qu'il secoua la terre. Les hommes chevauchèrent épouvantés ne sachant que faire quand reparut devant eux le petit homme qui leur cria:

"Saluez-moi, je vous conjure! Par la nature, par l'huile, le baume et le sel, par toute la création, je vous en conjure, saluez-moi!"

Huon lui dit: "Salut, mon gentil sire."

Aussitôt la tempête s'apaisa, les oiseaux commencèrent à chanter, les papillons à poursuivre les rayons de soleil et tout était joie et paix.

"Vous faites bien de me saluer," dit le petit homme, "je suis le nain Obéron, fils de Jules César et de la fée Morgue. Ma mère était belle, belle comme l'aurore qui paraît après la nuit. Une fée mécontente me jeta un sort me rendant petit à jamais mais elle se repentit et me donna aussi de don d'être le plus beau des petits hommes. Et voyez, je suis petit mais je suis beau comme le soleil. D'autres fées me comblèrent de dons, je vais vous les conter: je connais le cœur et les pensées des hommes. A mon signal il n'est animal dans la forêt qui ne me réponde. Je puis voyager d'un côté à l'autre de la terre en moins de temps qu'un oiseau voltige d'une branche à une autre. Quand les hommes entendent le son de mon cor, leur faim et leur soif s'apaisent et leurs souffrances disparaissent. A un autre son du cor ils chantent et ils deviennent heureux. Je ne vieillirai jamais. Je connais tous les secrets du ciel, et lorsque je m'assieds près du ruisseau j'entends les anges chanter!"

Après qu'il eût dit ces paroles, des larmes remplirent ses yeux.

The dwarf appeared before them and cried out:

"Men who pass through my forest, the King of the World greets you!"

But the men didn't respond at all because they were afraid of falling under his power, and they fled through the bushes.

A tempest suddenly struck. The highest trees were shaken and thrown to the earth, the wind drove the clouds at a wild pace across the black sky, and thunder reverberated so mightily that it shook the earth. The men rode their horses in fear, not knowing what to do, when in front of them the little man reappeared and cried out to them:

"Salute me, I entreat you! By nature, by oil, balsam and salt, by all of creation, I entreat you, salute me!"

Huon said to him: "Greetings, my gracious Sire."

At once the tempest subsided, the birds began to sing, the butterflies followed in the rays of the sun and everything was joyful and peaceful.

"You did well to salute me," said the little man, "I am the dwarf Oberon, son of Julius Caesar and the fairy Morgue. My mother was beautiful, beautiful as the dawn which appears after the night. A disgruntled fairy cast a spell making me small forever, but she repented and also gave me the gift of being the most handsome of little men. And see how I am small, but I am as beautiful as the sun. The other fairies heaped gifts upon me, and I will recount them to you: I know the hearts and the thoughts of men. At my signal, there is not an animal in the forest who will not respond to me. I can travel from one side of the earth to the other in less time than a bird flies from one branch to another. When men hear the sound of my horn, their hunger and their thirst is satisfied, and their sufferings disappear. At another sound of the horn they sing and become joyful. I will never grow old. I know all the secrets of the heavens, and when I sit beside the stream I hear the angels singing!"

After he had spoken these words, tears filled his eyes.

"Gentil Obéron," lui dit Huon "c'est merveilleux tout ce que tu me contes, mais dis-moi, pourquoi pleures-tu?"

"Huon mon frère," répondit-il, "je t'aime car tu es noble et loyal. Mais à présent tu vas partir et c'est comme si mon frère me quittait. Ne m'oublie pas. En repassant par la forêt, appelle Obéron, tu auras besoin de lui plus tard. Va, je ne puis plus parler!"

Le Jugement à la Cour De Charlemagne

Bien que Huon eût été vainqueur et que la trahison d'Amaury fût prouvée, Charlemagne ne pouvait pardonner à Huon d'avoir tué son fils car il avait au cœur trop de chagrin.

Néanmoins, comme Huon était revenu victorieux, le Roi résolut de ne point le faire tuer, mais de lui prendre son château, son duché de Bordeaux et toutes les terres que son père lui avait laissées.

Le jugement devait donc avoir lieu à la cour de Charlemagne.

Les nobles ducs et barons y étaient tous assemblés et le fier Huon entra dans la salle.

Le grand Charlemagne le regarda et ne put retenir ses larmes car il allait punir le plus vaillant des chevaliers de France.

"Huon," lui dit-il, "ta chevalerie a été bien prouvée, tu es victorieux d'Amaury mais, néanmoins, tu seras durement puni. Mon armée entrera dans Bordeaux et s'emparera de tes terres et de ton château aux grandes tours. Telle est la décision que je prends!"

Des murmures de révolte s'élevèrent et …

Huon parla.

"Grand Roi," dit-il, "bien cruelles sont tes paroles. Pourquoi semer la terreur dans les foyers des pauvres gens du pays ? Bien injustement seraient-ils punis. S'il est une punition que tu veux infliger à Huon, que ce soit lui seul qui en souffre!"

"N'a-t-on jamais entendu des paroles plus sages chez un home si jeune?" murmurèrent les nobles ducs et barons.

"Gracious Oberon," said Huon, "all that you have told me is marvelous, but tell me, why do you cry?"

"Huon, my brother," he responded, "I love you because you are noble and true. But now you are going to leave and it is as if my brother were going away from me. Do not forget me. In passing again through the forest, call Oberon. You will have need of him later. Go, for I can say no more!"

Judgement at the Court of Charlemagne

Although Huon had been victorious and the treason of Amaury was proven, Charlemagne was unable to pardon Huon for having killed his son, because he had too much grief in his heart.

Nevertheless, as Huon had returned victorious, the King resolved not to have him killed, but to seize his castle, his duchy of Bordeaux and all the lands which he had inherited from his father.

The judgement had to be held at the court of Charlemagne.

The noble dukes and barons assembled there, and proud Huon entered the chamber.

Great Charlemagne looked at Huon and was unable to restrain his tears, because he was going to punish the most valiant of all the knights of France.

"Huon," he said, "your chivalry has been well proven; you are victorious over Amaury, but nevertheless, you will be severely punished. My army will enter into Bordeaux and take possession of your lands and your castle with its great towers. Such is my decision!"

Murmurs of rebellion arose and....

Huon spoke.

"Great King" he said, "your words are cruel. Why sow fear in the hearts of the poor people of the country? Unjustly will they be punished. If it is a punishment which you wish to inflict upon Huon, let it be him alone who suffers!"

"Has one ever heard wiser words from such a young man?" murmured the noble dukes and barons.

Le roi réfléchit un instant.

"Eh bien," lui dit-il, "tu iras alors porter un message à l'Amiral Gandisse à Babylone au-delà de la Mer Rouge. Quinze de mes preux y sont allés, chacun à son tour, mais ils ne sont jamais revenus. Si tu reviens de Babylone, de duché de Bordeaux ne te sera point pris et tu pourras vivre en paix. Mais tu devras accomplir tout ce que je t'ordonnerai."

Huon écouta les commandements du grand Charles.

"Tu iras au palais de l'Amiral Gandisse. Tu y trouveras sa fille: la douce Esclarmonde et tu la prendras comme épouse.

"Tu parleras à l'Amiral Gandisse d'une voix si forte que tous ses chevaliers t'entendront.

"Tu lui diras que Charles, l'Empereur de France, lui mande de lui envoyer mille éperviers, mille lévriers, mille ours enchaînés, mille seigneurs de grande lignée, mille jeunes demoiselles parmi les plus belles du pays; et tu lui diras de m'envoyer aussi ses blanches moustaches!"

"Vous voulez donc la mort de Huon!" s'écrièrent les barons indignés.

"Oui, certes!" répondit Charles plein de fureur.

"Sire," dit Huon, "y a-t-il encore quelque chose que vous m'ordonnez?"

"Oui!" répondit Charles. "Si jamais tu retournes en France, ne mets pas ton pied dans Bordeaux avant de m'avoir vu. Malheur à toi si je t'y surprends! Ton frère Gérard gardera de duché pour toi en ton absence."

"Seigneur," dit le jeune Huon, "j'obéis à tes ordres. Il n'est peine au monde que je n'endurerai pour préserver la terre de mon père et te servir en loyal vassal. Accorde-moi seulement la faveur de laisser mes dix compagnons m'accompagner jusqu'à Jérusalem, la terre sainte."

"Qu'ils aillent jusqu'à la mer rouge!" s'écria Charlemagne, "mais pas plus loin."

Huon le remercia doucement.

The king thought for a moment.

"All right," he said, "you shall then go to carry a message to Amir Gandisse of Babylon beyond the Red Sea. Fifteen of my valiant knights have gone there, each in turn, but they never returned. If you return from Babylon, the duchy of Bordeaux will not be taken from you and you will be able to live in peace. But you must accomplish all that I command you to do."

Huon listened to the commands of great Charlemagne.

"You shall go to the palace of Amir Gandisse. There you will find his daughter, sweet Esclarmonde, and you shall take her as your wife."

"You shall speak to Amir Gandisse in a voice so loud that all his knights will hear you.

"You shall tell him that Charles, the Emperor of France, demands that he be sent one thousand hawks, one thousand greyhounds, one thousand bears in chains, one thousand lords of high lineage, one thousand of the most beautiful young maidens in the country; and you shall tell him to also send me his white mustaches!"

"You want Huon's death!" cried the indignant barons.

"Yes, certainly!" responded Charles in full fury.

"Sire," said Huon, "is there anything else which you command me to do?"

"Yes!" replied Charles "If ever you return to France, do not set your foot in Bordeaux before seeing me. It will be unfortunate for you if I surprise you there! Your brother, Gerard, will guard the duchy for you in your absence."

"Lord," said young Huon, "I obey your commands. There is no pain in the world which I would not endure to preserve the land of my father and to serve you as a loyal vassal. Only grant me the privilege of allowing my ten companions to accompany me as far as Jerusalem, the Holy Land."

"They may go as far as the Red Sea!" cried Charlemagne, "but no farther."

Huon thanked him graciously.

Les barons pleuraient amèrement. Le duc Naimes s'approcha de Huon, lui adressa mille recommandations, l'embrassa tendrement et de chaudes larmes ruisselèrent de ses yeux.

Puis s'approcha un des chevaliers, le cousin de Huon, un nommé Guichard de Chartres.

"Huon, mon cousin," dit-il, "je veux aller avec toi ; laisse-moi t'accompagner et ne me refuse pas cela."

"Beau cousin," dit Huon en l'embrassant, "je t'aime car ton cœur est bon et loyal ; nous nous en irons joyeux et fiers car le bon Dieu nous aidera et nous ramènera bientôt dans la douce France."

Les douze compagnons partirent et l'air retentit de leurs chants à leur passage. Cependant, au fond du cœur, Huon souffrait durement car il ne put revoir sa douce mère avant de partir.

Ils passèrent par les plaines, les forêts, et soudain en regardant les beaux rayons de soleil jouant parmi les feuilles, Huon se souvint d'Obéron, son doux ami.

"Où es-tu, Gentil Obéron?" s'écria-t-il. Et le petit roi apparut aussitôt. Huon descendit de son beau destrier et invita tous les preux à s'asseoir sous un chêne autour d'Obéron.

Huon lui raconta alors les commandements de Charlemagne.

"Beau compagnon," dit Obéron, "bien pénibles sont les épreuves que tu dois subir. Mais tu ne seras pas seul; Obéron sera à tes côtés, mais à une condition:

"C'est que jamais tu ne dois dire un mensonge. Si par malheur tu oubliais cela, Obéron ne serait plus ton ami!"

Puis le petit roi lui présenta une cruche pleine de vin. "Bois ce vin," lui dit-il.

Huon vida la cruche d'un trait et elle se remplit aussitôt à nouveau.

Les yeux d'Obéron s'illuminèrent de joie.

"Je le savais bien que tu es noble et loyal," dit-il, "car seuls ceux qui n'ont aucune mauvaise pensée au cœur peuvent boire

The barons wept bitterly. Duke Naimes approached Huon, praised him a thousand times and embraced him tenderly, as hot tears streamed from his eyes.

Then one of the knights approached, a cousin of Huon named Guichard de Chartres.

"Huon, my cousin," said he, "I want to go with you; allow me to accompany you and do not refuse me."

"Handsome cousin," said Huon, embracing him, "I love you because your heart is good and loyal; we will go joyfully and proudly because the Good Lord God will help us and we will soon return to sweet France."

The twelve companions departed, and the air resounded with their songs as they passed. However, at the bottom of his heart Huon suffered greatly because he was unable to see his sweet mother before leaving.

They passed through the plains and the forests, and suddenly, while looking at the beautiful rays of sunlight playing among the leaves, Huon remembered Oberon, his sweet friend.

"Where are you, Gracious Oberon?" he cried. And the little king appeared instantly. Huon dismounted from his fine destrier and invited all the valiant knights to sit around Oberon beneath an oak tree.

Huon then recounted to Oberon the commandments of Charlemagne.

"Noble companion," said Oberon, "truly painful are the trials which you must undergo. But you will not be alone: Oberon will be at your side, but on one condition:

"It is that you must never tell a lie. If by misfortune you forget that, Oberon will no longer be your friend!"

Then the little king gave Huon a jug of wine.

"Drink this wine." He said to Huon.

Huon emptied the jug in one gulp, and it refilled itself immediately.

Oberon's eyes shone with joy.

"I know that you are noble and true," said he, "because only those who have no bad thought in their hearts are able

de ce vin, et alors la cruche se remplit à nouveau; mais si un méchant venait à y mettre ses lèvres, le vin disparaîtrait de la cruche et elle resterait vide dans ses mains. Prends donc cette cruche avec toi, Huon, car maintes fois elle te servira.

"Je te donne aussi mon cor d'ivoire. Tu n'en auras pas plus tôt sonné que je serai à tes côtés avec cent mille chevaliers armés. Mais garde-toi de m'appeler à moins que tu ne sois en danger inévitable, sinon tu serais durement puni.

"Maintenant écoute-moi, tu iras avec tes compagnons à Brindes, le port aux mille navires. Là tu demanderas Garin le marinier. Bien nombreux sont ses vaisseaux qui franchissent les vastes mers. Il t'aidera et t'hébergera, toi et tes compagnons. De tous ses vaisseaux, il te donnera le plus beau. Va, Huon, le temps presse, il me faut te quitter!"

A ses mots le petit roi fondit en larmes.

"Obéron, mon doux compagnon," lui dit Huon, "que tu es bon pour moi! Mes chagrins ont disparu depuis que tu m'as parlé; mais rien ne me fait si grand peine que de te voir pleurer. Dis-moi donc la cause de ton chagrin."

"Je pense," répondit Obéron, "à toutes les souffrances par lesquelles tu devras passer, car tu es jeune et téméraire. N'oublie jamais, Huon, la promesse que tu m'as faite et sois toujours noble et loyal!"

Les compagnons partaient, il traversaient les grandes montagnes aux sommets blancs et purs. Enfin ils arrivèrent à Brindes, le port aux mille navires.

Il y avait là dans la ville un homme ayant grande allure et richement vêtu qui se tenait sous un dais somptueux.

"O Sire roi," dit Huon, "je vous salue."

"Je ne suis point roi," répondit-il. "Je suis Garin, le marinier, mais c'est avec grand cœur que je te salue, jeune seigneur, car tes traits sont nobles et je ne sais pourquoi, en te regardant, de doux souvenirs me reviennent à la mémoire. Comme tu ressembles à Seguin, mon gentil oncle, qui gouvernait Bordeaux!

to drink this wine, and then the jug refills itself anew; but if a wicked person places his lips on it, the wine disappears from the jug and it remains empty in his hands. So take this jug with you, Huon, because it will serve you many times.

"I also give you my ivory horn. No sooner will you sound it, then I will be at your side with one hundred thousand armed knights. But be careful to call me only if you are in certain danger, or you will be painfully punished.

"Now listen to me: you will go with your companions to Brindes, the seaport of a thousand ships. There you will ask for Garin the sailor. Many are his ships which cross the wide seas. He will help you and harbor you, you and your companions! He will give you the most beautiful of all his ships. Go, Huon, time is pressing. I must leave you!"

At these words the little king dissolved in tears.

"Oberon, my sweet companion," said Huon, "you are so good to me! My sorrows have disappeared since you have spoken to me; but nothing gives me such great pain as to see you cry. Tell me the cause of your sorrow."

"I think," replied Oberon, "of all the suffering through which you must pass, because you are young and daring. Never forget, Huon, the promise which you gave me, and always be noble and true!"

The companions left, and they crossed over great mountains with white and clear summits.

They finally arrived at Brindes, the seaport of a thousand ships.

In the city there was a man with a grand manner, richly dressed, who was seated on a sumptuous dais.

"O Sir king," said Huon, "I salute you."

"I am not at all a king," replied the man, "I am Garin, the sailor, but it is with a full heart that I greet you, young lord, because your features are noble and I don't know why, in looking upon you, sweet memories come to my mind. How you resemble Seguin, my gracious uncle who governed Bordeaux!

Il est mort il y a bien des années, laissant deux beaux enfants: Huon et Gérard."

"Seguin était mon père," s'écria Huon, "et je suis Huon, un des enfants dont tu me parles!"

"Tu es donc mon cousin," s'écria Garin en enlaçant le jeune Huon dans ses bras. "Où vas-tu ainsi ? Et quel bon vent t'amène dans ce port?"

Huon raconta à Garin les commandements de Charles.

"J'ai beaucoup de richesses," dit Garin, "et j'ai une femme et de beaux enfants, mais je laisserai tout cela et te suivrai, beau cousin."

Garin dit adieu à sa femme et à ses enfants.

"Ne pleurez pas," leur dit-il, "je reviendrai avec de beaux présents d'or fin et de pierreries."

Mais, hélas! Garin au grand cœur ne devait plus revenir.

Les compagnons entraient dans le vaisseau, ils levaient l'ancre et commençaient à naviguer.

La mer était bonne et le navire glissait doucement sur l'onde. Ils arrivaient bientôt en terre sainte.

Les nobles compagnons descendirent, s'agenouillèrent et remercièrent le bon Dieu de leur avoir donné un vent si favorable. Puis Huon se leva et leur dit:

"Compagnons, vous m'attendrez ici; je m'en vais seul à présent poursuivre ma route."

"Non, Huon," répondirent-ils, "nous irons avec toi jusqu'aux bords de la grande mer rouge."

"Comme il vous plaît," répondit Huon.

Et ils montèrent sur leurs beaux destriers et partirent chevauchant.

Bien étranges étaient les pays qu'ils traversaient.

C'était d'abord le pays de Féménie où seules des femmes vivaient. Puis le pays des Couains où il ne pousse pas de blé et on n'y mange jamais de pain. Puis le pays de Foi où mûrissent des raisins magnifiques et où poussent de beaux épis d'or et les habitants y sont si loyaux que les champs ne sont jamais gardés.

He has been dead for many years, leaving two handsome children! Huon and Gerard."

"Seguin was my father," cried Huon, "and I am Huon, one of the children you speak of."

"Then you are my cousin," cried Garin enfolding young Huon in his arms. "Where are you going? And what good wind led you into this port?"

Huon told Garin of the commandments of Charles.

"I have much wealth," said Garin, "and I have a wife and some handsome children, but I will leave all of this and follow you, noble cousin."

Garin said farewell to his wife and to his children.

"No weeping," he said to them, "I will return with beautiful gifts of fine gold and precious stones."

But alas! Great-hearted Garin would not return again.

The companions boarded the vessel, and they raised anchor and set sail.

The sea was kind, and the ship glided gently over the waves. They soon arrived in the Holy Land.

The noble companions disembarked, knelt down and thanked the Good Lord for giving them such a favorable wind.

Then Huon rose and said to them:

"Companions, wait for me here; I am now going alone to pursue my way."

"No, Huon" they replied, "we will go with you to the shore of the great Red Sea."

"As you wish," responded Huon.

And they mounted their handsome war horses and rode off.

The country through which they travelled was very strange.

There was at first the land of the Women, where only women lived. Then the land of Couains, where wheat didn't grow and where no one ever ate bread. Then the land of Faith, where magnificent grapes were ripening and where grew beautiful golden stalks of grain, and the inhabitants there were so honest that the fields were never guarded.

On cueille à foison de blé et des fruits; et dès qu'ils sont cueillis il en repousse aussitôt de nouveaux.

Ils passèrent ensuite par un pays maudit où le soleil ne se montre jamais, où il n'y a ni chant d'oiseau ni fleurs, ni vin.

Tout y est sombre et triste et les habitants ne rient jamais.

"Qu'allons-nous faire?" dit Huon à ses compagnons, "il ne pousse rien sur cette terre maudite ; comment allons-nous boire et manger?"

Soudain il pensa à la cruche qu'Obéron lui avait donnée, et ils pouvaient y boire tous car ils étaient bons et loyaux. Pleins de force et de courage ils poursuivirent leur chemin.

Ils passèrent par un bois et virent un beau vieillard à la longue barbe grise, si longue qu'elle lui arrivait aux genoux. Il était tout orné de galons d'or et construisait un chemin dans le bois. En voyant les preux, il poussa un cri de joie.

"Soyez les bienvenus!" s'écria-t-il. "Vous êtes les premiers hommes que je rencontre dans cette forêt depuis …. voilà bien trente ans."

Il accourut au devant d'eux et regarda Huon sans mot dire.

"Beau chevalier," lui dit-il ensuite, "comme tu ressembles à un noble duc qui gouvernait Bordeaux. Mon nom est Géréamine de la douce France. Il y a bien longtemps que je l'ai quittée. J'étais prévôt à Bordeaux et je suis parti au combat, laissant mon frère Quirre à ma place. Les Sarrasins m'ont fait prisonnier mais je me suis échappé et voilà trente ans que je parcours cette forêt en y construisant des chemins."

"Ami," lui dit Huon, "je suis le fils du Duc Seguin de Bordeaux."

Le vieillard, en entendant ces mots, se jeta, plein de joie, dans les bras de Huon.

Huon lui raconta ensuite toute son histoire et lui parla des commandements de Charlemagne. Géréamine se joignit à eux et ils poursuivirent leur chemin.

An abundance of wheat and fruits were gathered, and when they were harvested, they sprang up anew.

Then they passed through an accursed land where the sun never showed itself, where there was neither the song of birds nor flowers, nor wine.

Everything there was gloomy and sad, and the inhabitants never laughed.

"What are we going to do?" said Huon to his companions. "Nothing grows on this cursed land. How are we going to drink and eat?"

Suddenly he thought of the jug which Oberon had given him, and they were all able to drink because they were good and truthful. Full of strength and courage they went on their way.

They passed through a wood and saw a handsome old man with a long gray beard, so long that it came to his knees. He was adorned with gold lace and was building a path in the woods. On seeing the valiant knights, he uttered a cry of joy.

"Be welcome!" he cried. "You are the first men whom I have met in this forest since…a good thirty years."

He ran in front of them and regarded Huon without saying a word.

"Handsome knight," he said at last, "you resemble a noble duke who governed Bordeaux. My name is Gereamine of sweet France. It's a long time since I left it. I was a provost in Bordeaux and I went off to war, leaving my brother Quirre in my place. The Saracens made me a prisoner but I escaped and these thirty years I have been crossing through this forest and building roads.

"Friend, "Said Huon, "I am the son of Duke Seguin of Bordeaux."

The old man, hearing these words threw himself joyfully into the arms of Huon.

Huon then told all of his story and recounted the commandments of Charlemagne. Gereamine joined the company, and they proceeded on their way.

Tout en chevauchant, Huon raconta à Géréamine les merveilles que faisait Obéron, son doux ami. Il lui montra le cor d'ivoire et d'or.

"Je vais y sonner," dit Huon, "et tu verras aussitôt cent mille chevaliers armés."

Le sage Géréamine arrêta sa main.

"As-tu le droit, jeune ami, d'y sonner sans que tu en aies besoin?"

"Non, je n'en ai pas le droit," répondit Huon, "mais que m'importe! Je voudrais bien savoir si Obéron viendra vraiment si je l'appelle."

Ils s'assirent sous un arbre, étalèrent les mets, burent du bon vin de la cruche et Huon se mit à sonner.

Mais Obéron, en entendant l'appel du cor d'ivoire, poussa un profond soupir.

"Qu'avez-vous, gentil roi?" lui demandèrent ses chevaliers.

"Mon jeune seigneur, Huon, est en danger," répondit-il, "il me faut le sauver. Armez-vous mes chevaliers, et suivez-moi."

Huon vit alors descendre vers lui Obéron et les cent mille chevaliers. Mais Obéron lui lança un regard courroucé.

"Tu oublies donc si vite les promesses, enfant au cœur léger. Bien peu as-tu mérité ce cor d'ivoire!"

"Pardonne-moi, Sire" dit Huon, "j'ai essayé la cruche qui se remplit à merveille mais je n'avais point encore essayé le cor. Il me tenait beaucoup de voir si vraiment tu viendrais à mon appel. Pardonne-moi si j'ai douté de toi un instant; je sais maintenant que toutes tes paroles sont vraies; mais si tu veux me punir, voici mon épée, frappe-moi."

"Tu as parlé sagement," répondit Obéron en souriant, "je te pardonne. Et, pour que tu connaisses mieux mon royaume, je t'invite, ainsi que tes compagnons, à laisser ce frugal repas et à venir dîner en mon palais."

"Grand merci," dit Huon, "nous t'en saurons tous gré."

Aussitôt ils se trouvèrent devant un palais splendide.

Riding together on horseback, Huon recounted to Gereamine the marvels performed by Oberon, his sweet friend. He showed him the horn of ivory and gold.

"I am going to sound it," said Huon, "and you will instantly see one hundred thousand armed knights."

Wise Gereamine stayed his hand.

"Have you the right, my young friend, to sound it here without having the need to do so?"

"No, I don't have the right," responded Huon, "but what does it matter! I would like to know if Oberon will really come if I call him."

They sat down under a tree, spread out the food, drank the good wine from the jug, and Huon blew the horn.

But Oberon, hearing the call of the ivory horn, emitted a deep sigh.

"What is the matter, noble king?" asked his knights.

"My young lord Huon is in danger," he replied, "I must save him. Arm yourselves, my knights, and follow me."

Huon then saw Oberon and the hundred thousand knights coming down towards him. But Oberon pierced him with an angry glance.

"You forget your promises so quickly, light-hearted child. You have little deserved the ivory horn!"

"Forgive me, Sire" said Huon, "I tried the jug which miraculously refills itself, but I had not yet tried the horn. I was greatly seized by the desire to see if you truly would come to my call. Forgive me if I momentarily doubted you; I know now that all your words are true; but if you wish to punish me, here is my sword, strike me."

"You have spoken wisely," responded Oberon, smiling. "I forgive you. And, so that you may better know my kingdom, I invite you and your companions to leave this frugal repast and to come dine in my palace."

"Many thanks," said Huon. "We are most grateful to you."

Immediately they found themselves in front of a splendid palace.

D'immenses marches de marbre rose conduisaient à une vaste salle où, autour d'une table débordant de mets, étaient placés quatorze fauteuils et un trône d'ivoire et d'or que les fées avaient donné à Jules César.

Obéron prit place sur le trône. Huon s'assit à son côté, puis tous les chevaliers se placèrent à côté d'eux.

Puis Obéron combla tous les chevaliers de beaux présents. Il leur donna beaucoup de nourriture à emporter pour qu'ils n'aient jamais faim et leur fit de douces recommandations.

"Le chemin que tu vas prendre," dit-il à Huon, "te mène à Tormont. La ville est gouvernée par Eudes qui est un de tes oncles, mais il est devenu sarrasin et n'aime plus sa douce patrie. Si un français vient à entrer dans la ville, Eudes le fait arrêter aussitôt. Garde-toi donc d'y aller; passe à côté de la ville mais surtout n'y pose pas le pied!"

"Eh! Sire!" dit l'intrépide Huon, "voudrais-tu que je passe à côté d'une ville où règne mon oncle, sans même aller lui rendre visite? S'il veut nous causer du tort, j'aurai bien vite fait de me défendre!"

"Fais donc comme il te plaira, frère," dit Obéron, "mais garde-toi de sonner du cor à moins que tu ne sois en grand péril; maintenant va, mon enfant!"

Ils partirent et bientôt les tours de Tormont apparurent à l'horizon.

"Si tu veux m'en croire," dit Géréamine, "Huon, mon jeune seigneur, n'entre pas dans la ville."

"Je n'ai guère envie d'écouter des conseils," répondit Huon, "je ferai comme il me plaira."

Et il entra avec tous ses compagnons.

"Au nom de la France, je te salue," cria Huon au premier gardien de la ville.

Le gardien ouvrit tout grand ses yeux et posa un doigt sur ses lèvres.

Immense stairs of pink marble led to a vast chamber where, around a table filled with dishes of food, there were placed fourteen armchairs and a throne of ivory and gold, which the fairies had given to Julius Caesar.

Oberon took his place upon the throne. Huon sat down at his side, and then all the knights sat down beside them.

Then Oberon heaped beautiful presents upon all the knights. He gave them much food to carry, so that they would never hunger, and he gave them kind advice.

"The road which you are going to take," said Oberon to Huon, "will lead you to Tormont. The city is governed by Eudes who is one of your uncles, but he has become a Saracen and no longer loves his sweet motherland. If a Frenchman comes to enter the city, Eudes arrests him immediately. Be careful when you go there; pass around the city, and above all, do not set foot inside!"

"Ah! Sire," said the intrepid Huon, "would you wish me to bypass a city where my uncle reigns, without paying him a visit? If he wishes to cause us harm, I will very quickly defend myself!"

"Then do as you please, brother," said Oberon, "But at least be careful not to sound the horn unless you are in grave peril. Now go, my child!"

They left, and soon the towers of Tormont appeared on the horizon.

"If you wish to believe me," said Gereamine, "Huon, my young lord, do not enter this city."

"I have little desire to listen to advice," replied Huon. "I shall do as I please."

And he entered with all his companions.

"In the name of France, I greet you," cried Huon to the first guard of the city.

The guard opened his eyes wide and placed a finger on his lips.

"Gentil chevalier," dit-il, "ne dis pas d'où tu viens car si le gouverneur de la ville t'entendais, il te ferait mettre en prison!"

"Voilà bien des jours, ami," dit Huon, "que nous chevauchons par monts et par plaines et nous sommes fatigués. Nous voulons nous reposer ici; ne crains pas pour nous, car je n'ai guère peur de mon oncle Eudes."

"Beaux Sires," répondit le gardien, "je vais vous mener chez un homme qui aime la douce France; il vous soignera avec bonté."

Il les conduisit à la demeure du prévôt Hondré.

Le prévôt ouvrit bien grand ses portes et était tout joyeux de les voir. Dès qu'ils s'étaient installés, Huon enleva son cor, le confia à la charge du prévôt et appela Géréamine.

"Géréamine, mon ami," lui dit-il, "va chercher un bon crieur et dis-lui de crier par la ville que tous ceux qui veulent passer joyeusement la soirée, boire beaucoup de vin et manger de la viande à foison, se rassemblent dans la demeure du prévôt Hondré. Puis va chez les panetiers et achète tout leur pain; va chez les bouchers et achète toute leur viande ; puis chez les poissonniers et achète tout leur poisson."

Géréamine s'en allait dans la ville faire tout ce que son jeune seigneur lui avait dit.

Et il mena grande joie. Toute la ville accourut. Les coupes de vin étaient toujours pleines car la cruche se remplissait incessamment.

Mais ce soir-là le Duc Eudes n'eut rien à manger car il n'y avait ni pain chez les panetiers, ni viande chez les bouchers, ni poisson chez les poissonniers.

Et ayant entendu dire qu'un riche français avait tout acheté, il s'en fut chez le prévôt Hondré, bien courroucé.

"Bel Oncle," dit Huon, l'intrépide, "vous voilà bien emporté. Ne savez-vous pas que je suis votre neveu? Nous venons de la douce France et en son nom je vous salue."

"Noble knight," said he, "do not say where you are from, because if the governor of the city hears you, he will put you in prison!"

"These many days, friend," said Huon, "we have ridden over mountains and across plains, and we are tired. We wish to rest ourselves here; do not fear for us, because I have little fear of my uncle Eudes."

"Good Sires," responded the guardian, "I am going to lead you to the home of a man who loves sweet France; he will look after you with kindness."

He led them to the dwelling of Provost Hondre.

The Provost opened his doors wide and was overjoyed to see them.

After they were settled, Huon took up his horn, entrusted it to the Provost, and called Gereamine.

"Gereamine, my friend," said he, "go and search for a good town crier, and tell him to cry throughout the city that all who wish to pass the evening happily, to drink much wine and eat abundant food, should gather together in the dwelling of Provost Hondre. Then go to the breadmakers and purchase all their bread; go to the butchers and purchase all their meats; then to the fishmongers and purchase all their fish."

Gereamine went into the town to do all that his young lord had said.

And everything was accomplished with great joy. All the city came running. The wine cups were always full because the wine jug endlessly refilled itself.

But that evening the Duke Eudes had nothing to eat because there was no bread at the breadmakers, nor meat at the butchers, nor fish at the fishmongers.

And having heard it said that a rich Frenchman had purchased everything, he went to the home of the Provost Hondre, very angry.

"Good Uncle," said brave Huon, "You are quite overcome with anger. Don't you know that I am your nephew? We come from sweet France, and I greet you in its name."

"Ce sera bien ton dernier dîner," s'écria Eudes, "demain je vous ferai tous mettre en prison!"

"Nous verrons cela demain," répondit Huon, "mais ce soir asseyez-vous, mon oncle, et buvez de ce bon vin dans la cruche."

Eudes la porta à ses lèvres, mais la cruche se vida aussitôt. Il eut alors grand peur et ses mains tremblèrent.

"C'est parce-que tu es méchant," dit Huon, "car la cruche se vide dans les mains de celui qui pense au mal."

Eudes invita Huon ce soir-là à dormir dans son palais, mais au lever du soleil il fit entrer dans sa chambre dix chevaliers pour le saisir.

Hélas! Huon était assailli de tous côtés. Il chercha son cor et se rappela qu'il l'avait laissé chez le prévôt.

"Malheur à moi," s'écria Huon, "Obéron ne viendra pas à mon aide."

Mais soudain le prévôt, déguisé en sarrasin, entra dans la chambre et lui donna le cor. Huon sonna, et, au même instant, la ville fut assaillie par cent mille chevaliers aux écus étincelants, aux épées de fer luisant.

Eudes s'enfuit, épouvanté. Mais Huon le rejoignit et d'un trait de son épée lui perça la poitrine. Les français poussèrent des cris de joie et la ville fut délivrée.

Le bon prévôt Hondré fut alors nommé roi, et les fiers chevaliers poursuivirent leur chemin.

Obéron leur dit adieu et indiqua à Huon par où il devait aller.

"Lorsque tu verras un grand château aux murailles épaisses et dont la tour merveilleuse s'élève par-dessus la mer, détourne-toi de là et prends un autre chemin car dans ce château vit le géant terrible qui se nomme Orgueilleux.

"Il y a bien des années qu'il me ravit ce château. C'est mon père Jules César qui me l'a donné. Il avait mis vingt ans à le construire. Ce n'est pas tout, il m'a pris aussi mon haubert blanc, plus blanc que les fleurs blanches des prés!"

"This will be your last dinner," cried Eudes; "tomorrow I will put you all in prison!"

"We shall see about that tomorrow," replied Huon. "But this evening sit down, my uncle, and drink of the good wine in the jug."

Eudes brought it to his lips, but the wine jug immediately emptied itself. He was greatly afraid then, and his hands trembled.

"That is because you are wicked," said Huon, "Because the wine jug empties itself in the hands of one with evil thoughts."

Eudes invited Huon to sleep in his palace that evening; but at sunrise Eudes ordered ten knights to enter the bedchamber and seize Huon.

Alas! Huon was attacked on all sides. He searched for his horn and recalled that he had left it at the home of the provost.

"Woe is me," cried Huon, "Oberon will not come to my aid."

But suddenly the Provost, disguised as a Saracen, entered the bed chamber and gave him the horn.

Huon sounded the horn, and at the same instant, the city was besieged by one hundred thousand knights with sparkling shields and swords of shining iron.

Eudes fled in fear. But Huon overtook him and with a flash of his sword, pierced Eudes' breast. The Frenchmen gave shouts of joy, and the city was delivered.

Good Provost Hondre was then named king, and the proud knights continued on their way.

Oberon said farewell to them and advised Huon on where they should travel.

"When you see a large castle with thick walls and then a marvelous tower rising above the sea, turn away from there and take another road because in this castle lives the terrible giant named Arrogance.

"It has been many years since he seized this castle from me. My father, Julius Caesar, gave it to me. It took twenty years to build. And not only that; he also took my white hauberk, whiter than the white flowers in the meadows!"

"Eh! Gentil Sire!" s'exclama Huon, "crois-tu que je passerai de bon gré près de ce château sans châtier Orgueilleux? Mon épée lui percera les flancs et je reprendrai le château et ton beau haubert blanc."

"Tu n'y pourras point entrer," dit Obéron, "car la porte est gardée par deux hommes de bronze qui sont armés de faux tranchantes. Il n'est guère de géant même, qu'Orgueilleux n'ait abattu! Crois-moi, enfant, ce serait bien insensé d'y aller!"

"Tu m'aideras, Obéron! Si je suis en péril, je sonnerai ton cor."

"Tu pourras sonner autant que tu voudras," répondit le petit roi, "mais Obéron ne viendra pas!"

Et sur ces mots il disparut aussitôt.

Les compagnons se remirent en marche et chantèrent si gaiement tout le long du chemin, qu'ils avaient oublié tous les périls. Et, lorsque les ténèbres enveloppaient la terre, ils se jetèrent sur le doux gazon et s'endormirent.

Mais, à peine avaient ils ouvert les yeux le matin, qu'ils virent devant eux le château à la tour merveilleuse.

"Obéron, mon doux ami," s'écria Huon, "bien vraies sont tes paroles. Il n'est ni château ni tour au monde plus merveilleux que ceux-ci et tu me laisserais combattre seul sans venir à mon secours? Que m'importe! Je pars, et par ma foi, je conquerrai ton haubert blanc!"

Ses compagnons l'embrassèrent, le recommandèrent au bon Dieu, et l'attendirent dans les prés fleuris.

L'écu au cou et la bonne épée en main, il marcha vers le château.

Les deux hommes de bronze étaient là devant la porte.

"Comment entrerai-je?" pensait-il.

Mais au même instant une fenêtre s'ouvrit et une douce jeune fille s'y pencha. Elle vit Huon et pensa:

"C'est sans doute un jeune chevalier de la France." Et elle arrêta les hommes de bronze de frapper.

"Ah! Kind Sire," cried Huon, "do you believe that, in good will, I could pass near this castle without punishing Arrogance? My sword will piece his flanks, and I will retake the castle and your beautiful white hauberk."

"You will not be able to gain entry," said Oberon, "because the gate is guarded by two bronze men who are armed with sharp scythes. There is no other other giant whom Arrogance has not beaten! Believe me, child, it would be completely mad to go there!"

"You will help me, Oberon! If I am in peril, I will sound your horn."

"You can sound it as much as you wish," responded the little king, "but Oberon will not come!"

And with these words he instantly disappeared

The companions continued their journey and sang so gaily all along the way that they had forgotten the danger. And, when darkness enveloped the earth, they threw themselves on the sweet grass and fell asleep.

But, when they opened their eyes in the morning, they saw before them the castle with the marvelous tower.

"Oberon, my sweet friend," cried Huon, "your words are very true. There is neither a castle nor a tower in the world more marvelous than this one, and you will leave me to fight alone without coming to my aid? It doesn't matter to me! I go and, by my faith, I will win your white hauberk!"

His companions embraced him, commended him to the care of the Good Lord God, and waited for him in the flowering meadow.

With a shield on his back and a good sword in his hand, Huon marched towards the castle.

The two bronze men were there in front of the gate.

"How will I enter?" thought he.

But the same instant a window opened and a sweet young girl leaned out. She saw Huon and thought:

"This is without a doubt a young French knight." And she stopped the bronze men from striking.

Huon entra fièrement dans le château.

"Salut, beau chevalier," dit la jeune fille, "je vois par tes armes et tes nobles traits que tu viens de la douce France; mais, si tu m'en crois, ne reste pas ici. Retourne par la même porte par où tu es entré car si le maître du château se réveillait, tes jours, beau chevalier, seraient en grand danger."

"Ne crains pas pour moi," dit Huon, "car c'est pour voir le géant que je suis venu jusqu'ici. Mais parle-moi plutôt de toi, jeune demoiselle, comment se fait-il que tu sois ici?"

"Hélas!" soupira la jeune fille, "il y a bien sept ans que je suis prisonnière dans ce château. Auparavant je voyageais avec mon père dans un navire aux mâts puissants, mais une tempête s'éleva si forte que nous fûmes jetés sur ce rivage. Le géant tua mon père et m'enferma dans ce château. Voilà, beau chevalier, ma triste histoire."

"Pauvre enfant," dit Huon, "je vais bientôt te délivrer. Mais dis-moi, d'où viens-tu et quel est ton nom?"

"On m'appelle Sibylle," répondit-elle. "Mon père était le Duc Guinemer, frère du Duc de Bordeaux."

"Belle cousine," s'écria Huon, "sois la bien trouvée! J'ai grande joie de te revoir. Je suis Huon, l'enfant du duc de Bordeaux et je porte un message du grand Charlemagne à l'Amiral Gandisse à Babylone."

Et ils s'embrassèrent de bon cœur. Puis Huon alla trouver le géant.

Orgueilleux était grand comme quatre hommes à la fois. Il dormait encore. Huon le regarda.

"Ce serait bien indigne de ma part," pensait-il, "de l'attaquer pendant qu'il dort; mon gentil roi ne m'aimerait plus. Il me faut le réveiller, ce monstre d'Orgueilleux, et lui demander de bien vouloir s'armer. Après, je frapperai bien mon coup."

"Réveille-toi vieux coquin!" cria Huon, "Qu'est-ce que tu attends pour t'armer?"

Le géant sursauta à ces mots et de toute sa hauteur regarda l'intrépide enfant.

Huon proudly entered the castle.

"Greetings, good knight," said the young girl, "I see by your weapons and your noble character that you come from sweet France; but if you believe me, do not stay here. Return by the same gate through which you entered, because if the master of the castle awakes, your days, good knight, will be in great danger."

"Do not fear for me," said Huon, "because I have come here to see the giant. But tell me rather about yourself, young maiden, how did you come to be here?"

"Alas," sighed the young girl, "I have been imprisoned in this castle for seven years. Before then, I was journeying with my father in a strong-masted ship, but a great storm arose and we were thrown onto this shore. The giant killed my father and locked me within this castle. So that, good knight, is my sad story."

"Poor child," said Huon, "I am going to rescue you soon. But tell me, where did you come from, what is your name?"

"My name is Sibylle," she replied. "My father was the Duke Guinemer, brother of the Duke of Bordeaux."

"Beautiful cousin," cried Huon, "what luck to find you! I am overjoyed to see you again. I am Huon, the child of the duke of Bordeaux, and I carry a message from the great Charlemagne to Admiral Gandisse in Babylon."

And they warmly embraced. Then Huon set off to find the giant.

Arrogance was as large as four men. He was still asleep, and Huon observed him.

"It would be very unworthy on my part," thought he, "to attack him while he sleeps; my kind king would no longer love me. I must waken him, this monster of Arrogance, and ask him to arm himself. After that, I will strike my blow."

"Wake up, you old rascal," cried Huon, "why are you waiting to arm yourself?"

The giant jumped at these words and, from his great height, he regarded the brave youth.

"Que veux-tu de moi?" demanda Orgueilleux.

"Ce que je veux de toi," s'écria Huon, "c'est que tu ailles au diable et que tu ne retournes plus!"

"Eh! tu t'y prends à un bon moment, je n'ai point de faux et tu es bien armé."

"Et qui te dit que je te frapperai avant que tu ne sois armé? Va vite chercher ta faux et reviens me trouver."

"Ma foi," dit le géant, "je n'ai point vu de ma vie d'ennemi si courtois!

"Mais tu es bien fou de t'hasarder ainsi car, tel que le lion qui s'empare du chevreuil, je pourrai t'étouffer dans mes mains. Tu ne sais peut-être pas qui je suis. Mon nom est Orgueilleux et il n'est pas un diable en enfer qui ne soit mon cousin. Connais-tu peut-être Obéron? Tous ses pouvoirs magiques n'ont pas suffi à m'empêcher de lui prendre son château. En outre je lui ai ravi son haubert blanc. Personne ne peut le porter à moins qu'il ne soit absolument pur et loyal. Le haubert alors devient de sa taille et celui qui le porte est toujours vainqueur dans les combats. Pour mon compte, je ne l'ai même pas essayé, mais puisque tu as bien voulu me laisser m'armer, je te permets de l'essayer si tu veux. Va, je ne te ferai point de mal pendant ce temps."

Huon courut le chercher et le haubert lui allait parfaitement. Les yeux d'Orgueilleux devinrent rages de colère.

"Misérable!" s'écria Orgueilleux, "enlève ce haubert immédiatement. Si tu l'enlèves, je te donnerai cet anneau que l'Amiral Gandisse m'a donné pour que je ne lui fasse point de mal ; et avec cet anneau tu pourras entrer à Babylone sans danger car nul français n'a le droit d'y entrer. Et en outre, je te laisserai partir en toute tranquillité."

"Grand diable!" s'écria Huon. "Je l'aurai, ton anneau, et sans que tu me le donnes ! Tu pourrais m'offrir le monde entier et je n'enlèverai pas cet haubert! Je frappe, es-tu prêt, allons-y!"

Et Huon se jeta sur le géant.

"What do you want of me?" demanded Arrogance.

"What I want of you" cried Huon, "it is that you will go to the devil and never return!"

"Eh! You have chosen a good moment; I have no scythe, and you are well armed."

"And who says that I will strike you before you are armed? Go quickly to look for your scythe and come back to find me."

"My faith," said the giant, "I have never in my life seen such a courteous enemy!"

"But you are a great fool to risk yourself thus, because, just as the lion seizes the deer, I could choke you with my hands. Perhaps you do not know who I am. My name is Arrogance and there is not a devil in hell who is not my cousin. Do you perhaps know Oberon? All his magic powers were not enough to prevent me from seizing his castle. Besides this, I stole his white hauberk. No one can wear it if he is not absolutely pure and true. The hauberk then becomes his size, and the one who wears it is always the victor in battle. As for myself, I have not tried it, but since you have chosen to let me arm myself, I permit you to try it on if you wish. Go, I will do you no harm during this time."

Huon ran to search for it, and the hauberk fit him perfectly. The eyes of Arrogance became enraged with anger.

"You wretch!" cried Arrogance, "take off that hauberk immediately. If you take it off, I will give you this ring which Admiral Gandisse gave me so that I would harm him no more; and with this ring you will be able to enter into Babylon without danger because no Frenchman has the right to enter there. And in addition, I will let you depart in peace."

"Great devil!" cried Huon. "I will have your ring, and without you giving it to me! You could offer me the whole world and I would not remove this hauberk! I strike, if you are ready. Let us begin!"

And Huon threw himself upon the giant.

Il brandit sa faux pour frapper Huon, mais Huon s'échappa et elle s'enfonça dans un pilier. Pendant qu'Orgueilleux retirait son arme, Huon le frappa si fort qu'il tomba à terre, mort.

Huon appela alors ses hommes. Ils firent connaissance de Sibylle et menèrent grande fête dans le palais.

Mais le lendemain, Huon leur dit adieu car ils étaient arrivés à la mer rouge et, selon l'ordre de Charlemagne, Huon devait poursuivre seul le chemin.

Tous promirent de l'attendre aussi longtemps qu'il le faudrait. Ils le recommandèrent au bon Dieu et l'embrassèrent tendrement. Bien des larmes coulèrent ce jour-là.

Huon marchait au bord de la mer. Comment la traverserait-il? Il n'avait point de navire. Alors qu'il songeait tristement, un grand poisson surgit soudain des vagues et s'avança vers lui.

"Je suis Malabron, un thon de mer," cria-t-il à Huon. "Obéron m'envoie pour te porter à Babylone."

Huon, tout joyeux, sauta sur son dos et ils traversèrent la mer.

Bientôt Huon arriva aux portes de Babylone et y entra par le premier pont.

"Es-tu français ou sarrasin?" lui cria le portier.

Huon avait complètement oublié l'anneau du géant qu'il portait avec lui et avec lequel il aurait pu passer. Il oublia aussi la promesse qu'il avait faite à Obéron et il répondit au portier:

"Je suis sarrasin, laisse-moi passer!"

Soudain son cœur se serra. Il se souvint de sa promesse. C'était trop tard. Au deuxième pont le portier posa la même question. "Je suis français et je viens de la France," s'écria-t-il.

"Va, misérable," s'écria le portier, "je ne sais comment tu es passé par le premier pont!"

Au troisième et au quatrième pont il montra son anneau et passa.

Mais sitôt entré dans la ville, il s'assit sous un arbre et sanglota amèrement.

The giant brandished his scythe to strike Huon, but Huon dodged it, and the scythe embedded itself in a pillar. As Arrogance pulled out his weapon, Huon struck him with such force that he fell to the earth, dead.

Huon then called his men. They learned about Sibylle and held a great feast inside the palace.

But the next day, Huon said farewell to them because they had arrived at the Red Sea, and according to the command of Charlemagne, Huon had to continue alone on his journey.

They all promised to wait as long as it would be necessary. They entrusted him to the Good Lord and embraced him tenderly. The tears flowed freely on that day.

Huon walked to the edge of the sea. How would he cross it? There was no ship at all. While he sighed sadly, a great fish suddenly arose from the waves and advanced towards him.

"I am Malabron, a tuna from the sea," he cried to Huon. "Oberon sent me to carry you to Babylon."

Overjoyed, Huon jumped on his back, and they crossed the sea.

Soon Huon arrived at the gates of Babylon and entered by the first bridge.

"Are you French or Saracen?" the gatekeeper called to him.

Huon completely forgot the giant's ring which he carried, and with which he would be able to enter the city. He also forgot the promise he made to Oberon and he answered the gatekeeper:

"I am Saracen; let me through!"

Suddenly his heart shook. He remembered his promise. It was too late. At the second bridge, the gatekeeper asked him the same questions, "I am French and I come from France," he cried.

"Go, you wretch," the gatekeeper cried to him; "I don't know how you crossed over the first bridge!"

At the third and at the fourth bridge, he showed his ring and crossed over.

But as soon as he was inside the city, he sat under a tree and sobbed bitterly.

"Obéron, mon gentil roi, tu ne m'aimeras plus. Tu ne viendras plus aider Huon, ton ami. Hélas, j'ai menti et rien ne pourra réparer le mal. Aie pitié de moi, gentil sire, j'en souffre trop! Hélas, je n'ai pas pensé à ce que je disais. C'était de mauvais gré que je l'ai fait! Hélas, mon doux pays, ne te reverrai-je plus?"

Et il sonna du cor.

"Je saurai ainsi du moins si vraiment il ne reviendra plus."

Et au loin, Obéron l'entendit et baissa tristement la tête.

"Qu'as-tu?" demandèrent ses chevaliers.

"J'entends," répondit-il, "l'appel d'un pauvre misérable qui a menti. Hélas! Il est en danger mais je ne puis le sauver. Il souffre, pauvre enfant!" dit Obéron en sanglotant.

"Il ne vient pas," pensa Huon, "je suis seul à présent. Que m'importe! Advienne ce qui voudra."

Huon entra sans mot dire dans le palais. Au même instant les sarrasins, gardiens du palais, fondirent sur lui, mais il alla droit vers l'Amiral et lui montra l'anneau.

"Laissez-le!" s'écria celui aux hommes, "gare au premier qui le touche!"

"Qu'est-ce qui t'amène ici, jeune seigneur?" demanda l'Amiral.

"C'est le grand Charlemagne qui m'envoie," dit Huon. "Il est bien courroucé du peu d'égards que tu portes envers la France. Il te mande par moi de lui envoyer mille éperviers, mille lévriers, mille ours enchaînés, mille jeunes seigneurs de haute lignée, mille demoiselles parmi les plus belles, et, en outre tes blanches moustaches!"

"Il est fou, ton roi!" s'écria l'Amiral en éclatant de rire. "Pourrais-tu me dire, jeune homme, comment il se fait que tu aies cet anneau dans la main?"

"J'ai tué le géant Orgueilleux" répondit Huon, "et j'ai pris son anneau que voici!"

"Oberon, my kind king, you will not love me anymore. You will not come to help Huon, your friend. Alas, I have lied and nothing will repair the harm. Have pity on me, kind sire, I have suffered too much! Alas, I didn't think about what I was saying. I have done wrong! Alas, my sweet country, will I never see you again?"

And he blew the horn.

"At least, I will know if he will truly never come again."

And from far away, Oberon heard it and sadly lowered his head.

"Is something amiss?" asked his knights.

"I am listening," he replied "to the call of a poor wretch who has lied. Alas! He is in danger but I am not able to save him. He suffers, poor child!" said Oberon, sobbing.

"He will not come," thought Huon, "I am now alone. What will happen to me! Let come what may."

Huon entered the palace without saying a word. At the same time, the Saracens, the palace guards, discovered him, but he walked straight up to the Admiral and showed him the ring.

"Leave him alone!" the Admiral cried to the men, "Beware the first one who would touch him!"

""What has brought you here, young sir?" asked the commander.

"Charlemagne has sent me," said Huon. "He is very angry at what little respect you show to France. Through me, he commands that you send him: one thousand hawks, one thousand greyhounds, one thousand bears in chains, one thousand lords of high lineage, one thousand of the most beautiful young maidens, and your white mustaches as well!"

"Your king is mad!" cried the Admiral, bursting with laughter. "Can you tell me, young man, how it happens that you hold that ring on your hand?"

"I have killed the giant Arrogance," replied Huon, "and I have seized this ring!"

"Au diable!" s'écria l'Amiral, "tu vas attirer sur moi la colère de tous les géants, si on sait que tu es entré ici! Hommes, emportez-le, prenez son épée et jetez-le en prison."

Mais Esclarmonde, la douce fille de l'Amiral, avait tout vu. Et elle eut au cœur bien du chagrin.

"Un si beau chevalier," pensait-elle, "c'est grand dommage qu'il soit ainsi traité."

Chaque jour elle descendait donc vers le donjon lui porter de beaux mets et des fruits et lui parler doucement pour le soulager.

Un jour, le frère d'Orgueilleux se présenta devant l'Amiral Gandisse.

"Tu as dans ton palais un misérable qui a tué mon frère Orgueilleux et sur le champ je m'emparerai de ton royaume! Tu seras mon esclave jusqu'à la fin de tes jours!"

L'Amiral tremblait épouvanté.

Esclarmonde s'approcha alors de l'Amiral.

"Père," lui dit-elle, "il n'est chevalier au monde qui puisse combattre ce géant, sauf Huon que tu as emprisonné. Si tu veux, appelle-le et tu seras sauvé!"

Huon fut appelé. On lui rendit son épée et son haubert blanc comme neige.

D'un coup il abattit le géant.

"Voilà encore une tâche faite!" s'écria Huon. "Qu'as-tu à me dire maintenant, mon Amiral?"

"Misérable prisonnier!" s'écria Gandisse, "ce que j'ai à dire c'est que tu sois à cet instant même jeté en prison! Je n'ai plus besoin de toi!"

Les sarrasins entourèrent Huon et le menacèrent.

Il sonna à tout hazard de son cor et cette fois Obéron accourut.

Cent mille chevaliers armés envahirent la ville et des yeux d'Obéron se répandirent de doux rayons. Il entra dans le palais.

"The Devil!" shouted the Admiral, "You will bring the anger of all the giants upon me if anyone knows that you have entered here! Men, seize him, take his sword, and throw him into prison."

But Esclarmonde, the sweet daughter of the Admiral, had seen everything. And her heart was full of remorse.

"Such a handsome knight," thought she, "it's a great pity to have him treated like this."

Each day she descended to the dungeon carrying fine food and fruits, and speaking sweetly to comfort him.

One day, the brother of Arrogance presented himself before Admiral Gandisse.

"In your palace you have a wretch who has killed my brother Arrogance; and I will now take possession of your kingdom! You will be my slave to the end of your days!"

The Admiral trembled with fear.

Esclarmonde approached the Admiral.

"Father," she said to him, "There is not a knight in the world who is able to combat this giant except Huon, whom you have imprisoned. If you wish, call him and you will be saved!"

Huon was called forth. His sword was returned to him and his snow white hauberk.

With one blow, he killed the giant.

"Another completed task," cried Huon; "What have you to say to me now, my Admiral?"

"Wretched prisoner!" cried Gandisse, "What I have to say is that you will at this instant be thrown into prison! I have no further need of you!"

The Saracens surrounded Huon and threatened him.

In great danger, he blew his horn, and this time Oberon came running.

One hundred thousand armed knights invaded the city and Oberon's eyes beamed with gentle rays of light. He entered the palace.

"Homme de pierre," s'écria-t-il à l'Amiral, "tu voudrais emprisonner un homme qui t'as sauvé. Misérable! Ingrat! Tu seras durement puni!"

Huon se jeta sur lui et lui coupa ses blanches moustaches.

Huon et Obéron sortirent du palais.

"M'as-tu donc pardonné?" demanda doucement Huon au petit roi.

"Oui, mon enfant," dit Obéron, "mais ne recommence plus!"

Obéron lui donna un beau navire. Huon y conduisit la belle Esclarmonde et le vaisseau partit.

Bientôt il retrouva ses chers compagnons, et ils se racontèrent d'interminables histoires.

Puis ils entrèrent dans le vaisseau et prirent le large.

Le navire vogua doucement sur l'onde mais bientôt le ciel s'assombrit, les vagues se déchirèrent et une tempête terrible s'annonça.

Les hommes furent saisis d'une grande peur car les mâts du navire se déchirèrent, les cordes se rompirent et ils furent tous jetés dans les flots.

Huon prit Esclarmonde par le bras et pendant des heures il lutta contre les immenses vagues. Ils arrivèrent enfin sur la terre ferme mais le haubert blanc, la cruche et le cor d'ivoire étaient tombés dans la mer et Huon ne pouvait plus appeler Obéron.

Les compagnons luttèrent aussi contre les vagues et enfin arrivèrent sur un autre rivage.

Des hommes sauvages étaient venus sur la côte. Ils bandèrent les yeux de Huon et lui lièrent les mains. Ils emportèrent Esclarmonde et laissèrent l'enfant de Bordeaux seul sur le rivage.

Mais Malabron, le thon, entendit ses pleurs. Il lui détacha les bandes des yeux, lui délia les mains et le porta sur son dos jusqu'à un rivage où s'élevait un grand château.

Puis Malabron disparut dans les flots pour retrouver le haubert, la cruche et le cor, et les rapporta à son roi Obéron.

"Man of stone," he shouted at the Admiral, "you would imprison a man who saved you. Villain! Ungrateful one! You will be severely punished!"

Huon threw himself upon Gandisse and cut off his white mustache.

Huon and Oberon went forth from the palace.

"Have you then forgiven me?" Huon gently asked the little king.

"Yes, my child," said Oberon, "but don't do it again!"

Oberon gave him a handsome ship. Huon escorted beautiful Esclarmonde on board, and the ship set forth.

Soon he was reunited with his dear companions, and they told each other endless stories.

Then they boarded the ship and took to the open sea.

The boat sailed gently over the waters, but soon the sky darkened, the waves broke, and a terrible tempest arose.

The men were seized with a great fear because the boat's masts were breaking, the ropes unraveled, and they were all thrown into the waves.

Huon took Esclarmonde in his arms and for hours he struggled against the huge waves. At last they arrived on firm ground but the white hauberk, the cup, and the ivory horn were sunk in the sea, and Huon was unable to call Oberon.

The companions also struggled against the waves and finally arrived on a different shore.

Wild men came to the beach. They bound Huon's eyes and tied his hands. They carried off Esclarmonde and left the child of Bordeaux alone on the shore.

But Malabron, the tuna, heard his weeping. He removed the bandages from his eyes, untied his hands, and carried Huon on his back to a shore, where there arose a great castle.

Then Malabron disappeared in the waters to recover the hauberk, the flask and the horn, and he carried them back to his king, Oberon.

Huon errait tristement sur le rivage. Il n'avait plus sa bonne épée pour se défendre. Un vieux ménestrel, une harpe sur le dos, errait aussi près des rochers. Il s'approcha de Huon:

"Jeune homme," lui dit-il, "si tu veux porter cette harpe pour moi, je te donnerai deux deniers par jour et du pain à foison."

Huon mit la harpe sur son dos et suivit le vieux ménestrel, mais il avait bien du chagrin au cœur car, pensait-il: "ne suis-je pas le fils du Duc de Bordeaux? Et me voici réduit à servir un vieux ménestrel."

Ce soir-là, le Roi Inorin, qui gouvernait le pays, appela le ménestrel car son cœur était plein de tourments et il désirait entendre les doux sons de la harpe.

Le ménestrel se rendit au château et Huon le suivit.

Lorsque le roi vit Huon portant la harpe, il l'appela et lui dit:

"Jeune homme, ton visage est beau et noble. Comment se fait-il que tu serves ce ménestrel? Ne connais-tu pas d'autre métier?"

"Je sais," dit Huon, "monter à cheval et manier une épée dans les combats."

"Demain," dit le roi sarrasin, "je fais la guerre à Galafre, mon voisin, car il tient dans son palais ma nièce, la belle Esclarmonde. Si ton bras est fort, tu pourras venir avec moi au combat."

Huon y consentit de grand cœur et ils partirent à l'aube.

Les guerriers sarrasins lui donnèrent un pauvre vieux cheval et une épée qu'ils croyaient la moins bonne. Mais Huon la reconnut. C'était la sœur de l'épée Durandel, l'épée de Roland le preux.

Et il partit le cœur plein de joie en pensant à sa chère compagne qu'il allait retrouver.

Huon rencontra l'adversaire et sur le vieux cheval, fit mille prouesses éclatantes. Les compagnons de Huon étaient entrés dans la ville de Galafre et combattaient à côté du roi; mais lorsqu'ils virent Huon dans l'armée ennemie, ils se jetèrent dans ses bras, emportés de joie.

Huon of Bordeaux

Huon wandered sadly on the seashore. He no longer had his good sword to defend himself. An old minstrel, a harp on his back, also wandered beside the rocks. He approached Huon:

"Young man," he said, "if you would like to carry this harp for me, I will give you two coins a day and plenty of bread."

Huon placed the harp upon his back and followed the old minstrel, but his heart was filled with great remorse because he thought, "Am I not the son of the duke of Bordeaux? And here I am reduced to serving an old minstrel."

That evening, kind Inorin, who governed the country, called the minstrel because his heart was full of torment and he desired to hear the sweet sounds of the harp.

The minstrel went to the castle and Huon followed him.

When the king saw Huon carrying the harp, he called him and said:

"Young man, your face is handsome and noble. How is it that you serve a minstrel? Don't you know another trade?"

"I know," said Huon, " how to mount a horse and wield a sword in battles."

"Tomorrow," said the Saracen king, "I go to war with Galafre my neighbor, because he holds my beautiful niece Esclarmonde captive in his palace. If your arm is strong, you can come into battle with me."

Huon agreed whole-heartedly and they set off at dawn.

The Saracen warriors gave him a poor old horse and a sword which they believed to be the worst. But Huon recognized it. It was the sister of the sword Durandel, the sword of the valiant Roland.

And he set off with a heart full of joy, thinking of his dear companion Esclarmonde, whom he was going to find again.

Huon met the enemy and, on the old horse, performed a thousand brilliant deeds. The companions of Huon had entered the city of Galafre and fought at the side of the king; but when they saw Huon in the enemy's army, they threw themselves into his arms, overcome with joy.

Le combat se poursuivit et les compagnons furent victorieux, mais ils avaient perdu Garin au grand cœur, celui qui avait tout laissé pour les suivre, et Huon pleurait amèrement.

La ville se rendit.

Huon et ses compagnons coururent alors à la prison où la douce Esclarmonde était enfermée.

Ils ouvrirent les portes et retrouvèrent Esclarmonde. Bien grande fut leur joie de se revoir ! Puis ils se mirent en marche vers la vaste mer.

A l'instant même où ils arrivèrent sur la côte, un immense navire voguait à l'horizon.

"Il vient de France!" s'écrièrent les hommes, "voyez-vous les signes qu'il porte?"

Le navire s'approcha du rivage et jeta l'ancre. Des cris de joie s'élevèrent de tous côtés.

"Je suis Guirré, le prévôt de Bordeaux," s'écria le commandant. "Il y a deux ans que nous voguons sur les mers à la recherche de Huon et de ses compagnons."

"Nous sommes ceux que vous cherchez!" s'écrièrent les compagnons; et tous s'embrassèrent et il y eut grande joie.

Ils montèrent ensuite dans le vaisseau et prirent le large.

Huon parla à Guirré.

"Que se passe-t-il en France? Et dans Bordeaux, mon doux pays? Comment va Gérard, mon gentil frère?"

Guirré baissa la tête alors et parla tristement.

"Gérard a pris possession de Bordeaux et y règne en seigneur. Il a épousé la fille du traître Gibonard. Il a réduit les habitants à la misère et fait régner la terreur dans le pays!"

Huon écouta tristement ce récit.

Un bon vent souffla sur la mer et les porta bien vite sur le rivage de la douce France.

Comme ils étaient heureux de la revoir! Ils se remirent à cheval et parcoururent les champs et les forêts.

Bientôt les tours de Bordeaux apparurent au loin et Huon fut transporté de joie.

The battle continued and the companions were victorious, but they lost great-hearted Garin, he who had left everything to follow them, and Huon wept bitterly.

The city surrendered.

Huon and his companions then hurried to the prison where sweet Esclarmonde was imprisoned.

They opened the gates and rescued Esclarmonde. Great was their joy on seeing each other again! Then they marched toward the vast sea.

At the same instant when they arrived on the coast, an immense ship sailed across the horizon.

"It comes from France," cried the men; "do you see the flags it flies?"

The ship approached the shore and cast its anchor.

Cries of joy arose from all sides.

"I am Guirre, the provost of Bordeaux," cried the captain," For two years we have sailed on the seas in search of Huon and his companions."

"We are the ones you seek!" cried the companions; and everyone embraced and there was great joy.

Then they climbed aboard the vessel and set out to sea.

Huon spoke with Guirre.

"What has happened in France? And in Bordeaux, my sweet country? How is Gerard, my kind brother?"

Guirre lowered his head, then spoke sadly.

"Gerard has taken possession of Bordeaux and rules as lord. He has married the daughter of the traitor Gibouard. He has reduced the inhabitants to misery and has created a rule of terror in the land!"

Huon listened sadly to this account.

A fair wind blew over the sea and carried them quickly to the shores of sweet France.

How happy they were to see it again! They mounted on horseback and rode through fields and forests.

Soon the towers of Bordeaux appeared in the distance, and Huon was transported with joy.

Huon de Bordeaux

"Vois-tu, belle dame," dit-il à la douce Esclarmonde, "les tours du château de Bordeaux? C'est là mon doux pays que tu verras bientôt. Tu y porteras une petite couronne d'or et de longs cortèges te suivront par la ville. Mais nous ne pouvons pas y entrer avant d'avoir vu notre roi Charlemagne car ainsi me l'a-t-il ordonné."

Ils se rendirent à un couvent et s'y arrêtèrent pour passer la nuit.

Le bon moine les reçut de grand cœur et les combla de maintes bontés.

"Veux-tu," dit-il à Huon, "que j'envoie un message à ton frère pour qu'il vienne te trouver ici?"

"Bien volontiers, ami!" répondit Huon.

Gérard, en entendant la nouvelle, fut bien tourmenté. Il alla trouver Gibonard, son beau-père, et lui raconta la chose.

"Il est une façon de nous en tirer," dit Gibonard. "Ecoute, je me trouverai au lever du soleil dans la forêt avec mille hommes. Tu accompagneras Huon et dès que tu nous feras signe, nous nous jetterons sur lui. Nous l'amènerons à Bordeaux et nous les mettrons tous en prison. Puis, tu iras trouver le vieux Charlemagne. Tu lui diras que Huon est d'abord entré à Bordeaux et que tu l'as emprisonné pour avoir manqué de parole à l'Empereur."

Gérard approuva fortement cette idée. Il alla trouver son frère et dès qu'il le vit, son front rougit et ses yeux se baissèrent. Après que Huon l'eût embrassé, Gérard lui demanda maintes détails au sujet de ses exploits.

"Cher frère," dit-il ensuite, "allons nous reposer; tu dois être bien las cette nuit. Demain à l'aube nous partirons trouver le grand Charles."

Et ils s'embrassaient et allaient dormir.

Mais là, durant la nuit, Gérard ne dormit point. Mille mauvais desseins lui remplissaient le cœur. A peine le coq avait-il chanté qu'il réveilla tous les compagnons.

"Il n'est plus temps de dormir!" s'écria-t-il. "Debout, compagnons, l'Empereur nous attend."

"Do you see, beautiful Lady," he said to sweet Esclarmonde, "the towers of the castle of Bordeaux? There lies my sweet country which you will soon see. You will wear a little golden crown and a long procession will follow you through the city. But we cannot enter before having seen our king Charlemagne, because he has commanded me thus."

They arrived at a monastery and there they stopped to spend the night.

A good friar received them gladly and with great kindness.

"Do you wish me," he said to Huon, "to send a message to your brother so that he will come to find you here?"

"Very willingly, my friend!" replied Huon.

Gerard, hearing this news, was greatly distressed. He went to find Gibonard, his father-in-law, and told him the story.

"There is way for us to overcome this problem," said Gibonard. "Listen, at sunrise I will be in the forest with a thousand men. You will accompany Huon and as soon as you give us a signal, we will throw ourselves upon him. We will take him to Bordeaux and put them all in prison. Then you will go to find old Charlemagne. You will tell him that Huon has entered Bordeaux and that you have imprisoned him for having broken his word to the Emperor."

Gerard greatly approved this idea. He went to find his brother and upon seeing him, his face reddened and he lowered his eyes. After Huon had embraced him, Gerard asked him many details about his exploits.

"Dear brother," he said afterwards, "let's go to bed; you must be very tired tonight. Tomorrow at dawn we will leave to find great Charlemagne."

And they embraced each other and went to sleep.

But during the night, Gerard did not sleep at all. A thousand wicked schemes filled his heart. Hardly had the rooster crowed than he awakened all the companions.

"There is no more time to sleep," he cried. "Arise, companions, the Emperor awaits us."

Ils se levèrent et prirent la route.

Le cheval de Gérard l'emportait dans la forêt mais celui de Huon galopait doucement.

"Frère!" s'écria Gérard, "tu es bien heureux d'être de retour, mais qu'arrivera-t-il à ton pauvre jeune frère? Il n'aura plus de terres ni de château, et tu seras, toi, un grand seigneur."

"Ne crains rien, jeune frère," dit Huon, "je partagerai tout avec toi."

Gérard lança ensuite le signal et, de l'ombre obscure des bois, sortirent mille hommes armés. Un combat eut lieu et Huon fut jeté de son cheval car il fut durement blessé. On lui lia les mains et on lui banda les yeux. Puis, avant que la brume de l'aube ne fut dissipée, ils l'emmenèrent avec ses compagnons à Bordeaux, et les jetèrent tous dans le donjon du château.

Gérard se rendit ensuite au palais de l'Empereur.

Les ducs et barons y étaient tous assemblés, et Charlemagne à la barbe fleurie, siégeait sur son trône.

"Sire," dit Gérard à l'Empereur, "je viens vous apporter des nouvelles de Huon, mon frère. Il est de retour, mais, à en croire son silence, il est évident qu'il n'a pas vu l'Amiral. En outre, il vous a trahi car malgré vos ordres, il est entré à Bordeaux avant de vous voir. Je l'ai donc emprisonné dans le château par devoir envers mon souverain."

"Le menteur!" s'écria furieusement le Duc de Naimes. "A-t-on jamais vu homme trahir ainsi son frère? Je jure par ma foi que chaque parole de sa bouche est fausse. Je vous en supplie, O! Roi! ne l'écoutez pas mais allez plutôt vous-même à Bordeaux pour parler à l'enfant qu'on a lâchement emprisonné!"

"Préparez mon voyage!" dit le grand Charles, "je pars sur le champ! Ducs et barons, suivez-moi! Nous verrons qui aura raison!"

Ils arrivèrent bientôt à Bordeaux et les habitants, en voyant le grand Charles, les ducs et les chevaliers, se demandaient tous quelle était la cause d'un cortège si imposant.

They rose and set off on the road.

Gerard's horse bolted into the forest, but Huon's horse galloped gently.

"Brother," cried Gerard, "you are very happy to have returned, but what will happen to your poor young brother? He will no longer have lands nor the castle, and you will be the great lord."

"Do not fear, young brother," said Huon, "I will share all of it with you."

Gerard then gave the signal and, from the hidden shadow of the trees, came a thousand armed men. A battle took place, and Huon was thrown from his horse because he was severely wounded. His hands were tied and his eyes bound. And before the mist of dawn had disappeared, they led him and his companions to Bordeaux, and threw all of them into the castle's dungeon.

Gerard then went to the palace of the Emperor.

The dukes and barons were assembled there, and Charlemagne, with his flowing beard, ruled on his throne.

"Sire," said Gerard to the Emperor, "I come to bring you news of Huon, my brother. He has returned; but, in light of his silence, it is evident that he has not seen the Admiral. And furthermore, he has betrayed you, because in spite of your commands, he has entered Bordeaux before seeing you. I have thus imprisoned him in the castle out of duty to my sovereign."

"Liar!" furiously cried the Duke of Naimes. "Has one ever seen a man so betray his brother? I swear by my faith that every word of his mouth is false. I beg you, O King, not to listen to him but to go yourself, quickly, to Bordeaux to speak with the child who has been so disgracefully imprisoned!"

"Prepare my journey," said great Charlemagne: "I shall depart immediately! Duke and barons, follow me! We shall see who is right!"

They soon arrived in Bordeaux and the inhabitants, seeing Charlemagne, the dukes and knights wondered what was the reason for such an imposing procession.

Ils entrèrent dans le château au bruit des fanfares et Gérard ordonna que les tables soient remplies de mets et de vin clair pour honorer le roi, espérant que lorsqu'il aurait mangé et bu, il oublierait Huon.

Mais le grand Charles devina sa pensée. Il ordonna que les tables furent enlevées et que l'on amène Huon devant lui.

Alors Huon apparut et raconta au roi tous ses exploits.

"Grand Charles," lui dit-il, "j'ai accompli vos ordres, et grandes sont les souffrances par lesquelles nous sommes passés, mes compagnons et moi. Mais je ne vous les dirai point car il y aurait trop à raconter. Mon frère Gérard m'a trahi. Ses hommes nous ont assaillis et nous ont faits prisonniers. Les blanches moustaches de l'Amiral m'ont été prises durant le combat. Hélas, je ne puis donner ici de preuve, mais, par ma foi, je vous jure, o Roi, que toutes mes paroles sont vraies!"

En entendant ce récit, des larmes remplirent les yeux du Duc de Naimes et des barons.

Le grand Charles prit alors la parole:

"Enfant, tu a bien parlé mais tu n'as donné aucun témoignage pouvant prouver que ton récit est vrai. Un juge ne peut point juger s'il n'a pas de preuve sous la main."

Cependant, au loin, Obéron écoutait ces paroles et son cœur fut rempli de chagrin.

"Qu'as-tu, gentil roi?" lui demandèrent ses chevaliers.

"J'entends au loin," dit Obéron, "les pleurs du jeune Huon. Pauvre enfant, il a bien souffert. Je m'en vais, chevaliers, le délivrer."

Soudain s'illumina la grande salle où se trouvaient Charlemagne et ses chevaliers. Un rayon clair et beau entra par la porte et aussitôt apparut le bel Obéron à l'arc étincelant et ses cent mille chevaliers.

"Qui est donc cet homme?" s'écria Charlemagne. "Il est beau comme le soleil qui nous donne le jour!"

"Charles au fier visage!" dit Obéron. "Ecoutez-moi:

They entered into the castle to the sound of fanfares, and Gerard ordered that tables be filled with food and clear wine to honor the king, hoping that when he had eaten and drunk, he would forget Huon.

But Charlemagne guessed his intention. He commanded that the tables be removed and that Huon be brought before him.

So Huon appeared and recounted his exploits to the king.

"Great Charlemagne," he said to him, "I have fulfilled your commands, and in doing so, we have suffered greatly, my companions and I. But I will not tell you more because there is too much to tell. My brother Gerard has betrayed me. His men have assaulted us and made us prisoners. The white mustaches of the Admiral were taken from me during the battle. Alas, I cannot give them here as proof, but, by my faith, I swear to you, O King, that all my words are true!"

Hearing this account, tears filled the eyes of the Duke of Naimes and the barons.

Charlemagne then spoke these words:

"Child, you have spoken well but you have not presented any evidence to prove that your speech is true. A judge is unable to judge if there is no proof in hand."

But from far away, Oberon listened to these words and his heart was filled with remorse.

"What is the matter, noble king?" asked Oberon's knights.

"I hear from afar," said Oberon, "the weeping of young Huon. Poor child, he has suffered greatly. I shall go, my knights, to save him."

The large room where Charlemagne and his knights were gathered was suddenly filled with light. A clear, lovely beam of light entered through the door, and immediately beautiful Oberon appeared in a sparkling arc of light with his hundred thousand knights.

"Who is this man?" cried Charlemagne! "He is as beautiful as the sun that gives us day!"

"Il n'est homme sur la terre de qui je ne connaisse les pensées et je vous jure par toute la création que Huon a accompli jusqu'au dernier de vos ordres!"

Puis, s'adressant au traître, il lui dit:

"Maintenant parle, Gérard, devant ton souverain! Parle, Obéron t'écoute!"

Gérard tremblait devant les yeux rayonnants d'Obéron et ne pouvait rien lui cacher.

Il parla et les larmes l'étouffèrent.

"Oui, j'ai trahi mon frère!" s'écria-t-il, "mais c'est Gibonard qui m'a incité! Je m'en repens, croyez-moi, et m'en repentirai jusqu'à la fin de mes jours!"

Obéron parla alors d'une voix puissante :

"Selon la loi qui punit les frères qui ont trahi," dit-il, "je commande que Gérard soit tué!"

A ces mots Huon s'approcha d'Obéron et, les yeux pleins de larmes, il s'agenouilla devant lui.

"Mon gentil roi," dit-il, "aie pitié de mon frère, et, si tu veux me voir heureux, ne le fais pas tuer. C'est Gibonard qui l'a incité à me trahir. Pardonne-lui, je lui donnerai la moitié du royaume, nous redeviendrons amis et nous vivrons heureux!"

Obéron sourit et ses yeux se remplirent de larmes tant il fut ému en écoutant ses paroles.

Charlemagne pleurait aussi. Les deux frères s'embrassèrent, et tous les chevaliers se réjouirent.

Alors, Obéron prit Huon à part et lui parla doucement:

"Huon, mon frère," lui dit-il, "encore trois ans je vivrai dans mon château de Mohmur, mais après je quitterai la terre car le bon Dieu m'appelle dans le Royaume des Cieux.

"Huon, tu prendras alors mon royaume. Nous nous reverrons encore quelquefois sur la terre, mais après, nous ne nous reverrons plus!

"Adieu, Huon, sois heureux et si jamais tu es en peine, appelle toujours Obéron."

"Charlemagne of the proud face," said Oberon, "listen to me:

"There is not a man on the earth whose thoughts I don't know, and I swear to you by all of creation that Huon fulfilled every last one of your commands!"

Then, addressing the traitor, he said:

"Now speak, Gerard, before your sovereign! Speak, Oberon is listening to you!"

Gerard trembled before Oberon's radiant eyes and could hide nothing from him!

He spoke through his stifling tears.

"Yes, I have betrayed my brother," he cried, "but it is Gibonard who urged me! I repent, believe me, and I will repent until the end of my days!"

Oberon then spoke with a powerful voice:

"According to the law which punishes traitorous brothers," said he, "I command that Gerard be put to death!"

At these words, Huon approached Oberon and, with eyes full of tears, knelt before him.

"My noble king," said he, "have mercy on my brother, and, if you wish to see me happy, do not put him to death. It was Gibonard who urged him to betray me. Pardon him, I will give him half of my realm, we will again become friends and we will live happily!"

Oberon smiled and he was so moved by these words that his eyes filled with tears.

Charlemagne wept also. The two brothers embraced each other and all the knights rejoiced.

Then Oberon took Huon aside and spoke gently to him:

"Huon, my brother," said he, "for three years I will live in my castle of Mohmur, but after that I will leave the earth because the Good Lord calls me to the Kingdom of the Heavens.

"Huon, you will then take my realm. We will see each other again several times on the earth, but later, we will see each other no more!

Huon épousa la belle Esclarmonde et hérita bientôt du royaume d'Obéron. Il régna aussi dans son château de Bordeaux avec son frère durant quatre-vingt-dix-neuf ans. Après cela, il régna seul pendant mille ans le royaume que lui avait confié Obéron. Au bout des mille ans, il confia le royaume des nains et des fées à un bel homme au cœur pur et il alla rejoindre à jamais Obéron, son doux ami, au Royaume Céleste.

Love for all, all for love.

"Adieu, Huon, be happy and if you ever are in difficulty, always call Oberon."

Huon wed the beautiful Esclarmonde and before long inherited the realm of Oberon. He also ruled in his castle of Bordeaux with his brother for ninety-nine years. After that, for a thousand years he alone ruled the kingdom which Oberon had entrusted to him. At the end of a thousand years, he entrusted the realm of the dwarfs and fairies to a good man of pure heart and he joined his gentle friend Oberon forever, in the Kingdom of the Heavens.

Stories of Hope and Courage

Princess Wanda

MANY queens have reigned in Poland, many a princess has lived in the palace of Krakow, but none as lovely as the Princess Wanda; for never had the people of the country beheld such beauty, nor the people in yonder lands heard of such charm.

Day after day, the city of Krakow was crowded with envoys from distant lands. They crossed the icy northern seas and the stormy seas of the south to ask her for her hand.

One day, the streets of Krakow echoed with the blast of foreign trumpets and steel of armoured troops. The people rushed to the windows. It was an envoy indeed, this time from a neighbouring land, a land they called Germany.

Oftimes had the Princess Wanda heard tales about the king of Germany. The men in his gloomy country were forever at war. The people who worked on the land died of hunger, for all they reaped was taken away from them. And he loved not his people, nor did they love him.

Such were the tales told about the king of Germany, and Wanda resolved that she would never marry a king who loved his people so little. Thus she called the envoy and said: "Return to your king and tell him I cannot love him, for he loves not his people; and as I cannot love him, I shall not marry him."

Princess Wanda

The envoy returned to his country, the armoured troops and trumpeters following, and he delivered the message to the king.

The king rose from his throne, and the walls of his palace shook as he spoke.

"How many can we throw into the battle?" he shouted, "and how many has Poland?"

"Sir," replied the counselor, "ours are sevenfold."

And summoning the envoy, he said:

"Return this very day to Poland and tell Her Highness that if she accepts not my offer, we shall attack her country with forces sevenfold hers in number and weapons."

Such was the message delivered to Wanda.

The dusk was falling over Krakow, and the hour had come when all were gathered round the firesides. The city was happy indeed, and a great peace reigned over it. Wanda watched it as the thousands of little lights glimmered in the dark, she watched it as the moon bent over the city, and big tears rolled down her cheeks. Never, she thought, must Poland die.

Early the next day she called upon the royal gown makers. They came in haste and listened to her orders. "You shall make for me a wedding gown," she said, "of finest silk, embroidered with the flowers of Poland, the flowers I love."

But Wanda was sad as she spoke, and they knew not why; and the people of Krakow wondered and talked, and great was their impatience to know whether Wanda, whom they all loved, would marry the king they hated so.

Thus was Wanda clad in a gown of whitest silk, and the train bore real flowers in the folds.

She placed the crown upon her head and called her people.

They came in masses from the plains and valleys, and the trumpets blew so hard that they came from the hills and crowded on the banks of the Vistula River.

And Wanda spoke to them all.

"My people," she said, "a mighty enemy is at our gates. You all know him, for long have tales been told about him. He threatens to attack Poland if your Princess Wanda will not marry him. Can a princess marry a prince she cannot love?

"My people, I know you will fight whatever the enemy be, for you are sons of a brave and mighty country, but the enemy's forces are sevenfold ours in number and weapons. Therefore, my people, I have resolved to leave you, for having left you, he shall have no cause to declare war. I am young, it is true, and happy I would be to live with you for years and years to come. The fields of Poland are growing the first corn, and Poland shall be lovely soon; I must leave you, though, for the prince I marry must be noble and great.

"My people, as long as you live, Poland shall not die. If the whole world crushed it to dust, it would rise again through you. I must leave you now, but remember Wanda sometimes, perhaps at dusk when the old tales of Poland are told."

With these words, she bent over the Vistula like a pure white swan and disappeared under the waters.

The people wept bitterly and mourned for her. They built a mound there where she stood, so that Wanda should never be forgotten. But the people of Poland know that Wanda can never be forgotten, for the Vistula still repeats her words as it flows. "Poland shall never die. If the whole world crushed it to dust, it would rise again through you. Poland can never die."

English original by Noor Inayat Khan

The White Eagles of Poland

MY children, there is a country far, far away called Poland. You have heard about it. It is a brave country, a country of warriors and knights.

Have you seen their flag flying in the wind? Have you seen the proud eagle on the red background? Why is the red flag like the setting sun, and why is the eagle white? Just listen, and I shall tell you all about it.

Long, long ago, Poland was a very happy country. The knights who defended the land were so mighty that no enemy dared approach the Polish soil.

Have you ever seen white eagles? They lived in Poland long, long years ago, high up in the cliffs, and they were kings of the rocks. Their piercing eyes watched over Poland, and their wings spread out as wings of steel to protect it.

One day, long, long years ago, the knights of Poland were travelling through the country with their king, Boleslaw the Brave. The hour was late, and they halted awhile as their horses' mouths were foaming. The vast country lay below. They laid their spears and lances on the hot sand and looked upwards. The sky till the horizon was red as blazing fire. All was silent, not a leaf stirred; then, in a gush of wind, two white wings spread out against the sky. It was the white eagle. In one

The White Eagles of Poland

mighty glance he viewed the cities below, and a great majesty surrounded him.

Then, slowly descending, he flew towards the open space where they stood, for there lay his nest at the summit of the oak. There he gently spread his wings, glanced once more at Poland and laid down to rest.

"Indeed, this shall be our sign," said King Boleslaw, "Forevermore the white eagle against the sky of Poland shall be our flag, and as long as it flies our country shall not fall. Hawks cannot beat the white eagle nor can they live in its nest. We shall erect a castle on this spot, great and massive. It shall be called the nest. The knights of Poland shall dwell in it and as long as they live, Poland shall live."

Such were the words of the king and there where the nest lay, a castle and city were built. It was called Gniezno, which means the nest. It still stands massive and unchallenged as the years pass by.

The flag is now torn down, and the Eagle of Poland wounded, but it can never die. White eagles never die. As soon as its wings are healed, it will return to the nest, and Gniezno shall be full of knights with lances and spears, and Poland shall live again forevermore.

English original by Noor Inayat Khan

Perce-Neige

GRAND Soleil avait une fille qui se nommait Perce-Neige. Elle était belle, très belle, plus belle que toutes les petites fées au ciel. Elle avait des ailes de libellule, des cheveux de rayons d'or et des yeux scintillants comme des étoiles.

Et Grand Soleil l'aimait tendrement.

C'était alors très triste sur la terre. Il n'y avait rien, ni fleurs, ni verdure, ni rayons.

La fille de Grand Soleil se pencha sur les nuages. "Il pousse tant de pommes d'or et de fleurs ici!" pensa-t-elle, "c'est bien triste qu'il n'y en ait pas sur la terre."

Elle dit adieu à Grand Soleil et ce fut alors comme un tout petit rayon quittant le ciel.

Et elle descendit doucement pour rendre la terre belle comme le royaume de son père dans le ciel.

Sur la pointe des pieds elle sautilla sur le monde. A peine avait-elle fait quelques pas que tout devint joli. L'herbe poussa, les arbres se couvrirent de feuilles. Il n'y avait plus de triste terre. Tout était vert et or.

Perce-Neige se mit à danser, tant elle était heureuse, et plus elle dansait, plus les champs se remplissaient de pâquerettes et d'anémones, et il en poussa tant! Autant que là-haut au royaume de Grand Soleil.

Snow-Drop

GREAT Sun had a little daughter with sun-ray hair and sky-blue eyes, and Great Sun loved her dearly for when she played about in the clouds, the whole sky would ring with sweet laughter.

But one day, she peeped down from the white clouds and three little tears rolled down her cheeks. The big world lay down there so brown gloomy and Oh! It looked very sad indeed. And while Great Sun was not looking, hush! hush! Very quietly she flew down from the sky.

She skipped along the big big world, and as she went along, green blades of grass sprung up, hundreds of them, thousands of them, then daisies and golden cups. Even the ugly branches, the long lanky branches of the elms and oaks, the branches of all the trees in the world were suddenly covered with tiny green leaves.

How lovely! thought Great Sun's little daughter, and so happy was she that she sang and sang till all the birds in the world started to sing and all the big big world was full of song and joy. And so happy was Little Daughter that she danced and danced till little white rabbits came bouncing out from every hold, from every side, brown spotted ones, little woolly ones too.

Perce neige

Ce n'était pas tout. Il y avait bien des oiseaux sur terre mais ils ne savaient pas chanter. A peine Perce-Neige avait-elle chanté que tous les oiseaux au monde ouvrirent le gosier et ce fut alors des trilles interminables.

Tout était clair et beau. Grand Soleil souriait tant qu'il ne restait plus un nuage au ciel. Et tout le monde aimait Perce-Neige qui avait rendu la terre si belle.

Mais en ce temps-là vivait une fée aux longs cheveux blancs. Elle était courbée comme le saule qui se penche dans l'eau. On l'appelait Hiver.

Avant que Perce-Neige n'était venue, Hiver régnait toujours sur terre. Mais depuis, on l'avait oubliée et la vieille en était bien courroucée.

"Par ma volonté," s'écria-t-elle, "par la gelée, le sable blanc et la bise, j'ordonne que Perce-Neige disparaisse!"

Aussitôt apparurent une file de bonshommes aux sourcils froncés. Il y avait Gelée, Sable Blanc, Bise, Transparent....

"Ecoutez-moi, mes sujets," s'écria Hiver en les voyant. "Perce-Neige est venue me chasser de mon trône. Voyez, les arbres sont verts, la terre est en fleurs, Grand Soleil se moque de mes pouvoirs, il rit là-haut à en fendre le ciel. Au diable celle qui ose détrôner Hiver, la grande reine!"

Les bonshommes firent un grand salut et promirent de faire disparaître Perce-Neige.

Ils attendirent que vînt la nuit, la sombre nuit durant laquelle Grand Soleil dort et ne voit point ce qui se passe.

Et chut!......chut!......à petits pas, ils parcoururent le monde

> Perce-Neige où est-elle?
> Peu importe qu'elle soit belle
> Qu'elle soit douce ou qu'elle soit blonde,
> Elle ne verra plus le monde,
> Car avant que l'aube puisse naître,
> Perce-Neige doit disparaître.

Ainsi chantaient-ils et la nuit était noire, très noire.

Snow-Drop

Great Sun smiled from the sky as he had never smiled before, so happy was he to see how lovely his little daughter had made the world. And so happy was he, that he woke earlier every morning and went to sleep later every night so as to gaze longer at the lovely world where his daughter dwelt.

Everyone loved her dearly. Only one living being did not love Great Sun's little daughter. It was Queen Winter. For since Great Sun's daughter had come on earth, Queen Winter had no longer reigned over the world. She called her best guards, and…crack, crack, crack, along they came: Frost-Bite, Fog-Gloom, North Wind and all the others.

"Woo…oo…," said Winter, "mighty guards, the Kingdom of Winter is in danger. Great Sun's little daughter is loved by everyone and I, your queen, am being forgotten. If you wish that the kingdom of cold abide, Great Sun's little daughter must die."

"Woo…oo…!" said Frost-Bite.

"Woo…oo…!" said Fog-Gloom.

"Woo…oo…!" said the blasty North Wind.

"When Great Sun is asleep, you shall seize her and hide her under the earth, so far away that no soul can find her again!"

And when Great Sun had gone and all the world was fast asleep, tip-toe, crack….crack, they went into the woods.

The little girl was sleeping beneath the bough of a pine-tree.

No one saw them come up to the tree. No one saw little daughter frozen stiff by Frost-Bite; made invisible by Fog-Gloom; and carried away by North Wind, so far away that no-one could find her again. No one saw except two little robins who were sitting on the bough and they followed quietly behind. No-one saw them put Great Sun's little daughter under the earth except the two little robins. They hid and watched.

The world became very sad as the days went by.

The little green blades lost their colour and faded away. No one knew where the daisies and buttercups had vanished nor why the birds had lost their voice. The tall trees wept so hard

Tout dormait. Perce-Neige dormait aussi.

Ils la trouvèrent sur la mousse verte parmi les anémones et ils l'emportèrent silencieusement dans leurs bras.

Personne n'entendit ses pleurs sauf un tout petit rouge-gorge et il suivit les bonshommes en secret.

Pauvre Perce-Neige! Elle fut emportée loin, très loin. Rouge-Gorge suivait toujours mais il s'arrêta soudain car la terre s'ouvrit et Perce-Neige disparut dans un royaume noir et obscur où Grand Soleil ne pourrait plus la revoir.

Hélas! Sur la terre on n'entendit plus que soupirs. Les arbres baissèrent leurs branches et pleurèrent tant, que toutes les jolies feuilles tombèrent en larmes. Les fleurs se fermèrent et n'ouvrirent plus leurs petits cœurs et les oiseaux s'en allèrent, on ne sait où....

Tout devint silencieux. Grand Soleil ne riait plus. Il ne pouvait plus voir la terre où Perce-Neige, son enfant, ne dansait plus. Il se levait donc plus tard chaque matin, et s'endormait plus tôt chaque soir, car la terre ne l'intéressait plus.

Fée Hiver régnait maintenant toute glorieuse et toute la terre était couverte de blanc.

"Où es-tu, Perce-Neige?" murmuraient sans cesse les arbres. "Où es-tu, Perce-Neige?" répétaient les ruisseaux.

Hélas! tout était en vain.

Mais Rouge-Gorge le malin n'était point parti avec les autres oiseaux. Il gardait le secret au fond du cœur et lorsque toute la terre n'espérait plus la revoir, il ouvrit l'aile et retourna là où un jour la terre s'ouvrit.

"Viens Perce-Neige!" appela Rouge-Gorge, "Reviens sur la terre car Grand Soleil nous quitte tous les jours plus longtemps tant il a de chagrin de ne plus voir son enfant. Reviens Perce-Neige, sinon Grand Soleil nous quitterait tout à fait et il ferait toujours nuit sur terre, il n'y aurait plus de jour. Viens Perce-Neige, viens pour que Grand Soleil ne nous quitte pas!"

"Je ne le puis," répondit Perce-Neige, "car, si Fée Hiver me voyait, elle me tuerait. Mais si tu veux je reviendrai comme une

that all their lovely leaves fell to the ground. No more white backs came peeping out of holes. The air was full of sighs, and Great Sun awoke later every morning and went to sleep earlier every night so sad was he to look upon the big big world where little daughter was no more to be found. Sometimes he would hide his face for days behind the clouds and Queen Winter reigned over the earth.

"Where is she?" muttered the trees as they swayed up and down.

"Where is she? Twii! Twii!" asked the birds as they shook the frost off their wings.

"Where is she?" whispered everything.

One day, two little red-breasts sitting on the bough of a pine tree fluttered their wings and flew away, far away to the spot where Great Sun's little daughter was hidden under the earth.

Too…too… with the tip of their beaks, they tapped on the ground.

"Are you there, little daughter?" they called, "Twii! twii! are you there?"

" Yes, robins," she whispered, "I am here."

"Do come back, Little Daughter," they pleaded, "the big big world is so sad without you."

"I cannot, little robins," she whispered, "for if I did, Queen Winter and her guards would kill me."

"Do come back, Little Daughter," twittered the robins, "the tall trees have lost all their leaves, so hard have they wept. The birds sing no more. No one knows where the daisies have vanished, and the Great Sun is so sad that he rises later every morning and leaves us earlier every night. Sometimes he hides his face for days behind the clouds and if you don't return, Little Daughter, he may never come again."

"Hush! I will come!" whispered little daughter, "but I will come as a flower as tiny as a drop, and as white as the snow so that Queen Winter cannot see me."

toute petite fleur, blanche comme la neige, et alors elle ne me verra point."

Perce-Neige sortit toute petite et si blanche que Fée Hiver ne la vit point.

Mais Grand Soleil reconnut son enfant.

Bientôt on remarqua que Grand Soleil se levait plus tôt chaque matin et s'endormait plus tard chaque soir.

"Grand Soleil ne nous quitte donc pas!" pensèrent les grands arbres, "qu'est-il donc arrivé? Perce-Neige serait-elle retrouvée?"

Et tout le monde se mit à chercher.

"Chut! Elle est là!" murmurait Rouge-Gorge à voix basse. Tous les champs et les forêts se réjouirent tout bas pour que Fée Hiver n'en sache rien, et toute la terre était en fête car Grand Soleil qui quittait la terre revenait tous les jours plus longtemps, et Perce-Neige perdue était enfin retrouvée.

Snow-Drop

And Snow-Drop grew out of the snow but everyone knew it was Great Sun's little daughter. They whispered it to each other when Winter was not about. And new leaves grew on the branches again, and very shyly the birds sang again, and Great Sun smiled again as never before, and he woke earlier every morning and went to sleep later every night for his little daughter was found and all the big big world was happy once again.

English version by Noor Inayat Khan

Vilayat and Noor Inayat Khan

Memories of Noor

I remember. Yes, I remember! Yes she is always there, somewhere in my mind, in my soul.

I remember her wise intervention in our lives as children, her mothering us though when she was just two years older than me. I remember her love of flowers, of all things beautiful, her tears when our father (Abba) sang to us sacred songs, enraptured by their beauty.

We hardly ever saw our father except surrounded by his disciples or when he came to tell us a bed time story before going to sleep. He was the father of the entire family of his disciples. We could not understand our schoolmates speaking about their 'dad.' I remember her calling us, saying: did you see Abba's eyes this morning? As he opened the door of the oriental room to usher in the next mureed, we could not believe the light, the fire in his eyes! She used to listen with rapt attention when Murshid gave us his children's class in the garden. This deep impression flowered since in her *Jataka Tales*, the first installment of her project of writing the stories of the lives of the prophets of the world religions, which was unfortunately to be interrupted by the tragedy that followed. A smattering of poems tell of her deep kinship with the humble, the suffering, the beleaguered; her striving to honor children's candid dreams

of the future, upholding high ideals to overcome the sardonic cynicism of our societies. She even planned to start a newspaper for children called *the New Age*—a prophetic foresight into a catch-word that became a modern paradigm!

Who would have thought that the pallid shy girl who was voted 1st prize for camaraderie by the very schoolmates who had first ostracized her for her olive skin and whose hearts she won would turn out to be the war hero who defied the brutal Gestapo, outwitting their intelligence until betrayed by a would-be friend?

At the news of our father's death, our world was plunged into darkness. Our mother, so sweet, so loving, so fragile broke down and was committed to bed for eleven years until the portents of war crashed upon our family. Noor was our little mother; taking care of all the children's needs, nursing us through our colds, advising us in our quandrums. As we grew, music took over our ailing hearts as a saving grace. The house was vibrant with music. Noor played the harp, Claire the piano, Hidayat the violin and I played the cello. We adopted a genius of a violinist, Janksi,[1] age 15, whom the professors of the Conservatoire and the École Normale de Musique said they had nothing to teach. We studied under Nadia Boulanger, Stravinski, Prokofiev, Paul Dukas, Wanda Landowska, Thibaut. Noor and I accompanied my cello teacher Maurice Eisenberg to visit Pablo Casals at San Vicente, a sea-side resort on the Costa Brava in 1935. I spent time in the Swiss Alps at Champéry with her to tide over a difficult time.

Then came the dark foreboding clouds that were to disrupt our lives. We heard the brutal hysterical voice of Hitler on the radio: "my patience is exhausted"—if only he realized the millions of people whose patience he had violated, whose dreams of a better world he had flaunted. We still entertained hopes of a reprieve… but no, after the news of outrageous plunder, we heard the Nazi cannons at the gates of Paris. We had to decide

---

1 Janski Szegeti, nephew of violinist Joseph Szegeti

either to stay and knuckle under the ignominious regime or join the forces that were heroically resisting the evil tide.

Noor and I held a conference. In our service of the Message of unity we had been preaching respect of all religions, all races, the divinity in man. Now came the test: were these just words or were we going to stand up with our lives for what we pledged ourselves to? News of the dismal cruelty and abject contempt of the most elementary dignity of the human person in concentration camps had reached our ears. But, if you counter violence with violence, you are participating in the very violence that you purport to oppose! Truly we believed in Gandhi's non-violence. Here came the test. But, I said, supposing a Nazi with a machine gun is about to shoot eighty hostages and there were no way of saving the eighty hostages without shooting the Nazi; if you did not shoot the Nazi, you would be responsible for the death of the eighty hostages! We decided we would involve ourselves in a defensive role, valiantly, in the front line. My training as a fighter pilot, interrupted by an eye test was followed by training in minesweeping as an officer in the British Navy where I participated in the landing in Normandy. I never expected to survive the carnage of my mates in our tiny wooden E-boats in the front line under attack from the coastal cannons. Claire enrolled in the Auxiliary Territorial Service (ATS). Our mother served as a nurse. Hidayat's wife, being pregnant with Fazal, stayed in France. Noor volunteered for the most dangerous of all posts right inside the ruthless enemy's camp. She volunteered as a radio operator to secure the link between the British war office and the French Underground. She was right at the fulcrum of the conflagration, her messages decisive in the invasion tactics. She was betrayed to the Gestapo.

Noor's ordeal was beyond the limits of human endurance. As the Allies were advancing victoriously an order issued from Headquarters for her death sentence was carried out. Later the prison jailer said how sad he was for she had been an example and an inspiration which had won his reverence.

The only word she said (that brave girl) before shot from behind was "*Liberté.*" In that clamor through her "*Liberté,*" she was voicing the plea of umpteen trillions of people on our planet in this day and age, striving for freedom against oppression. That voice has echoed through the decades as we try to build a brave new world: the *nouvel age.* She was to be martyred in one of the very concentration camps whose victims she had pledged herself to rescue.

I remember her visiting me in London just before embarking. Imagine: she took time to tidy my room! She told me she could not reveal the secrecy surrounding her mission. Her one worry was the pain it would cause our mother. As I looked at her for a last time, I had a devastating hunch that I would never see her again—at least in her earthly garb. I do not know what the future has in store; but she is there ever-present in my mind, in my heart, in my soul.

I sometimes wonder if those who now live the opulent life or at least are enjoying the much-cherished political freedom of our modern societies realize that they owe this to the dedication of those who died and suffered torture for it. Her radio messages were decisive in the outcome of war.

Her spirit has inspired many women who see in her their archetype of the woman knight. Her spirit lives further whenever the call for freedom stirs our valiance.

Pir Vilayat Inayat Khan
1993

Selected Bibliography

Several books have been written about Noor or include her unusual story, including the following:

Basu, Shrabani. *Spy Princess: The Life of Noor Inayat Khan.* New York: Omega Publications Inc.

Fuller, Jean Overton. *Noor-un-nisa Inayat Khan (Madeleine).* London: East–West Publications.

Harper, Claire Ray and David Ray. *We Rubies Four; The Memoirs of Claire Ray Harper (Khairunisa Inayat Khan).* New York: Omega Publications Inc.

Inayat Khan, Noor. *Twenty Jataka Tales retold by Noor Inayat Khan.* Vermont: Inner Traditions International.

Princess Spy, a one-hour BBC documentary that appeared on 'Timewatch' in 2006.